Christmas
for the
VILLAGE
MIDWIFE

BOOKS BY TILLY TENNANT

THE VILLAGE MIDWIFE SERIES
The Village Midwife

THE VILLAGE NURSE SERIES
A Helping Hand for the Village Nurse
New Dreams for the Village Nurse
A Family Surprise for the Village Nurse

THE LIFEBOAT SISTERS SERIES
The Lifeboat Sisters
Second Chances for the Lifeboat Sisters
A Secret for the Lifeboat Sisters

AN UNFORGETTABLE CHRISTMAS SERIES
A Very Vintage Christmas
A Cosy Candlelit Christmas

FROM ITALY WITH LOVE SERIES
Rome is Where the Heart is
A Wedding in Italy

HONEYBOURNE SERIES
The Little Village Bakery
Christmas at the Little Village Bakery

STANDALONES
The Summer of Secrets

TILLY TENNANT

Christmas
for the
VILLAGE
MIDWIFE

bookouture

Published by Bookouture in 2025

An imprint of Storyfire Ltd.
Carmelite House
50 Victoria Embankment
London EC4Y 0DZ

www.bookouture.com

The authorised representative in the EEA is Hachette Ireland
8 Castlecourt Centre
Dublin 15 D15 XTP3
Ireland
(email: info@hbgi.ie)

ISBN: 978-1-80550-192-3
eBook ISBN: 978-1-80550-191-6

For my Mum and her never dull moments.

1

The tiny Cumbrian village of Thimblebury was on the countdown to Christmas. That morning, Thimblebury's midwife, Zoe, had turned the page on her calendar to December, and she was currently trudging down rows of snow-dusted firs with her boyfriend, Alex, looking for the perfect Christmas tree. The lines ran for miles, dozens and dozens of them, and beyond those, the windswept hillside dropped away to reveal a vista of gentle peaks and cavernous valleys, the majestic scenery of the Lake District, all white with early snow. She watched as her breath curled into a crystalline sky. A gap in the weather had brought intense sun and a cloudless horizon, but the forecast promised it wouldn't last for long and that more snow would be on the way. Despite being bright, it was bitterly cold, freezing the drifts beneath her feet so that they cracked and crunched as she walked.

'You wouldn't think it would be so hard to choose a Christmas tree,' she said as her gaze returned to the row. 'It's a tree, after all. They all look sort of...'

'Like trees?' Alex asked.

'I was going to say they all look basically the same – trunk, branches, needles. So how is it I like some more than others? Surely we ought to be able to walk over to the first one and go, *Right, that looks about the size – we'll take it.*'

'You wouldn't hear any objections from me if that's the way you want to do it.'

'And do you think it's a bit frivolous? Us buying two, I mean. I think we ought to get one for your house and leave it at that. Work's so busy, I'll hardly be home to look at mine.'

'I want to buy you a tree.'

'I don't need you to buy me a tree. I mean, it's a lovely idea, but I really don't. In all honesty, no tree at all is still better than what I had last year.'

'What did you have?'

'Some naff old plastic thing Ritchie's aunt had given to us when we first got married.'

'And that's precisely why I want you to have one this year. It's your first year in Kestrel Cottage.'

'I suppose so. In that case, I'm going to do Christmas lunch at mine. You and Billie can come over. That way, you both get a break, and we can all enjoy this tree you're insisting on buying for me.'

'*You* need a break too. You've barely stopped over the last couple of months, at work and out of it.'

'Well, if there are no babies, then there's no job, so I'm not going to complain about being busy.'

'Even so. Too busy if you ask me. Too much taking work home and, from a selfish point of view, not nearly enough time with me as I'd like.'

'You're unhappy about that?'

'I'd be lying if I said I didn't want us to see one another more, but I would never ask you to put me before your work. I know how important it is to you. As for Christmas, I want for you what you want for me. It's our first together. I want it to have good memories. I don't want to become that plastic tree your ex's aunt gave to you, something that makes you grumble in ten years' time when you think of it.'

'That' – Zoe took his hand and offered a bright smile, caught in the worlds of his soft brown eyes; she still felt giddy whenever she gazed into them, and she didn't think that would ever change – 'would never happen, tree or no tree. I only mean it seems a waste of money that you could be spending elsewhere.'

'Let me treat you, please. I want to. I've got to build new Christmas memories too. This is where I start.'

Zoe paused and then let out a resigned breath. How could she deny him that? He'd lost his wife around this time of year a few years previously, and he'd often spoken of his struggles in the short time Zoe had known him. However Zoe felt about the two-tree scenario, she had to admit that, in the end, it was only money. What the tree represented was a lot more significant than what it might cost.

'This one's nice,' he said, leading her to a slender, symmetrical specimen. I think it's about the right shape for the corner of your living room. That's where you're going to put it, right? By the window?'

'It seems the most sensible place to put it,' Zoe agreed as she pondered the tree. It *was* lovely, and she couldn't deny that she'd asked Ritchie for a real one almost every year they'd dragged the old plastic thing from the loft, only to be told he didn't see the point when they already had something that would do the job.

Do the job. That was Ritchie's attitude to everything. It didn't matter if it was right or not, as long as it did the job. Since their split, Zoe had begun to see that she'd fallen into that category too, a wife who wasn't perfect but would do the job. He'd pursued her to a point, even when she'd made it clear they were through, and for a while Zoe had believed the motivation for that had been love, but since their last meeting, when she'd finally put him straight, she'd come to see it hadn't been about love at all. She'd been the plastic Christmas tree, and he'd only wanted her because he didn't see the point in making the effort finding someone new would require.

'That one then?' he asked.

Zoe nodded. 'What about yours? Shouldn't we have brought Billie to look with us?' she added, troubled, and not for the first time that day, by the notion that his daughter hadn't come. She'd made a comment about not third-wheeling her dad, and though Alex had been content to leave it at that, Zoe wasn't convinced that staying away was actually what Billie had wanted. 'Maybe you should come back with her. We could just take mine for now.'

'She said—'

'I know what she said,' Zoe cut in. 'I don't know that she meant it. She probably felt she'd be in the way, but I bet she would want to come and choose. Like you said, we all need new Christmas memories, and maybe Billie needs them more than both of us.'

He smiled down as he smoothed a lock of dark hair behind her ear. 'How are you so good at this stuff?'

'I don't know about that.'

'But you get it, straight away. I don't know how, but you just look at a situation and you've worked it all out.'

'That's definitely not true!' she said with a self-conscious laugh.

'Well, things are better between Billie and me, and that's down to you.'

'It's down to you and the work you've both put in. I only said how I saw it, but you made the changes. Take some credit.'

'I will, when you start taking some too.'

Zoe laughed again.

'I love that,' he said.

'What?'

'Hearing you laugh. I hope I hear it every day for...' He blushed and cleared his throat. 'This one then?' he asked, going over to the tree.

Zoe smiled. 'What were you going to say?' she asked. 'Just then. You were going to say something and you stopped yourself.'

'I wasn't,' he said. 'It was nothing, just chat. You know what I'm like.'

'It wasn't nothing.'

'I don't even remember now,' he said, and whatever else Zoe did or didn't know, she could see when someone was trying to move a conversation on.

She hoped the thing he'd stopped himself from saying was a good thing. She was convinced of it. This relationship was so new, and they were both so uncertain of one another that it was all at once thrilling and yet fraught with possible pitfalls. There were things Zoe wanted to say that she hadn't dared for fear he'd think it too soon, and she was almost certain he felt the same. She was about to put it to him when she noticed a man in a puffa jacket and snow boots striding down the row towards them.

'Seen anything you like?' he asked cheerily.

Alex turned to Zoe. 'I think we've decided, haven't we?'

'Yes,' she said, going to the tree they'd chosen. 'I like this one.'

'Right,' the man said. 'I'll get it felled and wrapped for you, and I'll meet you back at the office to take payment. You know the way back, don't you?'

Zoe was trying hard not to laugh at every exclamation, but she didn't understand how someone could prick their fingers so badly every single time they went near a tree. The fir they'd chosen was wrapped in netting, and all they had to do was load it into Alex's car, but somehow they couldn't even do that.

'Ow!' he cried, yanking his hand away and almost letting the tree fall on top of her. 'Bloody thing! I swear it's out to get me!'

'Probably because you had it chopped down. It wants revenge.'

'I wanted you to have a nice tree.'

'I wanted a nice tree too but not at the expense of your fingers. Here, let me...'

'I've got it,' he said, wincing as he wrapped his arms around it and a branch poked through the netting and got caught in his hair.

This time Zoe couldn't help but giggle.

'My hero,' she said, clasping her hands to her heart and fluttering her eyelashes like a cartoon character as he finally got it into the boot.

Dusting off his hands, he grinned now too. 'We got there in the end!'

'Yes, we did, and well done.'

'Are you being sarcastic?'

'Only a bit. Thank you,' she added, reaching to kiss him. 'I can't wait to get home and decorate it.'

'We're decorating it together?' he asked. 'You said you wanted to—'

'Hold that thought,' Zoe cut in as she heard her phone ringing in her pocket. After pulling it out and seeing the caller ID, she answered, listened intently for a moment, and then rang off, giving Alex an apologetic grimace. 'Sorry, one of my mums has gone into labour. She's down for a home birth, and I said I'd attend, so it looks as if the tree is going to have to wait.'

'If I wasn't so in awe of how good you are at your job, I might start to resent all these interruptions.'

Zoe's head flicked up. Was that really a veiled complaint

this time? But he was smiling, and he didn't look as if he was complaining, and so she relaxed. It was so hard to know, and she longed for a time when she'd feel more certain of everything he said and did. It would come, though, so she just had to muddle through until then.

'It means one very good thing for us,' he added. 'Well, for Billie. It means she has the best midwife around.'

Zoe smiled now as he slammed the boot shut. 'I don't suppose you could get me back to the house sharpish? I could do with collecting my kit and getting to my birth before it's all done and dusted.'

'For my little heroine, anything. Come on, let's go.'

2

The front door was opened by one of the older Kovalenko children. Yana Kovalenko had five, and from the groans echoing down the hallway, number six was almost ready to make an appearance.

'Hello... um...'

'Alik,' the boy said. 'She's in the other room with Dad. He's just put up the pool. Olena is playing in it.'

Zoe paled. 'What?'

'Dad tried to get her out, but then Maria started to cry, and when he went to see what she wanted, Olena snuck back in again.'

'You're the oldest, right?' Zoe asked as he allowed her to come in and close the front door.

Alik nodded, in that sullen way that only teenage boys knew how to.

'I'm going to need a right-hand man until the baby's arrived, and it sounds as if your dad has his hands full. Do you think you could help me?'

'What do I have to do?'

'Boss your siblings around. Think you can manage that?'

'They don't listen to me.'

'Try... please. With a bit of luck it won't be for long.'

He nodded again and then showed Zoe into a dining room that had been cleared to allow space for a large blow-up pool. Yana's husband and the second-oldest son were filling it with buckets of warm water, while their four-year-old, Olena, splashed around laughing.

'Hello, Denys,' Zoe said. 'Coping?'

'I know she's not meant to be in there,' he replied, angling his head wearily at his daughter, 'but I'm trying to get this filled as quick as I can.'

'Where's your youngest?' Zoe asked, giving Alik a brief nod to galvanise him into action.

'I've got her in the playpen,' Denys said. 'Kateryna was watching her, but she had to go to her mum. I think the baby will come soon.'

'Hopefully,' Zoe said, noting how overwhelmed poor Denys looked amidst the absolute chaos of a home life that was not only dominated by five lively children, but had a sixth currently on the way, and his wife's fervent wish for a home water birth, which wasn't exactly the easiest thing to set up. 'You look like you could do with a cup of tea.'

'Make that vodka,' Denys said, 'and you're on.'

Any further niceties were drowned out by the protesting squeals of Olena as her brother tried to fish her out of the pool, and Yana yelling in Ukrainian from another room. Denys shouted something back and then turned a resigned look to Zoe.

'She wants to know if you are here and this is ready.'

'I'm coming!' Zoe shouted, following the sound of the reply.

She found Yana doubled over, pacing the living room, their third oldest child, Kateryna, rubbing her mum's back.

'How are we doing?' Zoe asked.

'Four minutes,' Yana said.

Yana had done this many times before, and she knew exactly how it worked. It was one of the reasons Zoe was happy to draw up a birth plan with her that she would definitely be more nervous about with a less experienced mother. For some, contractions four minutes apart might mean they still weren't that close to birth, though labour would have begun. But in Yana's case, Zoe was sure her instincts were reliable and that she'd been right to call.

'Can I get into the water?' Yana asked.

'As soon as it's ready. Denys is working like a trouper out there. Fingers crossed it won't take long.'

Yana blew out a heavy breath and then nodded, grimacing as she did.

'Another one?' Zoe asked.

'Yes,' Yana panted. 'My little Zoriana wants to come out now.'

'If she can be patient for just a bit longer' – Zoe opened her bag – 'that would be very helpful. Right, while we're waiting for your pool to be ready, let's have a quick look at you to make sure everything is well.'

An hour later, Yana was wrapped in warm, dry clothes, with baby Zoriana in her arms and the rest of her children gathered around, gazing at the newborn, clearly all besotted – even the oldest teens, who pretended to be so cool and above it all. Denys was making his wife, who hadn't eaten for over twelve hours, some food.

Zoe watched them all, a warmth swelling in her own breast. It was a bittersweet feeling – it always was. As much as she loved these moments, as much as they were the perfect eventuality that made her job so rewarding, she was always reminded of the fact that her own moment of holding a newborn son or daughter close had been robbed from her. Some days she found it easier than others to bear, but the love radiating from this family as they sat close together was so affecting, the emotions today had caught Zoe quite by surprise.

Yana looked up and smiled at Zoe. 'Thank you.'

'I didn't do much in the end,' Zoe said. She began to pack her equipment away. 'You had it all figured out by the time I arrived.'

'I'm still glad you were here,' Yana said. 'Perhaps I didn't need you so much, but I felt safer because you were here.'

'Well...' Zoe drew in a breath and tried to exhale her troublesome emotions away. 'I'm glad. It's what I'm here for. I'll be back to check on you tomorrow.'

'I hope the snow is gone for you by then,' Denys said, standing at the doorway with a bowl of soup on a tray. 'It's not easy to get around at the moment.'

'You should see the hill I live on too,' Zoe said cheerily. 'I'm thinking of hiring Rudolph to get me up and down there.'

'Rudolph?' Denys asked.

'You know, Santa's reindeer. One of them, at least.'

'Yes, sorry,' Denys said. 'I forgot.'

'I'm sure you must be tired – it's been a long day for you all,' Zoe replied.

'A happy one,' Denys said as he took the baby from Yana while Alik handed his mum the tray with her soup on. 'But,' he added, turning to his wife, 'perhaps this can be the last time?'

'It can be the last time if you stop making me pregnant,' Yana said, and the look of horror on the faces of their oldest children made Zoe burst into laughter.

'At this point,' she said, 'I think I'd better leave you to it.'

3

Zoe had arrived home to Kestrel Cottage exhausted after Yana's home birth. She'd promised to phone Alex if it was still early enough at that point to salvage their day, and even though it probably was, she messaged him to say she was too tired to be decent company and it might be better if they put off the tree decorating until the following day. Much as she wanted to see him, she reasoned there was no point if she was going to fall asleep ten minutes after his arrival.

The following morning was Monday, and even though she'd been on call over the weekend, technically it was a new work week. She never minded being called out, but sometimes, if there was a run, it could feel as if she hadn't had a weekend at all. Today was definitely one of those occasions. She couldn't stop yawning as she dressed, and let out an involuntary groan as she went to the window of her bedroom to see it had started to snow heavily again. To a point, it looked pretty, but it was making travel to her home appointments hellishly difficult.

Downstairs, the tree Alex had bought for her the previous day was standing in the porch to keep it cold and fresh until they could get to it. No fear of it staying cold, Zoe mused wryly as she passed it on her way out.

She closed the gate and waved at her neighbour and landlord, Victor, who was bang on time to give her a lift down to the village.

'It's really good of you,' she said as he opened the door of his old Land Rover for her.

'You'd never make it in your car,' he said cheerily. 'And it's no bother for me. Old Banger will make short work of the snow; she always does.'

It was lucky that Zoe had only one home visit to Yana on her list for that day and she could walk to her house if worse came to worst. She wasn't sure how she was going to cope if more came up later that week and the weather was still bad. She hated to cancel anyone but realised she might have to at least postpone one or two who lived further out until the roads were clear again. Hopefully that wouldn't be long.

'Never seen anything like this.' Victor started the engine. 'I've seen snow here man and boy, of course, but I can't remember the last time I saw it this bad and for this long.'

'At least it's not a regular thing then,' Zoe replied. 'I love snow, but I don't know if I could do this every winter.'

'I'm with you there, lass.' Victor yanked the gearstick and the car juddered, tossing Zoe so violently to one side she wondered if she'd have whiplash by the time they made it down the hill.

'Could you drop me outside the shop? I need to get a few supplies before I go to work. I can manage from there.'

'Whatever you like.'

There was a pause. Zoe couldn't help but smile because she was getting used to this pause, and she was beginning to recognise what it meant.

'Seen much of Alex?' Victor asked idly.

'Yes,' Zoe said, her smile growing. Victor loved to pretend he didn't gossip, but he was as interested in her new romance with Alex as everyone else. Perhaps more since he and Alex had become good friends. 'Quite a lot, actually.'

'Ah. So it's...'

'Going well,' Zoe finished for him. 'So far.'

'Of course,' he said gruffly. 'Early days and all.'

'Exactly. Early days. But I like to think we're off to a good start.'

A better start, she'd have said, but she didn't want to go over their rocky introduction with anyone who didn't already know about it. The fact was that anyone who'd witnessed Zoe and Alex's first few weeks from close quarters would have bet against them ever exchanging a civil word, let alone romance. It was funny, Zoe had reflected more than once, that life, as her grandma always said, could turn on a sixpence.

Wherever Zoe went, the same conversation was being had about the snow in wondrous tones. Some were happier than others, depending on how fond they might be of sledding or tubing or cross-country skiing, or hiking in snowshoes, or any of the other things people who often had lots of snow liked to do. Magnus, co-owner of Thimblebury's shop, being Icelandic, was rather nostalgic and very stoic about it all. The record-breaking snow currently falling on the Lake District reminded him of home, and he couldn't see what the fuss was about. Zoe could tell he was secretly enjoying the fuss anyway but not quite as much as he enjoyed telling people that snow wasn't nearly the obstacle to everyday life they all seemed to think it was. According to Magnus – who had no commute to his place of work, a nice electric heater at his feet behind the counter and an endless supply of tea brought to him by his partner, Geoff – snow was no issue at all if you simply found sensible solutions to it.

'Easy for you to say,' Flo huffed as Zoe leaned on the counter, checking the emails on her phone as she waited for her turn to be served. She'd been there with enough time to go through quite a lot because Flo had much to get off her chest, mostly about how neglected she was.

Zoe couldn't help but smile to herself as she caught snatches of the conversation, scrolling her messages with the absent patience of someone who was too tired to worry about it. And Flo was far from neglected – Zoe's friend and colleague at the surgery, Ottilie, made sure of that. She and her partner – Flo's grandson, Heath – went out of their way to look after her – not that anyone listening to Flo would know it.

'I could fall over in that snow and freeze to death and nobody would find me,' she said, pursing her lips like she was eating a lemon.

'Are you thinking of painting yourself white then?' Magnus asked with a subtle, blithe humour that Zoe had come to recognise since her arrival in the village.

'What's that got to do with anything?' Flo snapped.

'Well, I wondered how you wouldn't be seen in the snow. But then I thought, if you were painted white, then it would be camouflage. So I wondered if that was your plan.'

Flo narrowed her eyes. 'Don't be ridiculous. I can leave if you're going to be like that.'

'It's only a little tease,' Magnus said but looking somewhat sheepish with it.

'It's not fair, teasing an old lady for being afraid for her life. That's what's wrong with the world these days – no respect. No care for others. Everyone's a comedian at someone else's expense...'

'I'm sorry,' Magnus said, though he didn't sound all that sorry to Zoe. 'If I'm walking around, I'll be sure to keep a look out in case you are lying in the snow. I'll make sure Geoff does the same.'

Flo looked cynical but then seemed to decide that was the end of that particular conversation. 'Have you got my cheese in? The apple one?'

'Sorry, Flo, not yet.'

'You haven't had it in for weeks!'

'Not weeks, only a few days. The suppliers are struggling. It's the snow, I expect, having an effect on everything.'

'Oh!' Flo threw her hands into the air. 'Another thing ruined by this blasted snow! So when are you going to get it in?'

'We're doing our best,' Magnus said. 'As soon as we get some, I'll let you know.'

Flo frowned. 'I'm sure I don't know what I'm going to put on my crackers for tea.'

'We've got some nice smoked cheddar,' Magnus began, but Flo was already on her way to the door.

'I'll come back later to see if it's arrived...'

As the door slammed shut and Flo walked a cleared path, huffing as she went, Magnus turned to Zoe. 'What can I get for you, my love?'

'I want my apple cheese too!' She pretended to flounce out, and Magnus burst into laughter.

'Actually,' Zoe said with a grin, 'I need some waterproof plasters – I don't suppose you have any? I've looked at the first aid shelf, but I can't see them – probably right in front of my face, but...'

She followed Magnus to an area that held a scant and basic stock of first aid, and her grin spread as he put his hand straight onto a box. 'I said they would be,' she offered in an apologetic tone. 'Sometimes I worry about myself.'

'Some days are just like that,' Magnus said. 'Will these be all right for you?'

'Perfect.'

'Did you cut yourself?'

'Oh, Alex did yesterday trying to show me how manly he is

by wrangling a Christmas tree into a car. The tree came out best. I had to use the last plaster I had in my handbag on him and I thought it might be a good idea to get a replacement box in case he had more manly ideas.'

'Yes, manly ideas often lead to trouble.' Magnus smiled. 'Anything else?'

'Have you got any ground ginger?'

'That I can't help with, I'm afraid – we sold out yesterday. I take it you're thinking of entering something into the gingerbread house contest?'

'Me and everyone else in Thimblebury, apparently.'

'Every Christmas it's the same. Everyone wants to beat Corrine, of course, but they never do. Perhaps you'll be the lucky one.'

'I doubt that – have you even met Corrine? I think that woman was born with oven gloves on her hands. I'll have a go, but it's just for fun, really – an excuse to join in, you know? To tell you the truth, Alex and I have been talking about how we ought to make more of an effort to be a part of the community, and this seemed like a good place to start.'

'There's always plenty going on at Christmas that brings people together, that's for sure. And you've got lots of time for the competition.'

'Oh, I know, but I wanted to do a couple of practice runs beforehand.'

'You and everyone else... that's why the ginger is sold out.' He cocked an eyebrow. 'So you do want to win? Just a little?'

'Maybe a little,' Zoe said, laughing. 'I can't help it.'

'We all want to win a little,' Magnus agreed. 'If only to go down in Thimblebury's history as the person who finally broke Corrine's run.'

'You're going to bake something?'

'Naturally. I do something every year; Geoff too. We usually have some of them on display in the shop afterwards.'

'I'm looking forward to seeing them. So you don't know when you'll have the ginger in? If there are supply issues, I mean.'

'Different suppliers than Flo's cheese, my love. Geoff's at the wholesalers now; we should have it when he gets back.'

'Brilliant! If I pay you now, will you put some aside for me? I'll pick it up when I next come down to the village.'

'Pay me when you collect it.'

Zoe thanked him and left with the plasters and some other bits she'd picked up for work. The surgery staff took it in turns to fetch supplies of tea and coffee and snacks, and it was hers.

As she stepped out into the snow, she found it had restarted after a brief break. This time, however, the sky was heavy with it, falling in stuttering flurries. It was almost as if the weather itself was trying to apologise for the way it was behaving, or perhaps that it was uncertain what it was meant to be doing. Someone had cleared a path from the shop down to the road, and along the main street as far as the old stone cross that marked where the traders of old had sold their wares, but already the exposed ground was dusted with a powdery layer of fresh snow. Zoe didn't mind. She liked snow – at least down here where the terrain was flat and manageable. The hill going up to her cottage was a different matter, but she'd been lucky enough to have Victor and his Land Rover to take her up and down while the weather had been making the path difficult.

She drew in a lungful of clean, iced air, exhaling it as a great cloud that swirled up into the sky, and smiled. Life was good.

4

At the surgery, Zoe knocked at the door of Ottilie's office. From within, she heard her colleague's voice. More than a colleague, actually. Zoe and Ottilie went way back, all the way to the days when they'd shared a student house, both training to go into the health service. And with Ottilie's baby due in eight weeks, Zoe was also honoured to be Ottilie's midwife, which felt like the greatest and most important service she could give to repay her old friend for the kindness she'd shown when Zoe had needed it most. If not for Ottilie, who had seen what Zoe had needed and refused to give up on her, Zoe wouldn't have the incredible life she'd started to build in Thimblebury.

'Unless you have chocolate, you can bog off!'

Grinning, Zoe pushed open the door and put her head around it. Her friend was pinning a glittery Christmas card to a board already well populated by other festive cards of all shapes and sizes. Ottilie was popular in the village, but if anyone had been in doubt of that, the volume of cards here compared to what anyone else had in their rooms proved it. 'Sorry, no chocolate. Got to watch that blood sugar, after all. I've come to do your check-up before clinic starts.'

'I've done it all.'

'Blood pressure, urine—'

'Yes, yes...' Ottilie wafted a hand. 'It's all fine. Baby is kicking – boy, is baby kicking! I feel fine. Fat but fine. So you can go and get on with something more useful than worrying about me.'

'I wish all my mums were this easy.' Zoe leaned on the door frame and folded her arms. 'I'd work an hour a day and spend the rest of it watching reruns of *House*.'

'God, not that! Haven't you had enough of medical stuff by the time you go home?'

'*House* is not medical stuff... I mean, it is but not really. Anyway, I know you've got it all under control, but I think I ought to have a look myself, just to be certain. So come on – on the couch and let's have a look at that beautiful bump.'

Ottilie rolled her eyes but did as she was asked anyway. She'd only recently begun to wear a looser-fitting uniform, her progress coming all at once, but despite this, Zoe remarked on how much the baby had grown since the last review.

'It's all those huge dinners Heath keeps making me eat,' Ottilie said. 'I'm sure I'm eating for five, not two. I keep telling him I'm not having quadruplets.'

Zoe let her hands gently trace the shape of Ottilie's belly. 'You're blooming,' she said. 'Everything is progressing like a textbook pregnancy, as far as I can see. And if Heath wants to look after you, let him. You'll have enough to do when the baby comes.'

'Of course it's a textbook pregnancy,' Ottilie said wryly. 'I'm the most sensible, predictable woman in Britain – what else would my pregnancy be but sensible and predictable? I'm sure it's all very boring.'

'You can keep it boring for me – that's the way I like it. There...' She pulled Ottilie's tunic over her bump and stood back. 'All done with plenty of time to grab a quick cup of tea before your first patient.'

'I doubt that. It's Mrs Icke, and she'll have camped out overnight in her excitement to start complaining about every little thing that's bothering her.'

'Come to think of it, I did hear her voice when I came past reception.'

'Great... you could have warned me.'

'What, and have your blood pressure shoot up before we'd measured it?'

'Oh, Fliss has already had a go at doing that.'

'Why?'

'She's all grumpy about Simon being unavailable for clinic.'

'She agreed to it.'

'I know, but this is Fliss we're talking about. She's forgotten it's her replacement he's interviewing, and now she can only see how much extra she's got to do in his absence.'

'I'm sure she'll see it's worth it when things are sorted and she can finally retire properly. Anyway, what does she expect when she lands her news on everyone out of the blue and it's panic stations trying to find her replacement. Simon will be lucky to find someone who can do such a short notice period.'

'Hmm, try telling her that today.'

'No thanks. I think I'll just keep my head down until it's all over.'

'I don't blame you.'

'By the way, have you given any more thought to your own finish date? Fliss isn't the only one who'll have to be replaced, and you don't have long to go. Simon will also have to get cover for you while you're on mat leave. I'm surprised he's not more panicked about that.'

'I think he's preoccupied with Fliss's replacement. I've got ages yet.'

'You've got eight weeks until the birth, and even you can't work until the end. You can't keep putting it off.'

Ottilie waved a vague hand. 'I'm not; I just haven't had time to think about it. Anyway, Simon will be able to get agency cover for me. It's not like what I do is rocket science.'

'Hey, don't knock yourself down. It's going to take one hell of a nurse to cover what you do.'

'I don't know about that, but I remember what people around here are like when there's any kind of change. They don't like it one bit. I pity the poor nurse who covers for me, that's for sure.'

'Well,' Zoe said as she went for the door. 'You're going to have to decide soon, or you'll be having the baby on shift.'

'Shut up...' Ottilie said with a faint smile. 'You sound like Heath. You worry about your other mums; I'll be fine.'

Ten minutes later, Zoe was welcoming her first appointment of the day, Lara, who was ten weeks pregnant with her second child. It was their first meeting, and Lara had only confirmed the pregnancy a few days previously.

'You'd think I'd be used to all this,' she said as she sat down in Zoe's consulting room. 'But I don't remember it being this hard with Rhys.'

'Rhys is your little boy?' Zoe asked.

'Yes, he's six now.'

'I expect he's the difference. You didn't have all that extra work back when you were pregnant with him – there was just you to worry about. Is he active?'

'And then some. Never sits still. I'm knackered, and I don't know if it's him or the baby. Honestly, if the new one is half as bad, I've got my work cut out. I think that's why I kept putting off doing the test – I was dreading finding out because I knew things would get a lot harder.'

'Were you trying?'

'For a baby? Yes and no. We weren't putting any special effort in, if you see what I mean, but I wasn't trying *not* to get pregnant either. And I think it had been so long since Rhys I was wondering if I could get pregnant again – I mean, I'm thirty-six.'

Zoe smiled. 'Hardly ancient.'

'Yeah, I know, but they do say I'm an older mum, don't they? Anyway, with all that in mind, I didn't take a lot of notice until I started to feel a bit off in the mornings, and then I started to go off coffee and I was like, oh, this seems familiar. I don't know, but Rhys seems to be worse since we told him about the pregnancy. I think he's playing up deliberately. He's always been a handful, but he's just being so naughty. I had to go and see the head at school about him last week because he'd started giving his form teacher so much lip.'

'You're sure there isn't something else bothering him? You'll know him better than anyone, of course, but have you asked him if there's something bothering him?'

'I asked him why he was being such a little shit, but my other half says that's just showing him that playing up to get attention works. Anyway, I asked if he was upset about the baby, and I didn't get an answer either way – he just started to cry. I suppose that's my answer, isn't it?'

'I'm sure he'll come round to being a big brother when the baby arrives. I'd say give him plenty of attention and cuddles and maybe persuade your partner that's going to be more productive than ignoring the issue. Let Rhys know he'll always be number one whatever happens. He probably just needs reassurance.'

Lara looked unconvinced but not half as unconvinced as Zoe herself often felt when handing out words of wisdom to women who already had children, when she, despite her professional qualifications, had none. It was easy to regurgitate a training manual, but Zoe suspected that there was no substitute for lived experience, and she felt like a fraud for trying to hand out advice on a subject she had no lived experience of. Not out of choice, but that didn't change anything.

'Are you all right?' Zoe asked. 'In yourself? I imagine the whole thing with Rhys is stressful, but are you managing with being pregnant again? You're happy?'

'Now I'm getting my head around it, I think I am. I'm sure in a few weeks I'll be more excited.'

'You know you can talk to me about anything any time you need to,' Zoe said with a reassuring smile. 'It doesn't matter if I'm due to see you for a check-up or not. I'll let you have my mobile number before you go.'

'Thank you. I'll try not to ring.'

'Don't worry about that. Anything else you want to ask?'

Lara paused in thought before she spoke again. 'How much longer do I have to stay on the folic acid?'

'Only a couple of weeks more. Are you struggling on it?'

'Constipated like you wouldn't believe. I'm pooing out bullets! I'm surprised they don't crack the toilet bowl when they hit. That's another thing that seems to be worse than it was the first time I was pregnant. I don't remember it being this bad with Rhys. Can't I come off it early? I'm desperate.'

'I know, but it would be better if you could hang on. Two more weeks can't be that bad?'

'You're not the one sitting there for hours on end praying for a nugget to come out. I could have written a novel in the time I sit on that toilet every morning. I suppose I've come this far, so...'

'Is there anything else?'

'Mainly the folic acid, actually. I was hoping you'd say I could stop taking it.'

'Sorry to disappoint you, but I think it's better if you can stick with it. Have you tried putting something in your diet that might help ease things? Prune juice or something?'

'Not really. I know all about apricots and prunes and whatever, but I can't stand all that stuff.'

Zoe set about taking measurements to add to Lara's notes. They chatted as she got on with her checks, and the conversation turned to Lara's older son so often Zoe realised quickly that the issue there was far bigger than folic acid or anything else Lara had mentioned. There was no help for that, at least none that came from a clinical setting. Zoe only hoped that her offer to be on the end of the phone whenever Lara wanted to talk was some kind of help. As for the rest, Lara and her family would have to work it out, like so many before them.

The next appointment was a no-show, and when Zoe tried to phone, she discovered she had an incorrect number on her files. So she went through to reception to talk to Lavender about finding an alternative way of contacting them.

As she walked in, she was distracted by the sight of Simon, who was now their head GP, shaking hands with a woman at the doors of the surgery. There were a few warm words, then she left before Zoe could get a proper look. Even so, there was something familiar about her. From the brief glance Zoe had, she'd have said the woman was around her late thirties, early forties, attractive in a controlled way, very much giving the impression of someone who took a long time to choose her outfits in the mornings. There wasn't a hair out of place or an item of clothing that didn't perfectly coordinate, and the contrast between her and their retiring GP, Fliss, was almost comical. Fliss often looked as if she'd got up with two minutes to spare for work to discover someone had burned all her hairbrushes during the night.

'Is that one of the potential new doctors?' she asked Lavender as Simon strode back to his office.

'Yeah, she seems nice enough. He's got one more coming in before he decides. She's originally from Manchester, you know. Funny that, isn't it? With you and Ottilie moving here from Manchester. There'll be nobody left there soon – they'll all be in Thimblebury.'

'I feel as if I might know her from somewhere,' Zoe said. 'What's her name?'

'Emilia Dickens.'

Zoe paused and then shook her head. 'Don't think I know the name, but there's definitely something familiar about her. Maybe I've run into her working at the hospital in Manchester.'

'That's probably it,' Lavender said.

The surgery doors opened, and a heavily pregnant woman came in with a red-cheeked toddler.

Zoe smiled. 'Hello, Sam.'

'I'm a bit early,' the woman huffed. 'Wanted to give myself plenty of time to get here – don't move so fast these days, and it's slippery on the pavements with all that snow.'

'That's all right – seems sensible enough. And you're in luck: I'm free early if you want to come through.'

Corrine, as she often did, flung open the back door of Daffodil Farm to welcome Zoe before she'd even made it down the garden path.

'I saw Old Banger,' she said, ushering Zoe inside. 'Or rather, I heard it. Loud enough to wake the dead that engine is. Has Victor gone to put it away?'

'I think so,' Zoe said. 'I hopped out so I wouldn't get too wet in the snow. Shall I take my boots off?'

'No, no, don't bother. I've got to mop the kitchen floor anyway. Sit down. Tea?'

Zoe nodded, recognising a fragrant sweetness on the air. 'You've been baking? Or is that a silly question? Is that ginger I can smell?'

She decided immediately that it was a silly question because barely a day went by where Corrine didn't bake. And then Zoe noticed a structure of rare beauty out on the kitchen worktop, so intricate it was hard to believe someone had made it from food. Zoe got up to take a closer look.

It had steep eaves, with a tower and detailed tiles dusted with icing sugar, and high windows in the walls made from solid sugar slabs, and even delicate trails of ivy climbing the sides. A garden area was littered with tiny headstones and shrubs made from something that might have been edible paper but must have taken hours to fashion.

'This is your entry for the gingerbread contest? This is amazing!'

'Oh, it's just a trial run,' Corrine excused. 'I was trying out something new.'

'For the competition?'

'Yes. Can you tell what it is?'

'It's the church, right?'

'Well, that's something. I was worried it might not be recognisable.'

'It's brilliant, spot on! It's even got the little wicker gates and those gargoyle water spouts on the corners... and the graves and the war memorial... and the bit where the fence bends around that old oak. Corrine, it's... no wonder you win every year!'

Corrine blushed and wafted away the praise. 'I don't win *every* year.'

Zoe smiled. 'That's not what I hear,' she said, but it was typical of Corrine to be adorably modest about her talents. 'You ought to go on *Bake Off*, you know. You'd win that for sure.'

Corrine laughed. 'Heavens no! I couldn't stand all that pressure! The presenter would say one word to me and I'd be a mess. No thank you. I'll leave television to the people who can cope with it; I'm happy making cakes here in my kitchen for Victor.'

The back door flew open, and Victor kicked off his boots before stepping in. 'What's that? Is my name being taken in vain? What have I done now?'

'Corrine was just saying how she likes to bake for you,' Zoe replied.

'That's lucky' – Victor strode over to the gingerbread creation and studied it, hands in his pockets – 'because I like to eat them.' He reached out, pulled up a gravestone and then popped it into his mouth.

'Victor!' Corrine scolded. 'Not that one! I didn't say you could eat my gingerbread!'

'But it's a rehearsal! You said—'

'I know, but—'

'Then it won't matter if I have a nibble, will it?'

'I was going to take photos first.'

Victor had the decency to look guilty, even though it was wrapped in a grin. 'Sorry, love. What about I get the camera from upstairs and take some photos for you before any more graves go missing?'

'How about you show some self-control and there wouldn't be any more graves missing!' Corrine called after as he left the kitchen. Folding her arms, she turned back to Zoe. 'Honestly!'

'You should take it as a compliment. He can't resist your cakes.'

'He's like a big hairy child,' Corrine said, scowling, though there was a reluctant smile trying to break through.

Reflecting on what she knew of Victor, Zoe was inclined to agree. He was a gruff man, no stranger to his eighties, but he had the sweet tooth of a seven-year-old, a penchant for bad jokes and slapstick comedy, got along with people a quarter of his age far better than his peers, was excited by tractors, and his favourite hobby was making a fuss of a fluffy herd of alpaca that grew bigger by the week because he possessed absolutely no willpower when it came to refusing a rescue animal, despite running out of room. The evidence was overwhelming. Perhaps not so much a big hairy child, but definitely younger at heart than most men of his age. At least, the ones Zoe knew, which, admittedly, wasn't many.

'I thought I might have a go at the gingerbread contest,' Zoe said as they went to the table to sit down. 'Any tips from the reigning champion?'

'There's not so much to it so long as you get your gingerbread right. If that's good, you can build almost anything you like.'

Zoe was sure it wasn't quite that simple, but as she wasn't aiming to win (at least, she wasn't expecting to) she didn't push for more. 'Oh, and I hate to mention it, but there's a loose tile on the roof at Kestrel Cottage. I'm not sure if the weight of the snow has done it, but I thought I ought to say. A load of snow slid off, and there was a hole. I was worried it might cause more damage if we leave it, so...'

Corrine put a cup of tea on the table in front of her. 'I'll get Victor to have a look in the morning when we've got some daylight. Hopefully, the snow will have let up a bit by then too. Can you tell me where it is?'

'I'll draw a little diagram, if you like. Will it matter that I'm not in?'

'So long as you don't mind, it shouldn't be a problem.'

'I'll tidy up tonight, just in case you need to go inside.'

Corrine gave a knowing smile. 'Every time you say there's a mess, it's as neat as a pin. I'm sure it's fine, and we'd hardly kick you out over a few dishes in the sink.'

She opened a tin and pushed it towards Zoe, who peered inside to find it full of iced fruit cake. 'How's Alex?' she asked with a tone of innocence but an expression that was teasing and playful.

Zoe grinned. Corrine and Victor had been the first people in Thimblebury to find out she and Alex were dating, and rather embarrassingly it was because Victor had caught them in a steamy kiss at her gate the first morning after the first night before. And she still wasn't used to calling her nearest neighbour apart from them her boyfriend, though that was what he'd become. It seemed that the rest of Thimblebury, as they gradually found out, were as surprised and pleased as she was, and it never took long for the conversation to turn to him, especially here in Daffodil Farm, given Victor and Corrine liked him almost as much as she did.

'He's fine,' Zoe said coyly.

'Only fine? Well, that's disappointing.'

'Very fine,' Zoe added with a giggle. 'Very fine indeed.'

They both started to laugh but were interrupted by a bemused-looking Victor at the kitchen doorway.

'What's so funny?'

There was more laughter, and even if she'd wanted to explain the joke to Victor, Zoe was pretty sure she wouldn't be able to.

5

The nearby town of Keswick already looked festive, and Zoe couldn't wait to see how pretty it would look once the Christmas lights had officially been switched on. There was an air of expectation in the crowd that had gathered to see a local radio celebrity that Zoe wasn't familiar with do the grand lever pull. There was also a symphony of wonderful smells, of mulled wine and sizzling meat and tangy melted cheese and spiced sugared treats on sale at brightly lit stalls and vans parked around the perimeter. Christmas hits were blasting over a sound system, and Zoe grinned as Alex began to sing along.

Though she was warmed to see it, there was a touch of melancholy too. A couple of weeks previously, and not long after they'd got together, had marked the anniversary of his wife's death, and though he seemed positive now, at the time he'd struggled. He was so upbeat today that Zoe worried he was forcing it so he wouldn't ruin the night for her. She was simply happy to be there with him, and if he was a little sad in the background, she didn't mind him admitting it. In fact, she wanted him to because she wanted to support him in whatever way he needed, and she'd said as much, but he'd insisted he was fine. He was more than fine, he'd said, looking forward to a happier Christmas than he'd had since his wife Jennifer's last one, and he felt that his daughter Billie was too.

There was another reason he was upbeat, and it worried Zoe almost as much as the first one she'd been fretting about. His twenty-three-year-old daughter Billie, who'd announced some months before that she planned to have her baby adopted, seemed to be softening on the idea. Or rather, she didn't mention it as often, which had given Alex hope that she was going off it. Zoe felt the situation was far too complex to be so certain and that not talking about it didn't necessarily mean it wasn't going to happen. She was afraid of the bitter disappointment for Alex if Billie did follow through on her adoption plan after all.

'It's getting cold,' he said, fishing a pair of gloves from his coat pocket.

'But it looks so lovely with the snow everywhere. I know some people hate it – mostly me if I have to drive in it – but right now I don't want it to stop. It's making me feel very Christmassy.'

'I know what you mean. There's almost three weeks to go – it'll probably be gone by Christmas Day as well.'

'And if we've had it all now, that means no more until January, I expect. That's usually how it is, right?'

'We'll just have to make the best of it while we have it.' He wrapped an arm around her shoulder and kissed the top of her head. 'Want a hot chocolate while we're waiting for everything to start? I could go and get us one.'

Zoe glanced towards the trailer. 'The queue looks massive. The switch-on might happen while you're waiting to be served.'

'I'm sure it will be fine. I'll keep one eye on my watch, and if it looks like I won't get served in time, I'll abandon it and come back over.'

'Or I could come with you...'

'But you've got a great spot here. You said yourself you never get a decent view of anything at events because...'

'I'm vertically challenged?'

He grinned, reaching to smooth a lock of her dark bobbed hair behind one ear. 'You said it, not me. I'd say you're small but perfectly formed.'

'Just not perfectly equipped to see anything at a concert. Do you know what? It's just nice to be here. If I get a good view, that's great, but if I don't, I'll be happy just soaking up the atmosphere, so I'll come and queue up with you. I'd rather be with you when the lights go on than standing on my own. And the last thing I want to do is lose you in this crowd. Or you lose me, which is more likely because I make Thumbelina look like a giant.'

'I love that you're so tiny. It's adorable.'

'I'm hardly going to grow now, so you'd have to say that whether it's true or not.'

'Come on then...' He offered a hand, and she took it.

As they walked, her thoughts turned again to his wife, Jennifer. There were many questions she'd wanted to ask about her but hadn't felt able to. Silly things really, of no real consequence. Was she anything like Zoe? What were the things that had made Alex fall in love with her? She'd seen a photo on the wall in his house, but it hadn't really told her much, except that she'd had huge blue eyes and she'd been willowy, like Billie. She'd had a luminous smile – Zoe could see that even from an old photo. She looked like someone who'd loved life. And something in the way she looked at the camera, something coquettish, told Zoe that she'd probably had a sharp sense of humour too. Had she been smarter, sexier, funnier than Zoe? The thing with Alex was so new that, while she enjoyed being with him, there was still so much uncertainty that it sometimes caught her unawares, and then she'd doubt everything.

She tried to push the niggles away. There would be other,

better days to deal with them, days that wouldn't be ruined by their presence. This was an evening she wanted to remember in a good way. Their first Christmas together was something she wanted to be a happy memory for them both in years to come.

Alex's hand closed around hers, and in that instant every doubt was banished. He looked down at her, those dark, generous eyes filled with not only love, but admiration too. He'd told her often enough how proud he was of her, how proud he was to be with her, and if she had doubts about anything else, she had none about that. It was in everything he did.

She'd asked him what it was, what she'd done to make him feel that way, and he'd told her she hadn't done anything but be herself, which, in his eyes, was as perfect as a person could be.

She returned his smile now as they joined the back of the queue and Wham's 'Last Christmas' began to blast from a nearby speaker. Ahead of them, a young couple jigged a baby up and down between them, singing along and sending the infant into fits of giggles that were impossible to hear without wanting to join in.

'I really think Billie is going to keep the baby in the end,' Alex said, not for the first time, and those worries that Zoe had tried to banish crept back in. To a point, she understood the optimism for a different outcome, one where they kept his grandson living at Hilltop Farm, but she was afraid of it. If Billie went ahead with the adoption and Alex hadn't mentally prepared for that eventuality, she didn't know how he'd recover.

'You should wait to see before you make any plans,' she said carefully.

'I know – you're right. I'm not counting my chickens or anything.'

Except he was, and it seemed he wouldn't be warned that he might turn out to be wrong after all.

The baby further up the queue let out another adorable shriek of delight, and Alex watched wistfully.

'I'm going to get everything on my chocolate,' Zoe declared in a bid to bring him back to the here and now, a far more certain place for them to be. 'It's going to be disgusting. Can you cope with watching me drink it? I mean, it'll probably end up all over my face.'

'I'm going to have all the toppings too,' he said, and she was glad to see him back with her. 'I'll give you a run for your money, I bet.'

With her hands wrapped around her mug, fingers tingling as the warmth from it spread through them, Zoe turned her attention to the stage where the switch-on was about to begin. The pop music that had been pulsing from the speakers had stopped, and in its place a choir of small children were gathered on the stage, singing something jaunty about Santa being stuck in a chimney, a song Zoe vaguely remembered from her own childhood. It was all very cute.

Around the edges of the gathering, more children of all ages raced up and down, or pointed at things, or pulled on grown-up hands with excited wonder, or begged to be lifted up for a better view, or asked for sweet treats, all overwhelmed and overawed by an occasion that was possibly bigger than many of them had ever been to. There was a jolly Santa flanked by elves, working his way around with a collection bucket for local charities, someone offering the opportunity to get up close to a reindeer, a wishing tree where people could leave pinned messages of hope or love or condolence or all three, and a towering Christmas tree glittering with glass and tinsel. The brisk tang of pine rose into the frosty air to mingle with the sugar and spices of the refreshments and the breath of the crowds that curled up into the sky. From behind a bank of tumbling cloud, an iced moon made a brief appearance before being swallowed once again, and just as the countdown to the switch-on was about to commence, the evening's first fresh flakes of snow began to flutter down.

Zoe caught one in her hand and watched it melt. 'It's a good thing you booked that B&B room. If it starts to snow properly again, we'll be glad we don't have to drive back to Thimblebury.'

'And you said it was a waste of money.'

'I never said that! I only asked if it was a bit frivolous because I didn't want you spending all your money on taking me out. Because Christmas is coming, and you need the money for Billie and for other things.'

'And I said it's only one night, and we deserve it. *You* deserve it, for putting up with me.'

'Oh, it hasn't been all bad,' Zoe said with a smile as she pulled her scarf up around her chin. 'But it turned out to be a smart move, whatever the reason. We can have a nice drink and watch the snow fall as hard as it likes and not worry.'

'Do you think Billie will be all right on her own at Hilltop?' he asked, suddenly doubtful.

'Why wouldn't she be?'

'I don't know... She's vulnerable right now, and sometimes even I'm aware of how isolated Hilltop can feel when it's dark and cold and the rest of the village is down the hill below.'

Zoe offered a reassuring smile. 'With Corrine and Victor on standby? They'd be across that dividing field like a shot if she needed them. I'm sure she'll be more than all right. And she's got Griz for company. He's not much of a guard dog, but he's great at giving doggy affection. You can never feel lonely with Griz around, can you? Besides, I bet Billie's glad of the break from us. It'll be nice for her to have the house to herself. She can have a long bath, sit around in her fleece and watch whatever she wants to on telly. Whatever that is – I don't think I've ever had a conversation with her about what she likes to watch, so I don't really know.'

'Neither do I, and sometimes it's one of the things that

worries me. I wonder if I ought to know, like I ought to notice more than I do. But she's so...' He paused, searching for the right words. 'I don't know. She's hard to read sometimes, that's all.'

'She reminds me of Stacey's daughter a bit in that way.'

'Stacey... Geoff at the shop's sister?'

'Yes. I'm not sure if you've met her daughter, have you?'

'I don't think so.'

'You might not agree when you do, but she's closed, a bit like Billie can be. Only Billie's definitely not as miserable as Chloe. Then again, nobody could be that miserable. Ottilie says it's all a front with Chloe, and she's not so bad when you get to know her, but I feel like Chloe can destroy you with a look if she thinks you're annoying. But maybe we ought to introduce them – they could become friends; they've got a lot in common.'

'Billie doesn't really do friends.'

'I don't think Chloe does, come to think of it, but still... I think it would do them both good to open up a bit and accept some help and friendship. I guess people do what they want to – you can't force them to be a thing just because you think it would be good for them.'

Their discussion would have to wait because an announcement blasted out from the PA system, and then the countdown to the lights began. Everyone in the crowd joined in: TEN, NINE...

Zoe grinned up at Alex, transported back to her childhood for one glorious moment, where everything had been about fun and adventure, and there were no cares. Right now, she was here with Alex, looking forward to the sudden, magical illumination of the town and rush of festive joy, and she didn't want to think any further than that.

And then everywhere was flooded with light and thunderous applause, and Bing Crosby crooned about it beginning to look a lot like Christmas, and Zoe had to agree that it was.

6

Since her replacement was free to start work the following Monday, Fliss decided she wouldn't wait any longer and called time on her days as Thimblebury's GP. It felt like a momentous occasion, not just for the woman who had been a forceful personality in the village for almost forty years, but for the people who'd been under her care – some for their entire lives. Everyone understood that things had changed for her since the heart attack that had almost claimed her husband, Charles, but not everyone was happy about her decision to dedicate her time to him alone from then on.

There had been lots of goodbyes in various forms, and it had started to feel like she'd been in the process of leaving forever, so her final day turned out to be oddly flat. There had been hugs and tears, of course, but no real fanfare, and the fact was, Thimblebury was so small Fliss's colleagues were likely to see her on a regular basis anyway. She'd booked a last-minute grand tour of the Far East for herself and Charles, which meant they'd be gone over Christmas. Zoe wondered why she wouldn't want to celebrate her first Christmas as a free woman in her home village surrounded by her friends, but Ottilie had offered the opinion that, despite her decision to retire, the reality of it might be making her sadder than she'd admit, and that perhaps she needed a big adventure, filled with distractions and new sights and sounds, to help keep her mind off that – at least while she adjusted to the idea.

What was more of an event was the arrival of Emilia Dickens. Their new GP was far younger than Fliss – having just turned forty – and where Fliss was irreverent and gregarious, a larger-than-life character in every possible way, Emilia was considered and studious. She was softly spoken where Fliss was brisk and brash, and thoughtful where Fliss was reactive, and Zoe could see why their other GP, Simon, had chosen her as the colleague he wanted by his side to take the surgery forward. Emilia was far more like him than Fliss – who could be a loose cannon at times. The other factor in Emilia's favour was that she'd already worked a good portion of a notice period with her previous employers and so could take up her post quickly, allowing Fliss the pre-Christmas retirement she'd wanted.

All in all, Emilia seemed the perfect fit, though Zoe, Ottilie and Lavender agreed that the new regime would take some getting used to.

Emilia arrived promptly for her first day and shook the hand of everyone who was gathered in the reception to officially welcome her.

'Pleased to meet you. Looking forward to working with you,' was the mantra for each of them. It was safe and courteous, giving nothing away.

Lavender took some time to go through initial admin and IT procedures with her and then left her to have a quick word with Ottilie and Zoe in turn before retreating to her own room to set herself up. The only bump in the road was when Lavender informed her of the surgery's tradition of closing their doors at lunch to share food in the kitchen as a team.

'Really?' Emilia had raised her eyebrows in a way that

suggested a disapproval she didn't feel able to air yet. 'I don't think I'll be doing that. Of course, feel free to continue without me.'

Lavender hadn't been able to get into Zoe's office quick enough to relay the conversation with a pained expression. Zoe assumed she'd done the same with Ottilie. There hadn't been much of a window of opportunity for Lavender to really rant, but Zoe knew she'd have many things to say on the matter when they had time to discuss it properly. It was one of the changes she'd been afraid of. She'd long been a passionate guardian of their shared lunch, and she'd hate to see the tradition die out. Zoe did her best to smooth things over, seeing that there could be conflict between their receptionist and their new GP before she'd even sat in Fliss's seat, and when she had a second spare moment, she popped into Ottilie's office to get her opinion on the matter.

'Lavender will come round,' Ottilie said. 'And anyway, Emilia didn't say we had to stop.'

'No, but I think if she mentions it to Simon, he might start to think about it, and he might agree with her.'

'Even I agree with her a little bit,' Ottilie said. 'In principle, at least, though I like our lunchtimes far too much to say anything. But it's not standard practice these days, is it?'

'I suppose not, but I find it useful just to catch up on what's going on at the surgery. If we dress it up as a daily team briefing with chips... that could persuade him to keep it?'

'Maybe.' Ottilie smiled and then winced, rubbing her breastbone.

'Everything OK?'

'Indigestion,' Ottilie said. 'Happens a lot at the moment. No doubt you're going to tell me that's because the baby is taking up more room.'

'It's definitely got something to do with it. I'm sure you can sort what you need for it.'

'I can cope, don't worry.'

'I don't doubt it.' Zoe paused. 'You know, I really feel as if I know Emilia from somewhere. I can't put my finger on it, but she's so familiar to me I must have met her somewhere before.'

'Ask her – she might be thinking the same about you.'

'I could, but I'm sure she would have said something already if that was the case.'

'Perhaps she's the same – thinks she's either mistaken or embarrassed that she can't remember where she knows you from.'

'You could be right...' Zoe paused at Ottilie's door. 'I'll ask her later if I get a minute. Though it won't be at lunchtime. Apparently.'

'I know. Poor Lavender.'

'Do you think Emilia will push to stop the lunch-hour closing? Like you said, Simon's never been all that bothered about it, so if she put it to him, he might agree that we ought to stay open.'

'And upset Lavender? Simon's no fool – he wouldn't dare!'

Zoe got her chance in the kitchen as she went to get a quick coffee and found Emilia in there doing the same.

'You don't remember me, do you?' Emilia asked, and Zoe wondered if there was a hint of offence in her tone.

'I'm so sorry... I mean, I do, but I can't think where we've met. I've been racking my brain all morning.'

'You were best friends with my sister at primary school.'

'Georgia?'

Emilia nodded, and Zoe's look of apology became a broad smile. 'Georgia Capaldi! So you must be Emilia Capaldi!'

'I used to be. It's a funny way to say that, isn't it? Like you used to be a different person when only the name has changed.'

'No wonder I didn't recognise your name – you got married!'

'I'm sure I've changed a bit too. I was a chubby fifteen-year-old with no time to talk to my little sister, let alone her friends. I remember you being at our house a lot. Until you and Georgia fell out over that boy.'

Zoe's smile became more rueful than delighted. 'What a stupid thing to fall out over, eh? He didn't like either of us in the end, and then we went off to different high schools and that was that. How is Georgia? What's she up to nowadays?'

'She's...' Emilia seemed confused for a moment. Perhaps not so much confused as cautious about what she was going to say. 'She's been running a company with her husband.'

'Oh, what kind of company?'

'Oh, you know, investing, stocks, that sort of thing. I can't say I'm really sure what they do. But she's taking a break from all that anyway to have her first baby.'

'She's pregnant? How lovely! How far along is she?'

'Quite far – she's due in early January.'

'Aww... I'd love to catch up with her.'

'Well, I expect that will happen sooner than you might think.' Emilia spooned some coffee into a mug. She didn't hold Zoe's gaze at all as she finished her statement, and if it had looked to Zoe like she was holding back before, there was an unmistakable awkwardness in her now. 'They're coming to stay with me. They'll be arriving in the next few days, in fact.'

'That'll be so nice! Will they be staying long?'

'At least until Christmas.'

Zoe again sensed an awkwardness. It was the oddest feeling, but she couldn't shake the notion that there was more going on here than Emilia felt comfortable admitting. But then, as adults, they barely knew one another at all, so perhaps that was understandable. Perhaps she didn't feel it appropriate to be sharing the details of her sister's life with a woman who hadn't seen her since primary school, especially as her sister wasn't there. 'You'll have to let me know when she arrives. I'd love to see her again if she's not too busy.'

'Well...' Emilia began in that strangely evasive way again, 'I'm sure that will happen. She may need your care while she's here.'

'Of course. I'm only too happy to be on standby in case she needs some advice, but I assume she already has a midwife at home.'

'She does, yes, but the stay with me may extend beyond her due date. It's... it's a little open-ended.'

Zoe couldn't work out what the between-the-lines text was, but she couldn't deny it was there. So she simply smiled and nodded. 'It's not a problem. If she needs anything, she can come to me.'

'Thank you.'

'You're living in Simon's old house, aren't you?' Zoe asked, looking to find a new angle to connect with Emilia, but it really didn't seem as if Emilia wanted that. She simply nodded and picked up her coffee.

'I must get on, but I'll let you know more when Georgia messages me about her arrival.'

Emilia left the room, and Zoe was thoughtful as she made her own drink. It hadn't crossed her mind for years, but now she recalled vividly scenes from the argument between her and Georgia as if it had happened the day before. Though she barely remembered what had escalated it, she knew it had been silly. A huge deal at the time but in reality so inconsequential that when they'd gone their separate ways, it had faded into an incident that had once happened, a footnote in Zoe's life that had been overtaken by new friends, new experiences and growing up in general. She'd thought of Georgia in much the same way during that time, but they'd been close once.

How did she feel about the prospect of meeting up again

after all this time? They'd be very different people now, but perhaps enough of those two young girls remained in both of them that it would be a good experience. Not that she could avoid her anyway because it looked as if she'd be involved in one way or another in her capacity as midwife.

However she felt about it, the fact was, Georgia Capaldi was about to come back into Zoe's life.

7

Zoe and Alex had agreed on a quiet night at Kestrel Cottage. It was partly to save money after they'd splurged on the overnight stay in Keswick, but partly because while Billie was now far more supportive of their relationship, it still felt awkward spending time together at his place, where she was often pottering about, than at Zoe's. Tonight, Alex had brought wine and snacks, and she'd found a good film on a streaming service, and they were currently sitting on the sofa together, so wrapped up in one another that the wine was barely touched, the snacks unopened and the film running while nobody watched.

'We could go to bed,' Alex said in a hot whisper.

Zoe was breathless in her agreement. 'We could,' she said. 'What about the film?'

'What film? Were we watching one? I don't recall.'

'We were... something about a school and a Christmas play or whatever... I feel a bit guilty kissing like that in front of the children...'

Despite her so-called guilt, she kissed him again – a deep, long, insistent kiss that told him everything he needed to know.

Grinning, he pulled away to grab the remote control and

switched off the television. 'There,' he said, settling back into her, 'no need to feel bad now.'

After more increasingly frantic kissing, he stood and offered his hand. She took it, and he was leading her to the bedroom when the phone he'd left on the sofa began to ring. He suddenly looked torn, and Zoe decided to put him out of his misery. He clearly wanted to answer it but didn't want her to think she was second best. Slipping her hand from his, she went to peer at the caller ID and then looked up at him.

'It's Billie. I don't mind if you want to take it.'

'Sorry...' he groaned, but she wafted away the apology. She understood that neither of them were entirely free of obligations outside of their new romance, and that his daughter would of course always need to come first.

After swiping to answer, he listened in silence for a moment, his expression growing more troubled as Zoe watched. She couldn't quite make out what Billie was saying, but his responses were made with a tone that suggested he was trying to be understanding but was in reality frustrated by the turn of events. And then he finished by promising to go back to Hilltop immediately.

'It's Griz,' he said. 'Billie thinks he's eaten something from the fields and he's throwing up. She wants to know whether to call a vet, but I think I ought to go and see before she does that. I'm so sorry, but would you mind? I know it's cutting our date short, but—'

'Of course I don't! I'll walk with you.'

'You don't need—'

Zoe was already dashing upstairs to get her coat as she gave her reply. 'I want to. I might not be able to help, but at the very least, I'll get to see how Billie is. Hang on...'

She returned a minute later wearing her thickest coat and stoutest boots. Not exactly a sexy date outfit, but that was the reality of living in Thimblebury, she supposed.

Alex was already at the front door, lacing up his own Arctic-grade footwear.

'You're a star,' he said, looking up for a second. 'You know that, don't you? I don't know what I did to deserve you, but it must have been good.'

Zoe gave a soppy grin, too mesmerised by his dark eyes to think up a witty response. And then they stepped out into a night brittle with frost, with a sky so clear every star looked to be in touching distance. The snow had cleared in pockets and what was left crunched underfoot. Alex reached for Zoe's hand. It felt like instinct now to let him fold his fingers into hers, a thing he did that needed no permission, no explanation or thought, and on the rare occasion that he didn't take the initiative, she would find his in the same way, slotting her hand into his palm as if it was made to fit there.

'Are you worried?' she asked as they walked beneath a haloed moon.

'I'm sure it's fine. The thing is, she doesn't say it, but Billie loves that dog more than anything. I'm not going to let anything happen to him, not after the last few years. He's more than a dog; he's the only survivor of her old life, and I worry that something like that would send her over the edge.'

Zoe wanted to remind him that he was also a survivor of Billie's old life, but Alex himself had lost so much in that time that he was as emotionally delicate as Billie herself, and she wondered if it would be wise to remind him. So she simply nodded in the gloom. 'I can understand that.'

'But I reckon he's just eaten too much grass or something.' Zoe could hear the effort to be positive in his voice. 'He's a daft dog – he'll put anything into his mouth and give it a chew.'

'Don't they all do that? The dog we had as a kid was just the same.'

'Quite possibly.'

They were silent for a moment, and Zoe sensed his worry,

despite his efforts to hide it. And so she groped around for something to take his mind off his immediate concerns. In the end, all she could manage was a rather lame enquiry about his day, one that had seemed far too boring when he'd first arrived at Kestrel Cottage with romance very obviously on his mind.

'So now we're both paying attention,' she said into the gap, 'tell me about your day.'

'There's not much to tell. I had an interesting meeting with a guy from a company that provides ready-made camping pods. He's going to send me a quote for what I need. I'll be honest, I still haven't decided what our guest capacity might be – I think it will very much depend on how much the pods cost. I did a bit of research about advertising and stuff, went to see Victor, and that was about it. It was boring, really. How was your day?'

'I don't think it's boring. You might think mine was boring, but I think it was... if not interesting, certainly eventful. Our new GP arrived.'

'God yes, of course. You said she was due to start work, and I clean forgot. How was it?'

'Fine. She seems very nice, no drama. I actually sort of already know her, which was a weird coincidence I didn't see coming. I used to be best friends with her little sister, way back in primary school. I didn't recognise her at first, but she knew me. What's crazier is that her sister is coming to stay with her for Christmas. I mean, I haven't clapped eyes on the girl since we were eleven.'

'That's great!' Alex gave her hand a squeeze. 'You'll have so much to catch up on.'

'I know. I'm looking forward to it, sort of, but it's going to be weird too.'

'Why?'

Zoe shrugged. 'I suppose we're probably both completely different people than we were back then. Being friends as a kid doesn't mean being friends as an adult, does it? We might not even like one another now.'

'Don't be daft! How could anyone not like you? You're brilliant!'

Zoe grinned. 'All this praise! Careful, it might go to my head!'

'Good, let it. I'm not going to stop, no matter how much you ask me to. Someone has to tell you how special you are.'

She leaned into him, laughing lightly, and he planted a kiss on her head. But then the laughter faded as something else came to mind, something she hadn't yet aired to anyone, even though she'd thought it. 'I get the feeling there's something going on with her. Something not right.'

'Like what?'

'I'm not sure, but Emilia seemed cagey about what she told me. One thing she did ask was if I'd take care of her while she's here because she's about eight months pregnant.'

'Who, Emilia?'

'No, Georgia. That's her sister. But it's an odd thing because she has her own midwife already – presumably. So it makes me think her stay is going to be quite a long one. Open-ended – that's what Emilia said.'

'I suppose you'll find out when you see her.'

'I'm sure I will.'

'So when is she due to arrive?'

'Soon. Emilia said she'd be here over Christmas with her husband.'

'Emilia's husband or Georgia's?'

Zoe prodded him playfully through his padded coat. 'Are you being deliberately thick?'

He laughed. 'Honestly, no! It's just a natural talent.'

'Georgia's. I don't think Emilia has a partner at the moment, though she's definitely either divorced or separated because she has a married name now. That's why I didn't recognise her at first – I didn't make the connection with the name.'

'Right. Am I all caught up now, or is there more I need to know?'

They discussed Zoe's feelings on the matter some more, and then the conversation turned to Fliss's retirement before finally wandering over to Victor and his help with the search for more of the Bronze Age archaeology they'd accidentally found on Alex's land some months previously, subsequently taking a detour to Billie and how she was faring, before circling back to Grizzle and what might be wrong with him. By the time they'd covered all this ground, the lights of Hilltop were close. Zoe could see Billie at the downstairs window watching for them.

At their arrival, she opened the door with a tight smile. 'Hey, Zoe.'

'I thought I'd come for moral support,' Zoe said.

'Is he still throwing up?' Alex asked briskly as Billie stepped back to let them in.

'Not since I called you, but he doesn't look well,' Billie said. 'He's in his basket.'

'He must be ill if he's in his basket,' Alex said, attempting a reassuring smile for Billie that was fooling nobody. 'He hates being in his basket. I'd better have a look at him.'

They went through to the kitchen, where Grizzle was curled up looking very sorry for himself. His head rose at the sight of Alex, and his tail thumped a lame rhythm on the side of his doggie bed, but it seemed to be taking some effort to raise any enthusiasm, even for his favourite man in the entire world.

Alex kneeled beside him and ruffled the fur on his head. 'All right, trouble… what's going on with you then?'

Grizzle licked his hand as Alex looked him over, feeling at his nose and belly and then peering closely into the dog's doleful eyes.

'I feel like I'm pretending to know what I'm doing,' he said finally as he looked up at Zoe and Billie. 'Has he had much to drink?'

'A bit.' Billie wrapped her arms around herself, the sleeves of her bobbled cardigan pulled over her hands.

'That's good, isn't it?' Zoe offered.

'I think so,' Alex replied uncertainly. 'What do you think?' He glanced from Zoe to Billie and then back again. 'Keep an eye on him for the next couple of hours to see how he goes? If it looks like he's getting sicker after that, call the vet? I don't know what to do for the best.'

'Victor's pretty good with animals,' Zoe said. 'Should we ask him to come over? He might be able to tell us straight off if there's anything to worry about.'

'He is, but I'd feel bad dragging him out in this weather.'

'I'm sure he wouldn't mind. He's such an animal lover, I think if he knew there was a problem, he'd rather come and see.'

'I don't know...' Alex sent a doubtful look to Zoe, then to Billie and back again. 'I bet he'd come out like a shot. Perhaps it would put our minds at rest, eh, Bill?'

Billie nodded, total trust in her face that was obvious to anyone who cared to look. Since they'd become closer, Alex had often confided in Zoe that he worried Billie had too much faith in him and that he was bound to let her down eventually.

'I'll phone him,' Alex said. He looked at Zoe. 'Help yourself to a drink if you like... unless you want to call it a night and head home? I'd understand. This wasn't what we'd planned, and—'

'I'm happy to stay.' She could hardly be annoyed that their date had abruptly ended, given the circumstances. And she wanted to be on hand in case she was needed.

Taking off her coat, she turned to Billie. 'Want to come and help? You can fill me in on how you're doing at the same time.'

Alex shot her a grateful smile as he began to dial Victor's number, and she went to get cups.

Zoe and Billie didn't speak for a minute, both listening to

Alex fill Victor in on the problem and the response to his offer to come straight over. And then Alex went to put his coat away, leaving them alone.

'So,' Zoe said in a tone deliberately full of airy cheer. 'How's my favourite mum-to-be doing?'

'Oh...' Billie's glance went back to Grizzle in his basket, head listlessly resting on his paws. 'I'm fine,' she replied.

'He'll be all right, you know.'

Billie turned back to her. 'He looks so sad. I've never seen him like that.'

'Victor has loads of experience with sick animals.'

'Alpaca and sheep.'

'And dogs. Don't forget the family has sheepdogs too. He'll know what to do as soon as he gets here. I bet he already knows from what your dad's told him over the phone. He's just brilliant at all stuff to do with farms and animals.'

'What if he says to get the vet? Dad said the weather is bad and... well, he might take too long to get here.'

'There's no point in worrying about worst-case scenarios. Which I know isn't exactly what you want to hear, but it is true. I also know it's easier said than done, but you need to try. Worrying isn't going to do you or your baby any good.'

Billie looked as if she might want to argue but then let out a long sigh. 'OK. I'll try.'

'Your dad said you'd put the Christmas decs up,' Zoe said in a bid to lighten the tone and distract Billie from her worries. She gave the room an approving sweep. What Billie had put up was subtle and stylish and very Billie. She suspected that if Alex had been allowed to do it, the result would have been a lot more traditional and maybe even a bit cheesy – more or less what they'd both done at her house, once they'd managed to find the time, which had been difficult considering how busy she'd been. Still, Zoe loved how they'd decorated Kestrel Cottage. It was very her. Billie hadn't seen it yet, the weather being too bad for her to walk over. Once she did, however, she'd probably hate it. 'Did you order them online?'

'Yeah, there wasn't much in the shops around here. I mean, they're fine but a bit...'

'Old-fashioned?' Zoe asked with a wry smile.

'I didn't mean that, but a bit ordinary.'

'Traditional, yes, I know what you mean. But it's quite a traditional area in a lot of ways, so it's hardly surprising. Yours are a lot fancier than mine.'

Billie shrugged. 'How long do you think it will take for Victor to get here?'

'It depends on the weather. He'll come as soon as he can.'

'What if he gets stuck?'

Alex was back in the room to hear Billie's question. 'He's got a tractor and a Land Rover – he won't get stuck.' He went to Grizzle's basket and stroked his head. The dog gave his hand a listless lick in return. 'He said he'd come straight away, so we'll just have to sit tight.'

Half an hour later, there was a knock at the door. Alex rushed from the table to get it and returned thirty seconds later with Victor and a blast of cold, fresh air.

'Right then,' he said briskly, kicking off his boots and sending a brief nod to Zoe and Billie before going straight to Grizzle's basket. Ordinarily, the dog would have made some sort of fuss at Victor's arrival. Alex always said he wasn't much of a guard dog, but he'd always mark the arrival of a visitor by a lot of barking that was more excited than fierce. 'Let's have a look.'

He spent a few minutes examining Grizzle with more obvious purpose and experience than Alex had done, asking Billie questions about where they'd been, what she could remember seeing at the location, what his vomit had looked like afterwards and how long he'd taken to show symptoms. Eventually, he seemed satisfied, gave Grizzle a brief fuss and then stood up.

'Sounds like he's had a chew on something off the fields he shouldn't have done. But he's taking water, you said. Looking a bit sorry for himself but alert enough. I've got a little potion with me that I use for our Penny's dogs when they stick their nose where they shouldn't – I'll leave it for you. As he hasn't eaten for a few hours, it should be all right to give him a drop shortly. Try him with some little slivers of ice, and when he perks up tomorrow, give him some boiled chicken and rice instead of his usual food. I'd say it'll do the trick, but if he looks like he's getting worse... say tomorrow morning he still doesn't want to eat, then of course you'll need to ring the vet. You've got someone local? Because if not I can recommend a chap. He mostly deals with farm animals, but he'll take a look at a dog just the same, and he's very good.'

'That'd be brilliant, thanks,' Alex said. 'We haven't quite got round to registering him with someone local yet – you know how these things slip down the to-do list when you've got a million other things to take care of. I kept meaning to, but...'

'I understand. You've got a lot on.' Victor took a fizzy drink bottle from a deep coat pocket and gave it to Alex. 'Only a mouthful at first, just to see how he goes.'

'What is it?' Billie asked, her eyes wide, torn between wanting to trust Victor's assessment but clearly sceptical of what might be in the bottle.

'This and that,' he said. 'Mostly electrolytes and a spot of ginger – pretty much what you'd give to a person who was vomiting.'

'And that's it?' Billie asked.

'What else do you want to be in it?' Victor asked in a practical voice, not offended, but confident in his remedy despite Billie's obvious doubts. 'I'm sure the vet would come out and do something fancier, but he'd charge you an arm and a leg for it, and in the end, this will do just the same. It's never done me wrong yet with any of ours.'

'We appreciate it,' Alex said, shooting a glance at Billie that was obviously meant to reassure her. And it seemed to because she bent to fuss Grizzle and said no more about it. 'We really appreciate you coming over. I'd pay whatever it took to get him well, but even then we'd have to wait for hours for a vet to arrive.'

'Aye, that's true,' Victor said.

'Do I owe you anything for what's in there?' Alex asked.

'No, not a penny. It was all lying about the house, and to be quite honest, we've so much ginger lying around right now, I'm glad to be giving some of it away. I love Corrine's baking, but even I'm sick of gingerbread now!'

'So she's still practising like mad?' Zoe offered Victor a mug of tea.

'I'll say. She's not competitive, mind; it's not like that, though folks round here will say it every year because she always wins the contest. She's just a perfectionist. Likes to get it right. It's not her fault that her perfect is better than everyone else's.'

Zoe laughed lightly as she sipped at her own drink. 'No, I don't suppose it is. When you bake as much as Corrine does, you're bound to be better than everyone else. I'm going to have a go for fun, but I don't expect to place at all.'

'What's this?' Billie asked.

'The gingerbread house competition,' Zoe said. 'They have it every year here. And Corrine will win, just like she always does.'

Victor scratched his head through his hat. 'I don't like to say, but I'd save your money at the bookies if you're thinking of betting against her,' he said with a lopsided grin that was full of pride.

'From what I hear, I doubt you'd get good odds betting on her either,' Alex said.

'I've never made a gingerbread house,' Billie said. 'I've never even made gingerbread. Is it hard?'

'It is for me!' Zoe said with another light laugh. 'Still, the fun's in taking part, isn't it?'

'You fancy a go?' Alex asked his daughter, who shrugged.

'I might. Something to do, isn't it?'

'We could bake together,' Zoe said.

'That'd be good, wouldn't it?' Alex said to his daughter, who shrugged again.

She'd never been big on expressing her true emotions, and so it was hard to gauge her level of enthusiasm for the plan, but she hadn't outright rejected the idea, so Zoe saw that as a win. Anything that gave her an excuse to spend more time getting closer to Billie, for Alex's sake if nothing else, was something to be welcomed.

'We don't have a lot of time, though,' Zoe reminded her.

'Plenty of time!' Victor said cheerily.

'It doesn't matter,' Billie said. 'You all said Corrine was going to win anyway.'

'We said she normally wins, but as we've never seen what you can do, you never know.' Zoe gave an encouraging smile. 'You might have some hidden natural talent for baking that you didn't know you had. You might secretly be a gingerbread-house-constructing genius.'

'Or maybe I won't bother.'

'Oh, please bother!' Zoe said. 'Even if you only help me with mine. Because, believe me, they're so rubbish I need all the help I can get!'

'Maybe...' Billie's attention went back to Grizzle, who was now dozing. 'Do you think he looks better yet?'

'How long since he was sick?' Victor asked.

'A few hours, I think.'

'I expect he's on the mend then. Follow the plan and I bet he'll be right as rain this time tomorrow.'

'I can't thank you enough for coming over,' Alex told him, but Victor just waved a hand.

'Don't think on it for another minute. It's what neighbours do, isn't it? At least they do round here.'

'They do,' Zoe said with a smile. 'But especially round here, which is why I've started to think I'll never want to leave.'

8

Zoe had agreed to meet Ottilie and Simon's partner, Stacey, for a trek around the perimeter of the village. Stacey was still on the fitness kick Simon was encouraging her to be on (though she admitted it was hardly a kick and more of a limp flex of her toes) and was always glad of company. Ottilie was getting too pregnant to go far, though Zoe would have liked to have ventured out beyond the village, and in the end, the company was more important than the activity. There was a vantage point she'd heard about called Stanley Ghyll, not far from where they were, and she'd been meaning to go up and take a look, and had almost suggested it until she'd remembered how breathless Ottilie was becoming and how bad the weather was. It would have to wait, and it would probably be somewhere for her and Alex to explore alone when the spring came.

There were pockets of snow all over the hills, hardened like glass in hollows, while what had fallen on the roads and lanes of the village had become frozen slush, crunching underfoot as Zoe stepped on it. Some people had hung Christmas tinsel and baubles onto the bare branches of the trees outside their houses and on the lanes, and the village postbox was wearing a rather fetching knitted topper that depicted Santa and his reindeer pulling a laden sled.

So, eager to make the most of a few spare hours, the friends had settled on a circumnavigation of the village boundaries and a walk of a mile or two along the riverbank, if Ottilie was up to it.

She was on her way to the rendezvous at Stacey's house when she noticed a van outside Simon's old place. He'd rented it from Fliss for a time, but had now moved in with Stacey and freed it up for Emilia to take possession of. Zoe recalled a doubtful conversation with Stacey about that. She'd worried that he wasn't moving in with her because he wanted to but as a practical measure, a consideration for his new GP colleague. Of course, Ottilie and Zoe had told her not to be so daft, and that even he wasn't that much of a people pleaser, and though she'd told them they'd made her feel better, Zoe wondered if it had.

As Zoe approached, Emilia herself was in the doorway giving directions to the removal crew. At her side was a woman who could only be Georgia. Nobody could forget that distinctive flame-red hair, especially not Zoe, who had always been so envious of it and had always viewed her own as drab in comparison. Of course, Georgia herself had hated it, and perhaps understandably when it was often the source of bullying. But she seemed far more comfortable with it now, wearing it long and curled. She was also clearly very pregnant, her belly visible even beneath a heavy coat.

With a kick that was both excitement and trepidation, Zoe changed course and hurried over.

'Hi, Emilia...' she began and was about to address Georgia when the words were snatched from her mouth by a high-pitched squeal.

'Zoe! Oh my God!' Georgia flew down the path to fold Zoe into an enthusiastic hug. 'Em said you were here! Isn't that the craziest thing? Of all the places we could have moved to, we came to the exact village where you are!'

'I only moved here recently myself,' she replied, noting vaguely how Georgia had referred to her own arrival in a far more permanent way, but too distracted to process the information as she hugged her old friend again before holding her at arm's length to appraise her. 'Which makes it even madder! It's so good to see you – and you look so well!'

Georgia beamed. 'So do you. Incredible, in fact. Life here must suit you.'

Zoe nodded and then, smiling, sent a pointed look to Georgia's belly. 'And you're blooming nicely.'

'Waddling is more like it,' Georgia said with a laugh. 'Em tells me you're the surgery midwife. That's even crazier. So you'll be looking after me? Imagine telling us in primary school that this is where we'd be – we'd have thought it mental.'

Zoe laughed. 'Especially as I was rubbish at science. I had to take my biology exams twice to get on the course.'

'I'll leave you two to catch up,' Emilia said before going inside.

Georgia gave her a vague nod and then turned back to Zoe. For a second, Zoe was distracted by it. Something in both Emilia's and Georgia's expressions during the brief moment told her all wasn't well. But then Georgia spoke again, and she sounded so bright Zoe wondered if she'd imagined the tension.

'But you did it. Always were a determined one. Em says you're brilliant at your job, so you must have been better at biology than you thought. Anyway, what do exams count? Everyone knows they don't mean anything really.'

'I'm sure Mrs Crisp would disagree with you there.'

'Oh, that old cow! She'd disagree with anything that came out of my mouth – she hated me.'

'It might have been something to do with the impression she

caught you doing of her...?' Zoe lifted an eyebrow, and Georgia began to laugh again.

'Maybe.'

'So, I don't even know where we start, but how are you?'

'Well, we've got quite a lot of years to cover, so in answer to that question, I expect we'll need a decent night out together to get to them all. But in summary, I'm fine. Life throws its usual curveballs, but...' She shook her head, as if the thought of those curveballs had shaken her mood for a fleeting moment, before smiling again. 'How about you? Last I heard, you'd got married. You're still with him?'

'Actually, no. Ritchie and I split last year.'

'Zoe... I'm sorry to hear that.'

'Don't be. I'm not – well, I was at the time, obviously, but I'm not now. It wasn't meant to be, and I'm seeing someone else and he's lovely, so I think it worked out in the end. Emilia tells me you're married. Is your husband with you?'

Georgia nodded towards the van. 'Brett!' she called to one of the men who was moving things around inside it. 'Have you got a minute?'

'Yep, just— Careful with that!' he snapped to a crew member. 'It's over a hundred years old, and I can't just go to IKEA for another!'

Zoe tried not to frown, and she was too distracted by her current situation to dwell on what she'd later note with more curiosity. He'd told them to be careful with a side table that he'd claimed belonged to him. But if it was Emilia moving in properly and Georgia was only here on holiday, why was Brett moving his own furniture in?

Brett was blessed with thick dark hair, cut short and shot through with cables of steely grey. Zoe had never been very good at guessing ages, but she thought he looked older than Georgia, perhaps by ten years or so, though it may have been the grey hair giving that impression. There was some evidence of a fondness for beer hidden well beneath a thick sweater, but other than that he seemed strong and fit. Wiping his hands down his trousers, he leaped from the back of the van and strode towards the gate.

'Brett,' Georgia urged him over. 'Come and meet Zoe! I told you about her – remember? We were friends in primary school, and how crazy is it she's here? Like, in Thimblebury, where there's only about ten other people and Zoe just happens to be one of them!'

Brett offered a surprisingly formal hand for Zoe to shake. 'Ten other people and not one decent shop,' he said in a tone that seemed quite uncharitable to Zoe. 'How do you do? Pleased to finally meet you after hearing of nothing else for the past week.'

Zoe sensed some reservation, but she tried not to let it throw her. He knew nothing about her, other than the fact she'd been friends with his wife many years ago, so she supposed it wasn't as weird as she felt it was. And she had a history with Georgia that he might have heard all about, and Zoe couldn't be sure how Georgia had reported their falling-out. To Zoe it was all water under the bridge, and it seemed Georgia felt the same now, but it was hard to say how Brett might have viewed it.

'Georgia's really been looking forward to meeting up with you again,' he added.

'Me too,' Zoe said with a warm smile for her old friend. And then Brett took the opportunity to go back to the van.

'Have you got time to stick around?' Georgia asked her. 'We've got a bit to do here, but as I'm banned from carrying anything, I'm sure Em wouldn't mind if we have the kitchen for an hour to catch up.'

'I'd love to, but I'm meeting friends for a walk. I was on my way there when I happened to see you, so I'm afraid I really only meant to pop across for a minute. In fact, I'm probably already running late.'

'Oh, of course...'

Georgia's reaction was not what Zoe had expected. Mildly disappointed would have been normal, but Georgia's tone was suddenly so flat, if she hadn't thought it an overreaction, Zoe would have said she seemed almost crushed by her refusal to stay. And it wasn't really a refusal at all – it was simply that she didn't have the time at that moment.

'But I can totally do another day,' she added quickly. 'Just name it and I'll clear a space in my diary.'

'Oh, I will! How about tomorrow night?'

'Tomorrow...?' Zoe paused. It was sooner than she'd meant, but that didn't matter because she had nothing else planned, though she'd hoped to see Alex. Then again, she always hoped to see Alex, and Georgia looked like she really wanted to catch up. 'Tomorrow sounds good. Great. I'd like that. Shall I come here? Kestrel Cottage – where I'm living – is quite a trek, especially with all the snow, so it might be better for me to come to you. Or we can go out, if you're worried about being a bit upside down here. There's a lovely pub nearby, the Happy Greyhound. I expect it'll take a few days to put everything in order and—'

'Here is great; I'm sure we can make space... right, Brett?'

He stopped on the way past them with a lampstand in one hand and a box balanced on the other arm. 'Huh? Fine... whatever it is, I'm sure it's fine.'

'Perfect!' Georgia beamed at Zoe as he went on his way. 'About seven? Is that too early for you? Because I can—'

'Seven's fine. It's a date.'

'I can't wait to find out everything you've been up to since we last saw one another!'

'Me too,' Zoe said. 'Sorry, I've got to...'

'Oh, sure, of course. See you tomorrow!'

9

When Zoe arrived at work the following morning, Emilia was going over a request for an emergency appointment with Lavender in reception. They both turned to bid Zoe a good morning, and as they seemed busy, she returned it and then continued on to her own room. She'd wanted a quick word with Emilia to explain she'd had to hurry away the day before and hadn't been able to say goodbye before she'd left her and Georgia to move their things in, but as she went, she suddenly realised Emilia was following her anyway.

She stopped with a smile. 'I'm sorry, I thought you were busy with Lavender, and I didn't want to disturb you. Did you want me?'

'I only wanted to say thank you for coming to see Georgia. I mean, she tells me you're coming over later to catch up on old times.'

'Yes, but it's hardly a thing to thank me for. I'm really looking forward to it.'

'I know, but... well, I think it will do her good. She needs a distraction. As a family, we haven't had an easy time lately. I don't want to go into details at this point, you understand, but...'

'Oh...' Zoe said, wondering what else she was meant to say. Was she meant to ask, despite Emilia saying she didn't want to go into details? Was it one of those scenarios, like when you asked a neighbour if they were well and they said yes in a way that meant no and they wanted you to ask even though they'd implied they didn't want you to ask?

Emilia looked at Zoe meaningfully. 'I just wanted to say I'm glad she'll have a friend here.'

Georgia might not have had friends in Thimblebury until Zoe had made herself available, but she had a sister and a husband, and Zoe wondered what kind of hardships their family had endured that those two people were seemingly not enough? Emilia seemed sad and serious. She'd always come across that way to a certain extent – Zoe's recollections were that of a child, but she remembered Emilia as an earnest and introspective teenager. And yet, it seemed deeper and more profound than that now. She seemed like that young girl of many years ago but now burdened with genuine worry. Zoe had the distinct feeling there was a lot to unpack and at some point she was going to end up involved.

'I'm glad to have run into you both again,' she said. 'It'll be nice getting to know you as adults after all this time. There's a lot to catch up on – should be fun.'

'I'm sure it will be. Don't worry about me being around. I have a lot to do, so I'll probably be camped out in the study.'

'You don't have to stay out of the way on our account!'

'I don't, but I will. I think Georgia would prefer it, to be honest. I think she's probably due a break from me.'

Zoe wanted to ask where Brett would be, but then Emilia turned to head back to reception. 'I need to sort something with Lavender before the first patients arrive; I just wanted to catch you before you got busy.'

'Right. Will we see you for lunch?' Zoe asked, guessing what the answer would be.

'I don't think so,' Emilia said without turning around. 'I'm fasting today.'

Zoe frowned, but then decided not to ask and went to her own office to get ready for her working day.

An hour later, she went to call her next appointment through. Gemma was twenty weeks into her second pregnancy and was about as relaxed as any expectant mum Zoe had ever cared for. She had her ten-month-old in a sling as she sat scrolling on her phone. Zoe was delighted to see the door of the surgery open and Yana, her recent home waterbirth, come in with new baby Zoriana.

'Gemma...' Zoe dashed over. 'Give me one minute, would you?' Gemma nodded, and then Zoe went to Yana with a broad smile. 'You didn't take long to be out and about!'

'With five other children around, I don't have much choice,' Yana said with a light laugh. 'I can go out or stay in and go mad!'

'They're at school for some of the day at least,' Zoe said.

'Not enough,' Yana replied with a grin.

Yana had carried her daughter into the surgery in a car seat.

'I'm amazed you've managed to drive anywhere in this snow,' Zoe said.

'Ah, it's a good car,' Yana said. 'Not so much a problem.'

'She's absolutely gorgeous!' Zoe bent down to get a closer look at the baby. 'Perfect.'

'I think so, but of course I would.'

'I think they all are, but she is a pretty little thing. How are you doing? She's being good for you? It's just that I'm not meant to see you for your last review until—'

'I was in the village for other things so decided I would come to bring this,' Yana said, whipping out a large gift bag and offering it to Zoe. 'It's a small thank you for your help.'

'Ah, I didn't do all that much,' Zoe said, taking the bag and peering inside. 'You did the hard work.'

'You kept Denys calm – that's hard work too.'

'Chocolates!' Zoe said, closing the bag again. 'Thank you! I'll share these with the gang at lunch; I'm sure they'll go down well. I'd love to chat, but...'

'Of course.' Yana smiled. 'You're busy.'

'I'll see you next week, and if all's well, I can discharge you.'

'Denys is going snippety snip,' Yana said drily, 'so if all is well there, you won't see me again – not for babies, at least. I think six is enough.'

'Far be it from me to tell you what to do, but six is more than I could cope with, so I wouldn't blame you for wanting to call it a day. Thank you for the chocolates, and take care going home, won't you?'

Yana left, and as Zoe went to fetch Gemma, the door to the surgery opened again, and one of her young expectant mums, Maisie, came in with her mother, Bridget, both treading snow into the waiting room and causing Lavender, watching from her desk, to tut loudly.

'Hello.' Zoe smiled at Maisie, though it faltered as her gaze went to Maisie's mum. The last time they'd crossed paths at the village quincentenary celebrations, it hadn't exactly gone well. In fact, that was the understatement of the year. Bridget had torn a strip off Zoe, and in defending her, Fliss had threatened to take action against the family that included sanctioning their care. 'I'm not due to see you, am I?'

'No,' Maisie said. 'I've come with mum.'

'Seeing the doctor about my polyps,' Bridget said, 'not that it's any of your business.'

'Right,' Zoe said, the irony of Bridget's statement not escaping her. 'That's all right. I wondered if there'd been a mix-up somewhere.' She was about to leave them to it when something occurred to her. And once she'd noticed, she couldn't help but be bothered by it. 'Everything is OK with you, though?' she asked Maisie.

Bridget immediately snapped a reply in her daughter's stead. 'What's that mean?'

'It was a general query,' Zoe said. 'It didn't mean anything apart from being polite. You've got your twenty-week scan coming up soon, haven't you?' Zoe asked Maisie.

'Don't you know?' Bridget shot back.

Zoe resisted the urge to give an answer loaded with sarcasm and painted on a courteous smile. 'Not off the top of my head, no.'

'It's next week,' Maisie said.

'That's good.' Zoe shot a glance to where Gemma seemed content to continue scrolling on her phone. She was one of her less troublesome charges; even so, it was rude to keep her waiting. However, Zoe was convinced she needed a chat with Maisie sooner rather than later because the more she saw, the more concerned she was. 'Listen, I've got a lady waiting, but if you're still here after I've seen her and if your mum doesn't mind' – she glanced at Bridget, who simply glared at her – 'I'll have a quick word with you about how to prepare for it. I think you might find it useful.'

'What's to prepare?' Bridget asked. 'She goes, they scan her, that's it, done.'

'It's not quite that simple,' Zoe said.

Maisie nodded, shooting a wary look from her mum to Zoe and then back again, as if she couldn't decide who it was less scary to upset.

'Only if you're here and it's no trouble,' Zoe repeated. 'Otherwise, I'm sure the ultrasound department will send you instructions.'

It was a ruse. Bridget seemed suspicious enough that she might be able to tell, but Bridget, from what Zoe knew of her, was suspicious of everyone's motives in most things. Zoe didn't know if her plan would work, or even if it was necessary, but years in the job had given her a nose for problems, and her nose was going mad right now. She only needed a few minutes with Maisie alone to satisfy one way or the other whether she felt any intervention was needed.

'OK,' Maisie said finally. She and her mum continued on to the desk to book in with Lavender, and Zoe went to get Gemma.

'I'm so sorry you've had to wait,' she said.

Gemma looked up from her phone. 'What?'

'Sorry you had to wait.'

Gemma gave a careless shrug and got up from her seat, her other baby fast asleep in the sling strapped to her front. Zoe smiled at the little one, unbothered by anything going on around him, and decided nonchalance must be in the genes.

Luckily, Gemma was Zoe's last appointment of the morning, and fifteen minutes later she went back into reception to see Maisie was there without her mum. She seized her chance.

'Are you able to come through for a quick chat?'

'I think so,' Maisie said. 'Mum is with the doctor, but...'

'Lavender will tell her to wait if she comes out before we're done, don't worry.'

'OK.'

Zoe led the way, and Maisie was silent. When Zoe turned at the door to her room, she could see the young woman looked apprehensive and offered a reassuring smile. 'There's nothing to worry about. We won't be long... take a seat.'

Maisie did as she was asked, and Zoe pulled her own from behind the desk to sit alongside her.

'I hope you don't mind me saying, but you look a bit pale. Are you feeling all right? Not sleeping, perhaps? Something worrying you?'

'I'm sleeping, but I'm still tired,' Maisie admitted. 'Does that matter? Will they want to postpone my scan? You said you wanted to talk—'

'I was being a bit sneaky, actually. I wanted to speak to you without your mum there. Can I be plain, Maisie? You look thin. Are you eating properly?'

'Yes.'

'Maisie...'

'I'm not dieting!'

Zoe let out a sigh. Maisie's denial told her instantly everything she needed to know. They'd had conversations before around the food Maisie was eating and that time the young woman had expressed worries about putting on weight during her pregnancy. It seemed the issue hadn't been resolved in her mind, despite telling Zoe at the time that it was.

'Do you mind if I take some measurements? Because I think you look smaller than you should, and I do think you're thinner than you were last time I saw you. If you're not cutting down on your food, then it might mean there's a problem with your baby and I will have to refer you for more specialist care.'

Maisie shrugged awkwardly. 'I might have been on a bit of a diet.'

'Oh, Maisie, why?'

'I was trying to eat all the food you told me to, but I was still getting too fat.'

'Who told you that?'

'Nobody.'

'I thought,' Zoe continued, 'we'd sorted all that out. You need to eat well, and now is absolutely not the time to be on a diet. Tell me what you're eating and don't try to cover anything up.'

'I don't know. I eat different things every day. Mum says 800 calories is how much you need to eat if you want to lose weight.'

'People thought that in 1970 maybe! Nobody gives that advice now, not even to a woman who isn't pregnant!'

'But—'

Zoe shook her head. She always tried hard not to patronise the expectant mums in her care, and for the most part none of them needed it, but desperate times called for desperate measures. She could see she was going to have to spell it out for Maisie. 'You do realise you're putting yourself and your baby in danger? You'll be lacking in critical vitamins and minerals, and it has consequences. No wonder you're so tired; your body is fighting to keep you and another person alive – you need to nourish it, not deprive it...'

Zoe pulled a box of tissues from the far side of the desk and handed one to Maisie. 'I'm not trying to make you cry; I'm trying to look out for you. It's my job, but I'd want to anyway because you're one of my favourite clients.'

'I don't mean to keep messing up.' Maisie blew into the tissue.

'You're not messing up, but I wish you'd spoken to me before you'd started this diet business.' Zoe was thoughtful for a moment. 'I think,' she continued finally, 'that you and I ought to have more contact, so I'm going to ask you to see me a little more often. Not because you're messing up, but to put my mind and yours at rest. Could you come to clinic a bit more often? Failing that, perhaps we could have phone consultations?'

'I suppose.' Maisie dried her eyes. 'Do you still need to check me now? Only Mum will be waiting.'

'Could you come tomorrow?' Zoe asked, fairly certain she had a free slot but deciding she'd make time to see Maisie regardless. 'We'll take your measurements and chat a bit more about this diet. I understand you don't want to put on weight, but we need to have a frank conversation about how you can keep control in a way that is safe for you and baby. Would that be OK?'

'What time should I come?'

'Two?'

Maisie got out her phone and made a note. 'Two, got it. Should I tell Mum?'

'That's up to you. I obviously can't stop you from bringing her along either, but it might be better if you don't. I don't want her to be offended by anything we say, and—'

'She might kick off again, like she did before. I get it. I'll try to keep it a secret.'

'You don't have to do that.'

'I do. If I tell her I'm coming, she'll want to know why.'

'Is your mum...' Zoe paused, and then decided that they'd started out speaking plainly and they might as well continue. 'Is she encouraging you to cut calories? Was the diet your idea or hers?'

'Mine,' Maisie said emphatically, though Zoe wasn't convinced. Even if the idea had been Maisie's, there was a strong possibility that Bridget had somehow influenced it. Zoe and Maisie had been involved in a conversation like this once before, in the early days of the pregnancy, where Maisie had confided that her mum had been unhappy about how quickly Maisie was gaining weight and beginning to look obviously pregnant.

'Thanks for popping in,' Zoe said, choosing to leave things as they were for now. 'And for being so straight with me. Hopefully I'll see you tomorrow at two.'

Just before she headed to the kitchen for lunch, Zoe took a minute to message Alex. But rather than him texting back, her phone lit up with a call from him.

'Sorry,' he said. 'I know nobody phones nowadays – or so Billie loves to tell me.'

'What do they do then?' Zoe asked with a light laugh.

'You message or you're a weirdo... So call me a weirdo, but I wanted to hear your voice.'

'You did?'

'It does things to me, you see.'

Zoe giggled. 'In that case, hello. You sound happy. I take it that means Grizzle is on the mend.'

'He's almost back to normal. Whatever Victor gave him is miraculous. In fact, I'm sort of missing when Griz was ill already. The house was quieter. And tidier.'

'Aww, but he looked so sorry for himself it must be nice to see him all bouncy again.'

'Yeah, it is. I'm sorry we had to cut our date short.'

'That's all right. We're neither of us footloose or fancy free really, are we? People and dogs and all sorts of other things will want our attention sometimes, and I'm just grateful for any time we get together.'

'I couldn't have put it better myself. I'm the luckiest man ever for any spare minutes with you.'

'You say the nicest things, you silver-tongued charmer. Be careful, I might start to believe them.'

'How about we try again tonight?'

'I wish I could say yes, but I've made other plans.'

'Oh? That was fast...'

'I know, sorry. I'd say I'll try to undo them, but I don't think I can. Remember I told you my old school friend Georgia was coming to stay in Thimblebury over Christmas? Well, I bumped into her yesterday and promised I'd go to see her tonight to catch up. I don't know why, but I get the feeling she really needs someone to talk to right now, and I don't want to let her down.'

'She really needs someone to talk to, and why aren't I surprised that you think it has to be you?' he asked with wry humour in his tone. 'I'm disappointed, but how can I be mad about that?'

'You're sure? It's all right to say if you're a bit miffed. I'll make it up to you—'

'How can I be miffed? I'm sad I won't get to stare into those beautiful eyes, but I understand I can't have you all the time, even if I might want to.'

'Thanks for understanding. How about Wednesday? I'm busy tomorrow.'

'That'll work.'

'Perfect. You'll text me then?'

'I will, but if your date tonight stands you up for any reason, I want first refusal.'

'I'll remember that,' Zoe said, laughing. 'But I don't think for a minute she will.'

Zoe wandered down to the kitchen early for lunch, having a shorter morning clinic than normal, with the intentions of getting it set up for everyone else. She got there to find Simon sitting at the table with one of their regular pharmaceutical reps.

'Oh, hello!' The rep got up. 'I don't think we've met, have we? I'm Barry.'

'No, but I've seen you pop in,' Zoe said with a smile. 'I doubt you'd need to see me really; I'm the midwife.'

'Oh, yes, I've heard all about you from Lavender. Good things, mind. Very complimentary.'

'You'd have to say that,' Zoe replied, her smile growing.

'I would, but I can assure you it's all true.'

'What is?' Lavender's voice came from the doorway. 'All right there, Barry? Have you had a cup of tea?'

'Yes, Simon's looked after me. I've got something for you, actually.'

Lavender clapped her hands together. 'It had better be my

calendar! I've got dates to mark for next year already and no calendar!'

'Sorry, we had new printers on it and they've been a bit slow. Just goes to show, cheaper isn't always better... Here we are!' He produced a large envelope and handed it to her.

Lavender took it and opened it up, and then stared at it before gaping at him. 'What on earth is it?'

She turned the calendar so that the entire room could see. On the front cover was a mass of green blobs and what could only be described as tentacles.

'Yes, well...' Barry cleared his throat. 'I didn't design it. It's had... shall we say mixed reactions.'

'What's wrong with nice photos of birds? Or hills or Portugal or squirrels or something? What even is this?'

Simon peered at the photograph. 'Influenza, I'd say. Magnified a few times. It's fascinating, isn't it?'

'It's gross!' Lavender said. She opened up to the first page and then showed them another image, this time of red and purple tubes with what looked like hair all over them, floating in a sea of blackness. It looked like a weird alien landscape from an old sci-fi movie. 'Don't you have a calendar without photos of things that might kill me?'

'Sorry.' Barry gave an apologetic shrug.

Ottilie came in just as Lavender was displaying the page for March. She stared at it.

'What is that?'

'Norovirus, apparently,' Zoe said.

'Well, that's something to be reminded of as we sit down to lunch. I *was* hungry...' She went to the fridge and got out a large tub, then tipped it into a pan before taking it to the stove and setting it down to heat.

'That's done it!' Lavender said to Barry, giving the calendar and pretending to haul him from his chair. 'You can sling your hook, and take your calendar with you!'

Barry chuckled. 'Next time I'll bring a tin of biscuits then.'

'God no,' Lavender said. 'They'll come with pictures of bacteria or something!'

'I think we're about done anyway, aren't we?' Simon asked him. 'And I'm afraid it's lunchtime.'

'I think we are.' Barry checked his watch. 'And I've got another appointment to get to. If I don't see you all before, have a wonderful Christmas.'

'You too.' Simon offered his hand to shake. 'Thanks for the presents.'

'Merry Christmas,' Ottilie called from the stove. 'I don't know if I'll still be at work when you come again, so I'll see you when I see you.'

'Of course,' he said. 'In which case, all the best for your maternity leave...'

'Next time,' Lavender said, waving him off, 'don't bring us any more icky calendars!' She locked the door and then went to fill a jug with water. 'What is that, by the way?' She looked over Ottilie's shoulder. 'It smells amazing!'

'Thai green curry soup,' Ottilie said. 'I got the recipe from one of my new patients. Heath can't get enough of it.'

'I bet he can't,' Lavender said with a saucy laugh. 'But what about the soup?'

Everyone started to laugh.

'Right,' Ottilie said. 'If only I was in a state to oblige him. But he loves this soup, keeps asking me to make it, so I thought I'd try it out on you lot.'

'Try it out on me as often as you want if it tastes as good as it smells. There's bad news about the pud, though.'

Zoe laid the cutlery on the table. 'Don't we have any? I could go out and get some ice cream or something from the shop if—'

'No, we've got some.' Lavender grinned. 'But I'm sorry to inform you it's gingerbread.'

A collective half groan, half laugh filled the kitchen. All apart from Emilia, who had come for a glass of water but had made it clear she had no intention of staying. It was a shame, Zoe thought, because she could see that Lavender had looked hopeful as she'd walked in, and if Emilia would share just one lunch with them, it would go a long way to her being readily accepted as part of the team. Right now, she was offered courtesy, but it didn't really feel as if she was viewed as a colleague, and she kept such a distance that Zoe couldn't see how that was ever going to happen.

'I'm starting to hallucinate gingerbread,' Ottilie said. 'I dream about it, and not in a good way. Everywhere I go someone's baking it, cooling it, building with it or icing it, asking me to taste it. It's like the longest, most specific episode of *Bake Off* ever!'

Lavender glanced at Emilia with something like thinly veiled distrust. 'You're sure you won't stay to eat with us? There's enough.'

Emilia stood at the doorway with her water. She'd paused, listening to the conversation, and Zoe wondered whether it was because she'd been tempted to stay and join in. But then she shook her head. 'Thank you, but I don't think so. I've got a lot to do; I'm going to get back to my desk and plough through it.'

Zoe could tell Lavender was itching to pass some sort of judgement over Emilia's decision, probably a negative one, but she also clearly recognised her place in the hierarchy – such as one existed at Thimblebury surgery because Fliss had never been keen on that sort of thing. To her, colleagues were colleagues, and they were all equally as important when it came to keeping the surgery running. At this point, it was hard to tell how Emilia viewed it, but aside from her previous connection to Zoe, she hadn't seemed keen to be anyone's friend.

'If you change your mind, we'll be here,' was all that Lavender said, adding that she'd take some gingerbread to her at coffee break that afternoon, seemingly intent on ignoring the fact that Emilia wanted to fast.

'Thank you, but I don't think I'd eat it,' Emilia said before leaving them to it.

Lavender turned to the others with a sour look that left nobody in doubt that she was seriously struggling to keep her more extreme opinions to herself, and that were she able to air them, they'd be less than favourable.

'Don't worry,' Simon said, reading it. 'We've already had a conversation about the lunchtime close, and as I know how important it is to all of you – as, indeed, Fliss did – I've told her that nothing is going to change for the foreseeable future. We will carry on with our lunches as we always have if that's what you all want.'

'And she's all right with that?' Ottilie asked with obvious doubt.

'Yes.' Simon gave a brief nod before going back to his meal.

Ottilie, Zoe and Lavender exchanged a look. Whatever deal Simon felt he'd brokered, it was clear the other members of staff were thinking the same thing: how long would Emilia's agreement last? If today had been anything to go by, not long. Zoe also dreaded a conversation with Lavender that she saw looming on the horizon, one where Lavender asked Zoe to step in and use what influence she might have to change Emilia's mind. The fact was, Zoe had none, but Lavender might take some convincing of that.

10

Zoe had only been inside Simon's old house a couple of times, but it was still strange seeing someone else's belongings in there. As she approached, she noticed that the garden was hidden beneath a blanket of snow that hadn't yet melted, but the path to the front door had been cleared. It had gone from the roof apart from scattered patches. The houses either side had Christmas decorations in the windows and outside, draped from trees and shrubs, but Zoe noticed that there were none in Emilia's. But she'd only recently arrived and perhaps making her house festive wasn't on her list of priorities.

Inside, the place was cluttered – far more than was reasonable for one person. Simon had left furniture behind because it had never belonged to him in the first place – having been left for him by Charles, Fliss's husband, when they'd rented it to Simon – and even if he'd owned it, he wouldn't have needed to take it with him when he moved in with Stacey, who already had everything they might need. But even taking all that into consideration, the barely contained chaos that littered every surface and lined every wall suggested that either Emilia was a classic hoarder, or she had enough belongings to account for two or three people. Given the way Brett had been stressed out at the removal team, it was fair to assume that some of these things belonged to him and Georgia, which suggested they were planning to stay for an extended period of time. Hadn't Emilia said something about their stay being open-ended, now that Zoe thought about it? She'd been cagey about the details. Why?

Added to the request to care for Georgia for the remainder of her pregnancy, it painted a picture of... uncertainty? Perhaps a couple who weren't sure of their situation, both in the present and the near future.

If all this *was* going on, Georgia herself didn't seem troubled by it as she opened the door to Zoe. She met her old friend with a broad, open smile.

'Come in! I mean, come in if you can get in! We're a bit upside down...'

She led Zoe into a cosy sitting room, made even cosier by the reduced floor space that Zoe would soon notice characterising the entire house. After more initial greetings and apologies for the mess, Zoe noticed they were alone in there. She hadn't expected Brett or Emilia to stick around, but she'd thought they might have at least popped in to say hello on her arrival.

'Brett's gone for a walk,' Georgia said, answering the question before it was asked. 'Lunatic. It's freezing out there, not to mention there's black ice everywhere. I don't know what he expects to see in the dark. Still, he's a grown man and I can hardly stop him. Emilia's gone back to the surgery to do some bits and bobs. She says she won't be long, but we've all heard that one before.'

Zoe took a seat on the sofa while Georgia eased herself into an armchair. 'Emilia seems really dedicated.'

'That's one word for it. If you ask me, she'll work herself into a breakdown. Todd used to say— her ex,' Georgia said in answer to another unasked question. 'They split last year. He used to say her job was an obsession. Between you and me, I think her time at work had a lot to do with the marriage failing, but she wouldn't thank me for saying so. Perhaps don't mention that to her. She's weird about this stuff. Always was... I mean, I suppose she hasn't told you anything about it herself?'

Zoe shook her head.

'That figures,' Georgia said, shifting to get comfortable. 'Always was a secretive one.'

'I remember we were never allowed in her room, but, honestly, isn't that all teenagers?'

'I expect so. I couldn't say. But she's never grown out of it – if there was ever any growing out of it to do. Anyway, what about you? I want a full rundown... you know, previously on... like on the telly. What's been going on since primary school?'

'Blimey, how long do you think we have?'

Georgia laughed, shaking her hair free of her collar. 'OK, highlights then. Come on... what about this romance for a start?'

'Alex? Well...'

'He's new to the village too, isn't he? He's building holiday lets or something. He's found some treasure. Has a daughter... those are the things I already know.'

'Who told you all that?'

'I went to the shop for some dishwashing liquid.'

'Of course you did! And it was probably Magnus... although Geoff's been known to gossip every now and again. As long as you know it works both ways – they'll tell you what everyone is up to, and you'll be so entertained by it that you won't notice them collecting information to share with everyone else about you.'

'Oh, I'm cleverer than that – he didn't get anything.' She pointed to her swollen belly. 'Apart from the obvious, of course.'

'Speaking of which, how is the pregnancy? Not too stressful?'

'It's been stressful at times, but for reasons that are nothing to do with the baby. But you don't want to hear about that now; it's boring, and you're avoiding telling me about you. We'll get to my stuff later.'

'I'm not, and if I am it's only because there's nothing exciting to tell. I trained to be a midwife, became a midwife, got married, got divorced and then met Alex.'

'No kids in that lot?'

Zoe's pause had been unintentionally dramatic, but it telegraphed her sadness well enough that Georgia's smile faded.

'No,' she said. 'Not for the want of trying. I did manage to get pregnant eventually, but...' She shook her head and sucked in a steadying breath. She wasn't going to let that darkness in, not here and now.

'Oh, Zoe, I'm so sorry. Can't you have children then? Is that what you're saying?'

'I don't know. I don't think there's an obvious issue, but it seems less likely with every year that passes. It's all right – I'm happy enough. It's just how things are sometimes, isn't it? Do you know what you're having?'

Georgia looked conflicted. It was clear she wanted to ask Zoe more about her situation but perhaps sensed that Zoe didn't want to talk about it. In the end, she gave a smile that looked forced with her reply. 'No. I want it to be a surprise. Brett wanted to know, but he'll have to wait, won't he?'

'I think it's all right for you to call the shots, as you're doing all the heavy lifting. Thought of any names?'

'A few. I think there's a difference of opinion there too. In fact, I know there is and it's massive! Brett hates all of mine, and I'm not so fond of his. Do you think I'm entitled to call the shots there too?'

'I'd say yes, but I might be biased. So what have you got?'

'I like Melody for a girl, Miles for a boy.'

Zoe nodded as if giving the matter grave consideration. 'Solid names. Very nice.'

'Liar,' Georgia said with a grin. 'I haven't seen you for years, but I haven't forgotten that face. You don't like them.'

'Yes, I do... but it doesn't matter anyway, does it? I think most children grow into their names, however they sound to you at first. As they get older, you realise you couldn't imagine them being called anything else.'

'I know what you mean. So if I let Brett have his way, it might not be so bad – I might get to like them eventually?'

'What's he got?'

'What hasn't he got? He comes up with new attempts to win me over all the time, and each one is worse than the last! We got to Russell and Tina and I stopped listening.'

'I suppose they're quite old names – not very on trend – but they're not that bad, are they?'

'Really?'

Zoe grinned. 'OK, I'm not sure I'd choose them.'

'And do you remember Russell Stone from school?'

'Oh, I do! No wonder it has bad connections for you! BO that could take your eyebrows off and a stinky personality to match! So that's your reason for hating the name?'

'Does there have to be another? I don't want to think about rancid soup every time I call my kid in for tea.'

Zoe burst out laughing. 'You're still funny! So you could live with Tina? Or is there a Tina in your background doing the same job as Russell Stone? I don't think we had a Tina in our class, did we?'

'No, but I'll just be thinking about Tina Turner all the time.'

Zoe was smiling as she shook her head with wonder. 'Look at us – picking up like we never left off. I can't believe we ever fell out.'

'It was stupid, wasn't it? For what it's worth, I'm sorry we did. I missed out on a lot of years of fun.'

'Me too, though we were set to go to different high schools. We'd probably have lost touch anyway.'

'Probably. I'm glad we've run into one another again.'

'So am I. It's really good to see you.'

'So you're settling into village life?'

'Very much so,' said Zoe. 'I never saw myself living somewhere like this, but now I'm here, I love it. I never say for ever, but I don't think I'd be too upset if it was.'

'It seems friendly.'

'It's very friendly. I sometimes wonder if it's a bit too friendly at times.' She raised her eyebrows, and Georgia laughed.

'I expect I'll find that out for myself if the shop is anything to go by. But everyone has been lovely to me so far.'

'They are, and they'll help anyone with anything. It's a good community.'

'So you rent your place? I mean, you haven't bought it?'

'From Victor and Corrine who own the farmland it's on. They're the best – it's like having my mum and dad on the doorstep. And, of course, I have Alex on the neighbouring farm, which is lovely.'

'I bet. So how long have you been seeing him?'

'Not long at all – weeks. It was a rocky start, but it's brilliant now. I have a good feeling about it.'

'True love?' Georgia said with a waggle of her eyebrows. 'Or true lust?'

'It's too early to tell yet. I mean, absolutely true lust. As for the love... I'm hopeful. What about you and Brett?'

'We have our moments, but yes, I'm happy. Things haven't always been plain sailing, but, like you said, that's just the way of things, isn't it?'

'You can say that again. How long have you been married?'

'Only five years. It took me ages to find a good one and pin him down. I was beginning to give up hope before I met him.'

'Sounds like it was worth the wait.'

'It— Oh, blimey! I haven't even offered you a drink! I'm wittering on, and you're dying of thirst! I was so excited to see you...'

'So it's my fault?'

'Ha ha, yes, totally! So what can I get you? Tea? Coffee? Wine? Juice? I mean I'm not sure what juice we have, but I can check – Em is bound to have bought something healthy in.'

'Tea's fine. It's a weeknight, and as I assume you're not drinking and there's nobody else home, it's probably best not to open a bottle of wine. There's a danger I'd feel obliged to drink the lot.'

'I'm sure we could put a stopper in it and leave it for Brett, if you wanted some. He'd definitely drink it – have no fear.'

'That's just it – I'd be drinking and drinking and then I'd look and it would be gone. I'd be feeling guilty and have a lovely headache tomorrow morning. Best to stick with the tea, I think.'

'No problem. Come through if you want to carry on chatting while I make it.'

Zoe followed her into the kitchen, which was almost as chaotic as the other rooms in the house she'd seen, but it looked as if there had been some attempt at organisation here. Considering they'd want to cook, it made sense they'd try to get this one sorted first. But there were still boxes stacked in corners, labelled as food mixers and utensils and all sorts of other paraphernalia. Once again, there seemed like an awful lot for one person, so did some of it belong to Georgia and Brett?

Georgia chatted as she put the kettle on to boil and busied herself finding mugs and spoons. Mostly about how her pregnancy had challenged her and vague hopes for the personality of her baby when he or she was born. Then, on opening the fridge for milk, she let out a loud tut.

'Everything all right?' Zoe asked.

'Oh...' Georgia took out the milk and what seemed to have been a thunderous expression smoothed into something gentler again. It had happened so quickly that Zoe couldn't be sure she'd seen it at all. 'It's a good thing you didn't want the wine. We had a bottle of white in here a few hours ago, but someone seems to have laid waste to it. I couldn't say who.'

As Emilia was working at the surgery then surely Georgia knew it could only be Brett? And if it was Brett and it was their wine to drink anyway, why had Georgia looked so annoyed about it?

'Never mind,' she said, not knowing what else to say. 'It's done me a favour, whoever it is. The temptation is definitely out of the way now.'

'Biscuits?' Georgia held up an open packet. 'At least we still have those.'

Once again, Zoe sensed a subtext that she couldn't quite read.

They'd settled down, laughing more about old times than updating on new ones, when the sound of the front door slamming echoed through the house.

'Brett?' Georgia called. 'Is that you?'

'It's me.' Emilia came into the living room, looking anxious and tired. 'Sorry to disappoint you. Hello, Zoe.'

'Hi.' Zoe gave a sympathetic smile. 'Hard day?'

'A lot to get up to speed with. I'll have it sorted in a week or two. Fliss's notes were... well, she doesn't do notes like I do them.'

'I doubt she did anything like anyone else does it,' Zoe said with a light laugh. 'I didn't work with her for all that long, but she's a legend around here, and I'm not sure that's only for her skills as a doctor.'

'I'm beginning to see she had quite a unique take on the world. Where did you say she was right now?'

'Singapore, I think. At least that's where the trip was meant to start.'

'A bit too far away to have a chat about some of her patients then.'

As Fliss had retired, Zoe assumed nobody would be wanting to chat to her about patients. After all, it was no longer her job, but perhaps Emilia was finding her predecessor's way of doing things so difficult that she felt the need to. She certainly seemed stressed.

'Probably,' Zoe agreed.

'You want a drink?' Georgia asked. 'I can—'

'Don't get up – I can see to myself,' Emilia said. 'I think I'll open that bottle—'

'It's not there,' Georgia said quickly, flushing. 'Sorry. I'll get another one tomorrow.'

Emilia let out an impatient hiss and then seemed to check herself. 'Tea it is then. At least there's no danger of me developing a drink problem...' she continued as she left the room.

'Is she all right?' Zoe asked.

'Yes, I think so. It's all been a bit sudden, the move here and all the new patients. She thrives on order and routine, and so I think it will take some time for her to feel settled. But she said it herself – she knows she'll get there.'

Then the front door slammed again, and this time Zoe could hear a man's voice in the hallway. Then Emilia's, and then both of them faded as they went to the kitchen.

'I should...' Georgia began, but then the front door slammed once more. One of them had gone out again. As Zoe wondered which of them it was, Emilia came back into the living room.

'I hope you don't think I'm being rude,' she said to Zoe, 'but

I'm going to have a shower and then catch up on some reading upstairs. I'll see you at work tomorrow.'

'Not rude at all; I'm sure it's been a long day,' Zoe said.

Emilia gave a short nod and then was gone. When Zoe turned back to Georgia, she could see her friend looked worried. Given what she'd witnessed tonight, and what she'd gathered from it, Zoe was hardly surprised by that. This didn't seem like a very happy household at all.

11

From a small speaker on the reception desk, traditional carols were playing. It was possibly at a volume too loud for the space, and they'd undoubtedly get complaints from patients once the doors had opened, but one look at the surprisingly dark scowl on Lavender's face, despite the festive jollity of the music, persuaded Zoe that she shouldn't mention it. Besides, she was balanced on a stepladder tacking bright streamers to the wall, and so Zoe decided it was better not to distract her, not even with a good morning. But Lavender called down as Zoe walked past.

'You have no objections to me putting up Christmas decs in your room?'

'I don't see why I would. Good morning, by the way.'

'Only some people seem to think they're unhygienic. Honestly! It's not like she's performing open heart surgery in there.' Lavender came down the ladder and dug into a cardboard box on the floor, pulling out another garland. 'I mean, it's Christmas, isn't it? I've been patient enough – left up to me I'd have put them up weeks ago, but Simon told me to hang on. But people want to be cheered up, don't they? If you're ill at Christmas, you at least want something to take your mind off it. It's nice to see the place looking bright, isn't it?'

'Is it?'

'Of course!' Lavender held up some tinsel. 'This is not tacky! It's nice tinsel. It wasn't cheap – I ordered it online from John Lewis!'

'It's lovely tinsel...'

'And there's nothing migraine-inducing about a splash of colour, is there? And trees don't take up that much space, do they? Not a tiny three-footer! Zoe, you were over there last night, weren't you? I bet they don't have a scrap of tinsel up in that house, do they?'

'You mean Emilia's house?'

'Yes! Is the sister as miserable as her?'

'You mean Georgia?'

At this point, Zoe was reeling from the speed of Lavender's interrogation. She also hoped that Emilia wouldn't walk through at that moment and overhear any of the conversation she seemed to have been kidnapped by.

'I don't know what her name is. I'll leave, you know. I've had just about enough! Fliss didn't care for Christmas, but at least she let the rest of us enjoy it! At least she didn't suck the joy out of everything!'

'Well, I wasn't here last Christmas, so...'

Yanking the tinsel behind her, Lavender stomped back up the ladders. 'I don't have time to talk right now. I've got a load of tacky decorations to get up!'

Zoe paused, floored by the aftermath of Lavender's ire, and wondered what she could say to make it better. But as she watched Lavender tug the tinsel into place, she decided it was probably best to say nothing. Leaving her to it, she met Ottilie in the corridor.

'I see you're still in one piece,' she said with a wry smile.

'Lavender? Yes, apparently Emilia has issues with

Christmas decorations. She flat-out refused to have any in her room and told Lavender in no uncertain terms what she thought of it all. But she hasn't banned them from everywhere, has she? Lavender was putting them up in reception.'

'I think she would if she could, but I wonder if Simon has had a word. Lavender's threatened to hand in her notice at least three times this morning that I know of. He doesn't have a long history of working with her like Fliss did, but even he can see how good she is for the running of the surgery. It'd be chaos if we lost her – at least until we could get someone trained up, and to be trained to her standard would take months. Maybe even years.'

'What do you do when she's ill?'

'Panic,' Ottilie said with a grin.

'I hate to break it to you, but she's just threatened to hand in her notice with me too. You don't really think she'd go?'

'If you'd asked me a couple of months ago, I'd have said no way, but since Fliss left... well, we all know they were close, and Lavender was gutted when Fliss retired. I think under the radar it's been on her mind since then. She doesn't really need to work, you know. I think they'd manage all right on her hubby's money, but she likes coming to work because... well, I think it gives her purpose. But if it stops being fun, then why would she want to come?'

'I suppose so, but nobody *is* irreplaceable. One day she's going to retire as well, and then we'll have to sort things out for someone else to take over.'

'I know, but I don't fancy dealing with that any time soon. What she doesn't know about the running of this place really isn't worth knowing, and when the time comes for her to leave, it would be better if it was under amicable circumstances, ideally with a handover period so someone new can be trained.'

'Simon will smooth things over.'

'He could if—' Ottilie stopped, looking guilty as Lavender

appeared at the end of the corridor with a tattered old box in her arms marked *Decorations*.

'Are you going to tell me I can't do your room?' she demanded.

Ottilie gave her head a vigorous shake. 'God no! Please come and bless me with Christmas cheer because I'm afraid to refuse it!'

Lavender dropped the box with a crash and her hands went to her hips. 'Is that meant to be funny or something?'

'Sorry, no, it's not. Of course you can come in and do mine. I mean, I can do it if you're busy—'

'I'm always busy, but I still make time for stuff like this, even though it's not appreciated.'

'It's appreciated by us,' Zoe said. 'Very much.'

'Just give us a bit of warning before you come down to our rooms,' Ottilie said.

'I'm not stupid!' Lavender shot back before scooping up the box and marching back to reception.

'Bloody hell,' Ottilie said, blowing out a long breath. 'You don't happen to have a hard hat in your room, do you? The mood she's in today we'll need all the bodily protection we can get!'

Corrine handed Billie an apron. It was decorated with sprigs of holly and had deep symmetrical creases that suggested it had been recently purchased and only just taken out of the packaging. Zoe had brought her own over, one that had been gifted to her by Corrine shortly after her arrival in Thimblebury. Corrine wore her old splattered, faded, tested and true faithful, the same one she almost always had on whenever Zoe called in.

'I don't need that,' Billie said, holding it at arms' length. 'I won't make a mess.'

'I'm sure you won't, but just in case. I'd hate for you to stain that lovely top.'

Corrine gestured for her to put it on, and in the end Billie did, checking out the kitchen as if she hoped nobody really cool was hiding in a cupboard ready to jump out and laugh at her.

Zoe shared a secret look of amusement with Corrine. 'No Ottilie?' she asked. 'I thought she was coming.'

'She phoned to say she was feeling tired and wanted to stay in.'

'I don't blame her.' Zoe glanced at Billie. 'How are you doing there? Not too tired to bake?'

'I've done nothing but sleep this week,' Billie said. 'I'm all right. You're as bad as Dad, keeping on asking me every five minutes.'

'It's only because he cares about you,' Corrine said briskly. 'You'd have cause for complaint if he stopped asking, I'd say.'

To Zoe, Corrine's statement sounded a little like a rebuke and not like the usual gentle Corrine at all. She couldn't deny, however, that there was some truth in it, and, as Billie didn't reply, it seemed she thought so too.

Perhaps Corrine thought she'd been a little harsh, however, because her next enquiry was much more like her old self. 'Do you bake at all?' she asked Billie.

'Not really. Don't have time. I mean, I didn't used to.'

'Not even with your mum?'

'No,' Billie said, as unflinching at the mention of her dead mother as Corrine was in addressing her.

Zoe was used to that reaction now. Billie had built a wall around her grief – for both her mother and Luis, the boyfriend she'd lost tragically, shortly before she'd discovered she was pregnant with his child. She kept it locked up tight, and Zoe understood better than most that it was a coping mechanism, the only way she'd learned how to function in the face of so much heartache.

'Mum ran the business with Dad,' she continued. 'She didn't have much time for cooking. We ate out a lot in Spain. It was cheap and pretty good.'

Corrine looked sceptical, as if the notion of someone who didn't cook must be a lie. But then she gave a practical nod. 'So I'll start at the beginning and you won't feel I'm teaching grandma to suck eggs. Righto, that's all I needed to know.'

Zoe and Billie went to wash their hands while Corrine got various tools and bowls from the cupboards. From the corner of her eye, Zoe spotted what she presumed was Corrine's latest gingerbread test run sitting on a board. If it were possible, it was even more impressive than the one Zoe had seen before.

'Corrine... this is amazing!'

'Well, it's better than the last one,' Corrine said, coming up behind her and giving it an ultra-critical once-over. 'Yes, I think it's getting close to something reasonable now.'

Billie came to see what they were looking at. 'That's what I've got to do?' she asked, staring at Corrine's creation with uncharacteristic awe. It wasn't often Zoe saw her impressed, and that had to be impressive in itself. 'There's no way!'

'Don't be downhearted before you've even had a go,' Corrine said. 'You don't know what you're capable of until you try.'

'I know I'm not capable of that!'

Zoe herself was fully aware of her own severe shortcomings, but she intended to have fun trying. 'As long as it tastes good, I won't worry too much if mine doesn't look perfect,' she said.

'That's the spirit,' Corrine said with an encouraging smile. 'It'll all look the same once it's gone down.'

'Easy for you to say!' Billie replied, eyeing Corrine's baking with serious doubt. 'That looks amazing and probably tastes amazing too.'

'Come on,' Corrine chirped, ushering them back to the area

she'd set up as their work space. 'Let's get started and see what we can do!'

No matter how often she was met with a blank stare or a silent response, Corrine kept Billie in her sights. Zoe, on the other hand, she left largely to her own devices, and it was clear that she had a good reason for this. Corrine, ever perceptive, ever empathetic, knew what Billie needed. She could see that there was a happier person beneath that quiet, serious exterior, someone who'd been damaged, who'd had the heart ripped from her and feared the world because of it. She was cautious and cynical, but Zoe knew from Alex that she hadn't always been that way. And it seemed that what Zoe knew as fact, Corrine sensed instinctively.

'Some are born knowing how to bake,' she said as Billie measured her sugar, then her ginger and then tossed them together before dabbing a pinky into the whole thing to taste. She paused then added more ginger.

Zoe glanced down at the recipe book they were sharing. 'It doesn't say to mix them together like that.'

Corrine gave a nod of approval as Billie looked up, the concentration on her face morphing into a look of sudden doubt. 'Oh, have I done it wrong?'

'If you think it's right, then that's fine.'

'But what if I've ruined it?'

'I don't think you have.'

'I don't know…'

Billie started towards the bin, bowl in hand.

Zoe leaped to take it from her. 'Don't throw it away! We don't have enough ginger for you to start again!'

'We can always send Victor out for some more,' Corrine said serenely. 'But I think you ought to trust your instincts a bit more, Billie. I think they're serving you well so far.'

'Will you taste it then?' Billie asked, and Zoe was thrown by an expression that said Corrine's opinion really mattered. 'To check it's all right.'

'If you like, my love.' Corrine went over and dabbed a finger into the bowl as Billie had done, and then nodded. 'Oh yes, that'll do. I'd say crack on with that and let's see what happens when it's been in the oven. We've got all the time in the world. If it comes out wrong, we'll just try again.'

Before Billie could reply, Zoe dropped her wooden spoon onto the floor and let out a sweary hiss. Corrine tutted, as if to chastise her, but she was smiling with it.

'Sorry, Miss.' Zoe laughed as she bent to retrieve it and then went to get a cloth to wipe the floor.

'Let me,' Corrine said, going to the sink and taking it from her. 'Here' – she opened a drawer and took out another spoon, which she handed to Zoe – 'you carry on while I clean up.'

When Zoe turned around, she noticed Billie looking thoughtful as she allowed her gaze to wander to Corrine's spice rack.

'Do you think any of these will make it taste better?' she asked nobody in particular.

'Depends how pregnant you are,' Zoe said, laughing again. 'I'm not sure I'd go with the oregano or the parsley.'

'Sorry...' Billie turned away from the rack. 'I was just wondering how to make it...'

'Interesting?' Corrine threw her cleaning cloth into the washing machine before coming to join her, and then they both paid full attention to the tiny jars lining the shelf. 'You could certainly get bonus points for doing something creative with your flavours, especially if you're not the most skilled in presentation. How about zesting an orange or something?'

Billie turned to her. 'What about a lemon? Like that tea you buy. Dad got some for me – it helped me to stop feeling so sick when I first got pregnant.'

'Lemon and ginger. Yes, you could do that. You could even try black tea or coffee in there. Have a play around and see what you think works.'

'What are you putting in yours?'

'Me?' Corrine smiled. 'I'm not imaginative in that way. I'm a traditional old bird – it'll be the same old spices I always use.'

'What are those?'

'Ginger, obviously. Sometimes I'll play around with a little nutmeg or some cloves or cinnamon, or a touch of honey, that sort of thing. I often find it all comes together with the icing, and that's where I'll get a lot of my flavours in. There's no reason why you shouldn't dream up some new flavours, though.'

'Lemon sounds good,' Zoe called over, red-faced as she mixed.

'Maybe I'll try the orange after all,' Billie replied as she went to the fruit bowl.

Corrine exchanged a sly smile with Zoe and went back to her own bowl.

'Did you bake much as a nipper?' she asked out loud.

'Me?' Zoe asked, wiping her brow with a sleeve. 'Not really. We lived near a cake shop so I was like, "Why would I?" Their cakes were really good, better than I could have made.'

'I'm surprised to hear you say you haven't done much,' Corrine said to Billie as she returned with two oranges. 'Looking at you today, you're like a duck to water.'

'But you're not surprised to hear me say it,' Zoe cut in. 'Rude. I get the message; I look hopeless, and it's obvious I don't bake a lot.'

Corrine smiled. 'You're doing just fine. And I know you bake now – you've told me as much.'

'Not all that often,' Zoe said. 'I probably would do more if I had time. I'm not the world's best, but I do find it quite relaxing.'

'Is that why you do it all the time?' Billie asked Corrine.

Corrine's smile grew. 'Relaxing? I couldn't say. I think Victor would leave me if I stopped making cakes for him.'

'It doesn't bother you?' Billie asked. 'That he makes you do all the cooking and he wants cakes all the time?'

'Oh, I don't really think that,' Corrine said. 'Ignore me – it's just daft things I say. I like doing the cooking. It's a bit old-fashioned, the way we do things, but it's the way we've always done them, and the way it works best for us. I like to see him enjoy his food. I suppose it's the way I show him my love.'

'They do say the way to a man's heart is through his stomach, right?' Zoe added.

'That's what they say,' Corrine agreed. 'It's certainly true in Victor's case.' She wiped her hands on her apron and turned to Billie. 'How are you doing there?'

Billie was rubbing an orange vigorously over a grater. She shrugged. 'I don't know. Is this right?'

'Looks all right to me. You doubt yourself a lot, but you really shouldn't. I think you have a knack for it, you know. You're a natural, I can tell. Some people just are.'

'I always think it's like chemistry,' Zoe said. 'If you're good at that, then you'll probably be good with food.'

'I was rubbish at chemistry at school,' Billie said.

'Were you good at art?' Corrine asked.

Billie shrugged. 'I was all right. I got an A.'

'There you go then. Baking isn't only chemistry; it's art too. It's as clear as day to me you have art in you. The way you put your flavours together, it's like an artist mixing his colours for the right shade.'

'What's all this?' Victor ambled in, used mug in his hand. 'Art and paints. It's just cake, i'n't it?'

'You wouldn't understand,' Corrine huffed. 'Great heathen lump that you are. You've never mixed a cake batter in your life.'

'Ah, but I've eaten enough of them.'

'Your belt's telling me that,' Corrine said with a wink at Billie. 'Had to put another hole in, didn't you?'

Victor began to protest that it wasn't his fault and that Corrine had told him at the time not to worry and he was still slim and handsome and then stopped as she began to laugh. 'Rotten, that's what you are.'

Corrine was laughing as he took his mug to the kettle for a refill, and when Zoe chanced a quick look at Billie, she caught the merest ghost of a smile.

A couple of hours later, Corrine stood with her arms folded, studying Billie's gingerbread house. It was far from perfect – messy joints, off-centre decorations and blackened edges where the gingerbread had caught, but even Zoe could see it oozed a certain creativity. 'Not bad,' Corrine said. 'Not bad at all for your first go.' Then she moved over to Zoe's house, looking as though she was stifling a grin. Although, Zoe had decided it was less of a house and more one of those bomb shelters you used to see in old public information films about what to do in the event of a nuclear attack. One of the walls had already fallen off, and the roof looked ready to collapse at any moment.

'I'm sure it will taste all right,' Zoe said.

'I'm sure it will,' Corrine agreed, still trying to keep that grin under control. 'Shall we try some?'

Zoe snapped a corner from her fallen wall and then put it into her mouth. 'I was wrong – it doesn't taste all right either.'

'I'm sure it's not that bad,' Corrine said, taking some from her.

Zoe watched Corrine's face as she chewed laboriously. It was dry, too stringent, the heat of the ginger overwhelming and there wasn't enough sweetness from the sugar. Zoe couldn't tell where she'd gone so wrong, but had to assume that at some point she'd messed up on the measurements and not noticed her mistake until it was too late.

'It's a... ummm bold flavour,' Corrine said, and Zoe had to laugh.

'It's that all right! I did try to warn you!'

'Don't be so hard on yourself,' Corrine said. 'It's really not that bad.'

'I'm a big girl,' Zoe replied. 'I can take the truth. I don't know how I got it wrong – must have missed something off the instructions, maybe.'

'Maybe when Dad phoned as you were measuring, it put you off,' Billie said.

Corrine nodded. 'That'll be it.'

'Should I try it?' Billie asked.

Zoe shook her head with a rapidly widening grin. 'As your midwife and friend, absolutely not! There's no telling what it will do to you. And as everything you eat gets passed to your unborn baby, it might count as child cruelty. Come on – let's try yours instead. I bet it's as nice as it smells.'

Billie chewed on a piece she had left over from her construction. 'It's OK,' she said. 'Fine, I think.'

'Wow, that's good!' Zoe exclaimed through a mouthful. 'The orange really works!'

'Do you think?'

Corrine snapped off a corner and bit into it. 'Yes,' she agreed. 'It works very well. Did you put a little honey in too?'

Billie nodded. 'I mean, you said about honey, and I thought...'

'I did, and I'm glad to see you trying different combinations. It's very nice,' Corrine said. 'Delicious, in fact.'

At that moment, Victor returned to the kitchen, armed with the same dirty mug to be refilled a third time with tea. 'All done in here?' he asked.

'For today,' Corrine said. 'And yes, there's spare for you, you great greedy gannet.'

'That's not why I came down,' Victor said, and when Corrine lifted her eyebrows so high in disbelief they might have left her head entirely, Zoe burst out laughing again. The day had been good for her soul, if not for her baking confidence, because she realised then that she'd laughed an awful lot. She'd even seen flashes of contentment in Billie's expression at points during the evening. She couldn't wait to tell Alex.

'I'd avoid that one,' Zoe warned him, pointing to her tray.

'Righto,' Victor said, eyeing it briefly before, apparently, deciding he ought to take Zoe at her word. He moved along the counter and snapped a corner from another tray. 'Ooh, that's nice,' he said as he munched. 'Very tasty. And let's see...' He then went to a second tray and did the same. 'Lord above! Corrine – you've outdone yourself! I think this is the best you've ever made! Sorry, ladies' – he grinned at Zoe and Billie as he stuffed another chunk into his mouth – 'but the crown's not going anywhere this year.'

'As it happens,' Corrine said mildly, 'that's Billie's.'

Victor stared at the young woman. 'Yours? Ruddy hell, lass! I didn't know you could bake!'

'I don't.' Billie looked confused. 'It's nice then?'

'Nice? I'll tell you how nice it is – I'm going to take the rest, and I'm not going to apologise for it!'

Billie's gaze went back to the construction. 'It doesn't look very good, though.'

'Practice makes perfect,' Corrine said. 'That's all you need. You've got the basics, so that's halfway there.'

'I think she might be in with a chance this year,' Victor said to Corrine, who nodded, shooting Billie a look of pride that was heartening. Ever generous, Zoe suspected Billie winning would mean more to Corrine than winning herself, simply for the confidence it would inspire in the younger woman. 'A bit of beginner's luck is nowt to be sniffed at, eh?'

'That's not beginner's luck,' Corrine said. 'It's a God-given talent.'

Billie shook her head, but Zoe saw something that perhaps even Billie herself didn't know she was showing. A brightness, a tiny moment of epiphany so imperceptible that it might not have been there at all, but Zoe had spent enough time with Billie now to recognise a change in her demeanour when she saw it. Had Corrine inadvertently stumbled on the catalyst for Billie's recovery? She'd lived for so long in the shadow of her grief for the man she'd lost, the man who hadn't ever known about his baby, and in fear of what her life might be raising that baby alone, that Zoe had never known her without it.

'It's all a bit of fun anyway.' Corrine moved her creation to one side to make a space on the worktop. 'It's only to raise money for charity; in the end, it doesn't really matter who wins as long as lots of people join in. Now then...' She took off her apron, tossed it into the washing machine and then took a clean one from a drawer, fastening it over her dress. 'Who's for a bite to eat? I thought I'd make some ham sandwiches and a nice cup of tea.'

12

The following evening, Zoe slipped off her coat, red-cheeked from her walk over the fields to Hilltop Farm. Alex took it from her to hang up with his own while Zoe kicked off her boots, the chill of the stone floor of Hilltop's kitchen seeping through her socks. It wasn't unwelcome. They'd walked quickly and despite the freezing conditions outside, she'd worked up a sweat. 'Something smells good.'

'It's probably Billie,' Alex called as he returned and took off his own boots to sit at the back door. 'Are you in?' he called to the empty room.

Grizzle rushed through, wagging his tail and leaping around them in circles.

'Hello!' Zoe bent to fuss him.

A moment later, Billie's voice made her look up. Alex's daughter was taking a glass to the sink.

'Have you been baking again?' Alex asked.

Billie nodded. 'I tried some different things in the ginger-bread. I've been watching some cooking videos. I asked Corrine about vanilla and she said it might be nice. She'd never put it with ginger before, but I wasn't so sure when I made some. I did some with caramel too, and that was all right.' She gave an aimless shrug. 'The thing is, I don't know if I'm tasting stuff right.'

'How can you not taste stuff right?' Alex asked.

Billie shot him a withering look. 'Because I'm pregnant. Everything is weird when you're pregnant.'

'She's got a point,' Zoe said.

'OK.' Alex grinned sheepishly. 'The man will shut up now.'

Billie took a seat at the table. 'Anyway, there isn't that much time to keep messing around now. I'll have to decide soon because it's in a few days, isn't it? And I still need to get the hang of building the house. I mean, I know I'm not going to win or anything, but I don't want it to be embarrassing.'

'Don't worry, I'll do the embarrassing for you,' Zoe said. 'I can't see anyone else having to worry about winning the booby prize.'

'Yours didn't taste that bad,' Alex said.

'Liar,' Zoe replied with a grin, and he grinned back, not even trying to argue.

Billie ruffled Grizzle's fur as he rested his head on her lap, his huge brown eyes staring up at her with adoration. 'I'm not going to get my hopes up either.'

Zoe exchanged a brief look with Alex. He'd been encouraged to hear how well things had gone the evening they'd spent learning to make gingerbread with Corrine at Daffodil Farm and noted for himself how she'd returned home with a cautious enthusiasm. They'd discussed how good it would be for her to have something to do that would take her mind off her worries. It was only a silly village event, but Zoe suspected it meant much more than that. Perhaps it would signal the start of Billie's rehabilitation. Perhaps she would finally begin to enjoy life again and move on from the bitter losses of the past couple of years. And perhaps she might finally begin to see herself as a capable young woman. Who knew what that might mean for her future and that of her baby?

It seemed, in one way or another, that many of Zoe's expectant mums had been on her mind. Since her impromptu chat with Maisie in her clinic, Zoe had been pondering what to do about her too. Maisie had dutifully returned the following day, and they'd had another frank conversation about nutrition, and Zoe had – yet again – issued her with recipe cards and pamphlets full of information, but she still wasn't certain that her advice would cut through the noise coming from everyone else in Maisie's life. In particular, Maisie's mum, Bridget, seemed to have too much influence. Ordinarily, Zoe had no issue with supportive family members – in fact they were mostly to be encouraged – but Bridget had some odd ideas, and not all of them, as far as Zoe could tell, had Maisie's best interests at heart.

Maisie was younger than Billie but only by a couple of years, and the one thing Billie had that Maisie didn't was a stronger sense of herself. She wasn't swayed so easily by the opinions of others, and she had a more mature, practical outlook. Zoe had toyed with the idea of setting up a village support group for her pregnant mums, but she'd wondered whether it would be a waste of time. She had enough to keep her busy in clinic, but whether the numbers willing to be part of such a group would be enough to make it viable was a different matter. She'd suggested to one or two they go along to the existing mum and baby group run by Stacey at the village hall, but was aware it probably wasn't what they needed, especially if it was a first baby who hadn't yet arrived.

The idea occurred to her now, as she turned her gaze back to Billie. Maybe Billie and Maisie could be good for one another. It wasn't exactly a support group in the strictest sense, but they might be able to offer support to one another – albeit in very different ways. Billie needed something to restore her confidence and sense of worth, and Maisie needed someone who would encourage her to stand up for herself, perhaps to show an example with a little more common sense than the people she currently had around her. She needed to find a way to frame it that might persuade Billie it was a good idea, and that was the first problem Zoe could see with the plan.

'The shopping arrived,' Billie said, breaking into Zoe's thoughts. 'I put it away.'

'I said I'd do it when I got back,' Alex said. 'You shouldn't have strained yourself.'

Billie rolled her eyes. 'It's hardly straining myself. The heaviest thing in there was a bag of peas, which would have been defrosted if I'd left them in the bag for you to put away. I can still do stuff, you know, Dad.'

'I know. I worry you'll—'

'I won't,' Billie cut in. 'Stop fussing. Did you see Victor's girls?'

'We did,' Zoe said. 'They're as cute as ever.'

'And greedy,' Alex said. 'Love their treats.'

'A bit like Victor with Corrine's cakes then,' Zoe said with a grin. 'They say dogs look like their owners, but maybe alpaca behave like theirs?'

'Dogs look like their owners?' Alex eyed Grizzle. 'God help me then.'

'I didn't like to say anything, but now that you mention it...' Zoe grinned at Billie.

'Oi!' Alex said. 'Who's to say it's me who looks like Griz?'

'Everyone,' Billie said. 'Because you do.'

'Thanks a bunch. So, enough of that. What shall we eat?' Alex asked as he went to the fridge. 'It looks like everything is here. No substitutes?'

'Don't think so,' Billie said. 'I thought I'd cook, actually.'

'You don't have to...' Billie met his protests with a deep

frown, and he smiled. 'All right, that sounds nice. What were you thinking of?'

Billie turned to Zoe. 'You like curry, right?'

'I like everything,' Zoe said.

'OK, cool. So I thought I'd make a chicken curry.'

'Want some help?'

'Nah, I'm better doing it on my own – I'll only get annoyed at someone being in the way.'

'Trust me,' Alex said as Zoe looked set to argue. 'I know from experience that's true. Best to sit in the other room until she's done.'

Billie stood up. Zoe had noticed it was taking a little more effort for her to move around over the past week or so, but it was understandable as she was in her third trimester and the baby was getting big. However, as she still wasn't finding pregnancy unduly difficult and, despite Alex's concerns, seemed to have plenty of energy, she was happy to let Billie get on with things. On a selfish note, it meant more time for her and Alex to chat in the living room, and she didn't think she could ever get enough of talking to him – no subject was too boring as long as he wanted to discuss it. If she could have seen herself, she'd have probably told herself to stop being so soppy. It was a good job, in that case, that she couldn't.

Not yet, though. Zoe's thoughts were occupied by the problem of Maisie, and as she hadn't yet found the right way to frame her proposal to Billie, perhaps the only way was to come straight out with it.

'Billie, I've got an expectant mum who comes to clinic,' she began slowly, 'and I must admit I'd appreciate your take on her situation.'

Billie stopped at the door, frowning. 'My take? Are you even meant to talk about other people to me?'

'Well, it's a grey area in this case...'

'You're hardly going to report her, are you?' Alex put in.

'Ordinarily, I'd say you're right,' Zoe continued. 'The point is she's younger than you and not nearly as clued up. I won't say who it is or give you any medical details, I just want to know what you think of an idea I had to help her.'

'Why me?'

'Because you're smart and you have good ideas.'

Billie retook her seat, and Zoe was glad to see she was giving her full attention.

'As I said, she's a couple of years younger than you and a bit naïve even then. Her support network... well, let's just say they mean well but they cause more problems than they solve. The trouble is they're all she's got, and they're dishing out a lot of flawed information and advice, and of course I can't be there all the time keeping an eye on things. I worry they'll unintentionally cause real harm.'

Billie was silent for a moment, and as Alex opened his mouth to offer an opinion, she finally spoke. 'I don't know what I'm supposed to do about it.'

'Nothing,' Zoe said. 'Not unless you want to.'

'What does that even mean?' Billie asked.

Zoe took a moment before starting again. 'You're right – I'm not doing a very good job of explaining the situation. I had thought about starting a support group for my mums, but in a place as small as Thimblebury, I'm not sure it would work. But it might be that some of you, in a more casual way, could offer support to one another.'

'You want me to sort her out?' Billie asked, her tone straying into impatience.

'Doesn't it sound familiar, though?' Alex asked. 'A first-timer with a family who doesn't have a clue what you need?'

'It's hardly like that for us,' Billie said. 'You're a bit clueless, but you're not putting me in danger.'

'I might have done, if not for Zoe's advice.'

Zoe shook her head. 'That's not true. Billie's right about that

– it's not the same at all. And I'm not expecting anyone to *sort her out* – I just think talking to someone in a similar situation might help her.'

'We're both pregnant, but that doesn't mean we have loads in common.'

'She doesn't have the dad around either. Of course,' Zoe added hastily, 'it's a very different situation to yours, but the fact still stands. You're way more clued up than she is, and if she could be half as savvy as you, it would make my life a lot easier.'

Billie looked doubtful. 'I don't know what I'm doing half the time.'

'Neither does she. In the end, it might be that she helps you as much as you help her.'

Billie paused for a moment and then gave her head an emphatic shake. 'No. I'm not getting involved.'

'I understand,' Zoe said with a small smile. 'It was worth a shot, though. I need to find a way to dilute her mum's influence, that's all.'

'At least she has a mum,' Billie said. 'And just because you don't rate what her mum has to say doesn't mean it's wrong.'

'Billie!' Alex began to admonish her, but Zoe cut across.

'It's all right. I know what Billie means. I sound like an interfering professional, and perhaps I am.' She turned back to Billie. 'It's not a problem. I'm only trying to do whatever I can to help her. I thought a friend who understands some of what she's going through might be the answer. I'll think of something else, I'm sure.'

'You could at least give it some consideration,' Alex said but was met by stony silence from his daughter.

'Leave it,' Zoe said, afraid that pushing the request would sour the atmosphere. She wanted to help Maisie but not at the expense of her fragile new relationship with Billie. 'It was unprofessional of me to ask; I realise that now.'

'I'm going to cook,' Billie said, leaving the room before anyone had time to comment on her plan either way.

Alex turned to Zoe with a look of unnecessary apology. It was hardly his fault, and Zoe was already beginning to regret trying to involve them.

Alex was loading the dishwasher after their meal while Billie and Zoe went into the living room. Billie flicked idly through the TV channels.

'The curry was really good,' Zoe said. 'You're a brilliant cook.'

'We had a neighbour in Spain who taught me how to make loads of things.'

'Oh. Well, they did a good job.'

'Yeah, thanks.' Billie turned off the television and tossed the remote down. 'This girl.'

'Which... You mean Maisie?'

'That's her name? The clueless one you were telling me about earlier.'

'I wouldn't go as far as to say clueless, but... well, you could say she's a bit... inexperienced.'

'I've been thinking, and if you want me to talk to her, I will. Don't think we're going to be best friends or anything, but I'll meet with her. I can't make any promises, though.'

'I don't want you to. Nobody would expect you to spend time with someone you don't gel with. I do appreciate you giving her a chance, though.'

'What do you want to do about it?'

'I hadn't got that far yet. To be honest, the idea only occurred to me earlier on, and I haven't thought much beyond asking you. I'm not even sure I'm meant to be doing it at all.'

'If you want, you can give her my number and say I'm new and I've got no mates here or whatever, and it'll look like she's doing me the favour and you're just trying to find me a friend. What does it matter if I look like a loser? Sounds like I can't be a bigger loser than she is.'

Zoe couldn't help but grin. That wasn't how she'd put it either, but she was starting to recognise statements like this as Billie's humour.

'Thank you,' she said. 'I'll message her tomorrow. I think it will really help.'

'We'll see,' Billie said. 'She might not want to talk to me.'

'True, but nothing ventured nothing gained. I'm just glad of the offer.'

They both looked towards the door as Alex came in, rattling a tin at them.

'Dad!' Billie groaned. 'Those are the Christmas chocolates!'

'It's almost Christmas,' he said with an impish look. 'Technically it starts at the beginning of December, doesn't it, so technically *it is* Christmas. Or like pre-Christmas?'

Billie shook her head with such resignation that Zoe had to laugh. 'There's no hope for him, is there?'

13

If Zoe was worried about Maisie's reaction to her suggestion that she might like to connect with Billie, she needn't have been. On her lunch break the following day, she made a quick call with the concocted story, and Maisie seemed flattered by Zoe's request. It was difficult to know what that meant for how it would play out, and Zoe wondered if she'd come to regret putting these particular wheels in motion, but she passed on Billie's number anyway and decided to let the two young women work it out for themselves. The rest of her work day was routine, but it was still busy, and by the time she'd seen the last appointment out and cleaned her room, she was ready for a hot bath and a night in front of the television. She and Alex had agreed on at least two nights a week where they didn't meet up, and though they were both finding those nights torture, she agreed it was a good idea to have some time apart – if only so Billie didn't start to feel neglected.

She'd just arrived home, courtesy of a lift from Victor through snow that was frozen into hard drifts on the roadsides, when a text from Georgia came through.

How do I know if I'm having Braxton Hicks or the real thing?

Trust me, when you have the real thing, you'll know! It won't be long now! Do you need me to come over?

Yes, but only because I'm bored and I need you to entertain me. Where have you been all week?

You saw me three days ago!

Feels like forever. Am I on rations now? Come over. I have crisps. Lots of crisps. I need help eating them.

What about Brett?

He's out. Emilia is working. I'm so bored I might go into labour right now.

Zoe gave a small smile. She didn't reply immediately. She was tired and felt grubby from a day in an office where the heating had been set far too high, and as much as she wanted to oblige Georgia, she also needed some time alone to decompress. It was something that had felt in short supply recently, scarcer and scarcer as she became more deeply involved in the lives of Alex and Billie, and now Georgia. Not to mention the expectant mums in her care and all her other new friendships. Her visits to Ottilie, Stacey, and Corrine and Victor might have been more casual, but collectively they all ate into the time she had simply to exist as herself.

However, she had always found it almost impossible to ignore a call for help, and the more she thought about it, the more she recognised a subtext to Georgia's messages. Bored meant lonely. Brett was out again, and Emilia was working late. Did neither of them see that Georgia needed their support? Emilia had said as much to Zoe, and yet she didn't seem to be doing her bit. As for Brett... Zoe was beginning to see that he was rarely around. When she'd visited that first time, he'd been absent, and every time Georgia texted in the days since, there would be some hint – if not explicitly said – that he wasn't there with her. What was he doing? Where on earth could he be sneaking off to all the time? It was especially perplexing when Zoe thought about how close Georgia's labour was – most men would be making the effort to be around more, not less, on standby for the big event. Georgia was due on New Year's Day, so in her case the big event was extremely imminent.

After another moment of indecision that she decided was a bit on the uncharitable side, she texted back.

> *Can you give me an hour? Need to shower and get my head on straight, then I'll call to see you.*

> *If you're tired, there's no pressure. You don't have to. Sorry, I didn't think. I bet you've had a hard day.*

> *Honestly, it's fine. It will be lovely to chat, and you can tell me all about your plans for when the baby arrives! See you around 7.30?*

> *I'd love that, thank you!*

By the time Zoe showed up at Emilia's house, Brett had returned from wherever it was he'd been. He was polite as he greeted her but tense, and it looked as though Georgia had been crying. Zoe wanted to ask but realised it might not be the right moment – if it was even her business at all.

Despite this, Georgia gave Zoe a broad smile and a warm hug. 'You know you really didn't have to come out in the cold if you didn't feel like it, but is it bad that I'm glad you did?'

'Aww, no, it's not. Sometimes I need a kick up the backside – it's too easy to stay home and rot. I'm glad I came out. I can't stay late, though, if that's all right. Alex dropped me off. He says I can phone him to come and get me in a few hours.'

'Alex?'

'He was coming down to the village anyway, and he knows I'm not fond of driving down that hill in the dark. I can't say I'm always fond of walking it – it's so steep! I mean, I get on with it when I have to, but it's nice to have a lift.'

'Alex doesn't need to come out – Brett and I can take you home.'

'It's fine. I can—'

'I insist! Brett – we'll take Zoe home later, won't we?'

Zoe decided, looking at Brett's face as he put the can of beer he'd just taken from the fridge back with a barely disguised sigh of impatience, she'd rather go up to Kestrel Cottage blindfolded on roller skates than have him drive her. He nodded stiffly before she had time to protest again.

'Of course we will. Tell your boyfriend not to worry about it. It's not like I've got anything else to do...' he added as he left the kitchen.

Perhaps he'd assumed it was under his breath, but Zoe heard well enough. She watched him go. She was no expert on body language, but she'd seen more positive-looking examples of that too.

Once he was gone, she turned back to Georgia with a painted-on smile. 'So you're making the most of your time in the Lakes? Brett certainly seems to be enjoying being out.'

'He's walking a lot.'

'He likes walking?'

'He's been known to. It wears me out at the moment, so I don't go. And I think he appreciates some quiet time. Let's face it, there'll be precious little of that in a few weeks.'

'Newborns do tend to liven things up. Does he have any paternity leave lined up?'

'No. I mean, yes, he'll have time at home. Probably. It's all a bit up in the air at the moment.'

Zoe wanted to ask why, but again, she couldn't tell if it would be a welcome enquiry or not.

And then Georgia lowered her voice and it seemed the mask finally slipped. 'Things are a struggle right now.'

'For you?'

'For us both. I might as well tell you... I don't know why I was bothering to hide it, really.'

'The pregnancy's been hard?'

'Among other things...' Georgia paused and seemed about to share something significant with her, but then – and it was hard to be sure – seemed to change tack. 'Emilia is helping to look after me, which is more than a lot have. She's been so kind, more than we deserve. I should be grateful I have her. I suppose it's the baby making me feel down, and I really have no right to...'

'It's all right. You don't owe anyone an apology for how you feel. I'm here if you want to get it off your chest.'

'I know, and it's so kind of you, especially when we haven't seen one another for so long.'

'That makes no difference. Old friend, new friend, absent-for-a-while friend... it's still a friend.'

Georgia's eyes filled with tears. 'Look at me – all hormonal!'

'I think you can be forgiven for that. I'm here now if you want to talk. You're welcome to make good use of me.'

'I would, but...' Georgia's gaze went to the door Brett had just left by.

Zoe nodded. 'Maybe next time we can arrange to go out. If the weather improves, at any rate.'

'I'd like that.'

'Not far, of course. We could drive out somewhere, have lunch. Have you been far since you got here? There are some beautiful little towns, and right now they look even prettier with the snow and the Christmas decorations. In fact, Alex took me to Keswick not long ago for the light switch-on, and their decorations are amazing. If you're up to it, we could have a few hours there, get some food, take a look around, maybe get coffee – nothing taxing, of course.'

Georgia gave an enthusiastic nod. 'That sounds lovely. I'd like to see a lot more of the area.'

'You haven't done much exploring yet?'

'None. Brett's been for a few walks, but, like I said, I'd get too puffed out by that so I don't go. And Em's been too busy to take me out in the car. She's got a lot to do, at the surgery, getting straight here... you know.'

'Sounds like it's been boring. There's not much to do in Thimblebury itself other than walking. Hasn't Brett fancied a day trip out?'

'I don't think he's been in the mood for that sort of thing. He's got a lot on his mind.'

Zoe was going to ask more about Brett's worries when the sound of smashing glass reached them from another room. It was followed by Brett swearing. The colour drained from Georgia's face, and the air was suddenly stiff with tension. He wasn't even in the same room as them and yet Brett's mood – whatever it was – overshadowed everything.

14

Someone had whacked the heating in the village hall up so high Zoe was currently stripped down to a T-shirt and was still sweating. What was it with this village and heating?

Ottilie had laughed when they'd been in the shop together and she'd asked the question, having endured yet another overheated day at the surgery, courtesy of Lavender, who'd insisted they had to keep the patients warm. And what with the mood Lavender had been in since her showdown with Emilia over the Christmas decorations, even Zoe realised it was wiser to suffer in silence than challenge her on it. There had been a freezing fog hanging over the hills for days, sure, but, as Magnus had pointed out, anyone would think the world had been plunged into a new ice age the way everyone had gone rushing to their thermostats. Zoe wasn't often one to agree on things like that, but even she was beginning to think people needed to calm down. As people filed in for the gingerbread house competition, shedding coats and hats and scarves and instantly red-faced as the heat hit them, if Lucifer himself had wandered in wearing a pair of Speedos and asking for a bag of ice to cool down, she wouldn't have been a bit surprised.

There were Christmas decorations that had clearly seen a fair few winters pinned to the walls and ceilings, while a lopsided plastic tree, propped up by planks of wood to stop it toppling over, was taking up an entire corner of the room. Lavender had complained about that too, the previous day, having been in to help put the decorations up in readiness for the event.

'There's money for a real one,' she'd grumbled. 'There's money every year, and yet they get that motheaten thing out. I'm surprised it hasn't had an asbestos warning slapped on it by the council, it's so old. I told them I'd go and find one and chop it down myself if it meant I could bin that thing. I have night-mares about it every year until about February.'

Zoe was beginning to think Lavender might take Christmas just a bit too seriously. This had been confirmed earlier that week by Emilia – walking through reception to see a patient out – earning a glare from Lavender, who hadn't forgiven her for not allowing her consultation room to be decorated. Either to her credit, or to her detriment, whichever way you wanted to look at it, Emilia hadn't backed down, not even under the pressure of Lavender's most burning glowers. And when Lavender had snuck in one night after surgery was done and plonked a mini tree on her desk, Emilia had come in the next morning, silently put it on the reception desk in front of Lavender and had then gone back to her office without another word. That had led to Lavender turning up the volume of the Christmas carols playing in reception that week so loud that in the end Mrs Icke had marched to the desk and complained that it was interfering with her hearing aids. So much for the time of peace and love and goodwill to all men.

Zoe turned her attention back to the hubbub in the hall. There were long tables running the length of one of the walls, and on each had been draped a different, Christmas-themed tablecloth. Not a one matched, and some didn't fit the table they were supposed to be covering. The tables weren't exactly even either, and as she looked, Zoe could see Magnus and Geoff trying to stabilise a corner of the one they'd been allocated by shoving an empty folded crisp packet underneath the rogue leg.

As they arrived, other residents found their spot and began to set up. Or not, depending on how secretive and protective they were feeling about their creation.

Stacey, however, had no qualms whacking her gingerbread castle out and pointed to it with a grin. 'Brilliant, eh? Like someone who'd never seen a house and someone who'd never made gingerbread wrote an instruction manual on how to make a gingerbread house and I accidentally used it.'

'It's not that bad,' Geoff said.

Stacey laughed. 'Oh, shut up, you moron! Of course it is – it's horrible! I don't know why I put myself through this every year.'

Still laughing to herself, she wandered off to the urn that was being manned by someone from the playgroup to get a cup of tea.

Magnus, on the other hand, once he and Geoff had secured their wonky table, kept his creation in a plastic storage box, and though he took the lid off and peered inside, he quickly put it back on and stood with his arms folded, scanning the competition as they unpacked around him. Geoff went to take the lid off again, and Magnus slapped his hand away.

'It's not time yet!' Zoe heard him say. 'Someone might knock it!'

Geoff let out a sigh loud enough for her to hear at the other side of the room and then followed Stacey to get a cup of tea of his own.

Magnus wasn't the only one acting like aliens had replaced them with a copy. People who were usually calm – not that Zoe knew the wider village all that well – were nervy and short-tempered as they arrived and set up their space. Zoe watched all the mini dramas unfold – neighbours going to greet one another, gushing praise for their entry followed by a sneaky look that wondered if theirs was better. What was even more interesting was that all this competitiveness was for nothing. The prize, such as it was, was hardly worth having at all. Regardless, she couldn't deny it was hard not to get caught up in the drama, and Zoe hadn't yet put her own house on display, choosing to leave it in the box for a while, if only because she didn't want people coming over to examine it and leaving with a smug, gloating look on their face when they saw she would be no threat at all.

'You'd think the prize was a million pounds,' Billie said coolly as she took the lid from a plastic box. She glanced over at Zoe's, still sealed. 'Aren't you going to get yours out?'

'I will... in a minute.'

'It's not that bad,' Billie said. 'You made a new one, right? It's not the one you showed me the other day?'

'Why?' Zoe asked with a wry smile. 'Was the one I showed you that bad?'

'No, it was good.'

'Liar.'

'It was... I mean... so you brought that one?'

'I didn't have time to make another.'

'Oh. Well, it's fine.'

'Hmm, I'm not sure the judges will agree, but thanks for trying to make me feel better.'

'Anyway, I thought you said it was for charity and it didn't matter.'

'That was before I got here. Now everyone's looks way better than mine and I don't think I like it.'

'There ought to be a prize for coming last. Or for being the best attempt or whatever.'

'Like at school when you'd get a gold star for effort in wood-work, even though all the legs had fallen off the chair you'd made?'

'I never did woodwork.'

'I bet you were annoyingly good at pretty much everything else though.'

'I don't know. You'd have to ask Dad. Can I get a hand with this...? I'm scared I might drop it or knock a bit off.'

'Yes, of course...' Zoe helped Billie to lift her creation from the box, giving a low whistle as it emerged. She'd seen one of Billie's practice runs, and she'd tasted some of her flavour experiments, but this was the first time she'd seen the end result.

'It looks all right?' Billie asked.

'It looks great! You did all this by yourself?'

'Dad held some bits for me while I stuck it together, but yeah, more or less.'

'By the way, did Maisie call?'

'She sent me a message.'

'And?'

'It was fine. We might meet up, but it's all been messages so far.'

'Right. Do you think you might get on?'

'Who knows?' Billie said carelessly. 'We will or we won't – no point in stressing about it.'

'I suppose so. I'd feel better just knowing she had someone other than... well, someone to confide in.'

Zoe decided to close the subject for now. It probably wasn't the time or the place, though Maisie's predicament was often on her mind and she'd hoped Billie would have arranged to meet her by now. It was then she turned her attention back to the room and noticed one or two other competitors looking their way. Some seemed surprised to see Billie's entry, some less than pleased and some merely resigned.

Zoe turned her gaze back to it. In a sense, it was quite traditional and basic in construction. Since she'd been here, Zoe had seen ambitious attempts at fairy-tale castles, Santa grottoes and hobbit holes. Someone had built a church –

though it was nowhere near as good as the one she'd seen in Corrine's kitchen the time Victor had been eating the gravestones – and someone else had built a model of the village school, complete with marzipan choristers lined up in the grounds. She had yet to see Magnus's with her own eyes, but Ottilie had told her that Stacey had seen it and said it was a replica of the iconic cathedral in Reykjavik and the best she'd ever seen Magnus build.

Billie's was a house like any other – four walls and a roof, a chimney and a garden. But there was something so precise about it, so delicate and detailed that Zoe could see immediately the artistic flair that Corrine had spotted in her right at the beginning. Not only that, but Zoe already knew it would taste amazing.

As Billie checked it over, Zoe noticed Corrine arrive, Victor trailing after her with a huge box in his arms. After greeting a few people, they both made their way over, Corrine's allocated spot being next to Zoe's. A little unfair, Zoe had felt, but perhaps someone on the organising committee had a sense of humour.

Zoe smiled their way, but Corrine was peeling her coat off, tense and grumbling in a way Zoe wasn't used to seeing. It was clear that, despite what she'd said in the lead-up, this contest meant more to her than she'd let on.

'Someone needs to go and tell them about the temperature in here! The heat will have everyone's icing melting! I don't know why they didn't do it in the church like they did last year. It's far colder in my kitchen, so I don't know what that'll do to my joins!'

'I don't think you're the first person to say so,' Zoe replied. 'At least that's what I heard. Perhaps they'll do something about it.'

'Want me to have a word?' Victor asked, and at least he was his usual amiable self.

'Flo will be here shortly,' Corrine said. 'She'll have something to say about it.'

'Fair enough.' Victor put the box down, examined his palm and then licked it.

Corrine stared at him. 'What on earth are you doing?'

'Icing. On my hand. I'm not going to let a blob of icing go to waste, am I?'

'Icing?' Corrine flew to the box and opened it, peering in with an expression that, if Zoe hadn't known better, might have looked like borderline panic. 'Where's it from?'

'I think some went on the table when you dusted last thing – must have got on the bottom of the box.'

'Icing sugar, you clown!' Corrine put a hand to her chest. 'Don't do that to me! I thought something had broken off!' But then she paused, finally noticing Billie's entry. Her face transformed in an instant, impatience replaced by a huge smile. 'This is yours, my love?'

'I love how you automatically assume it's Billie's and not mine,' Zoe said wryly.

Corrine turned to her in some confusion. 'Oh, I'm sorry, Zoe. It's yours?'

Zoe had to laugh at the utter disbelief in her tone, even as she asked. 'No, it's Billie's. I wish it was mine. I'll tell you one thing this experience has taught me – there's no point in me applying for *Bake Off*.' She glanced at her own box. 'I might as well get this out now. Standing next to yours and Billie's, what's the use in even pretending it's not an actual embarrassment?'

'Oh, Zoe...' Corrine said, shaking her head. 'I'm sure it's not that bad.'

'It is.' Zoe opened the box. 'But it's all about the taking part, remember? A bit of fun that doesn't matter.'

'Of course it is.'

Zoe and Corrine took theirs out at the same time, and Zoe realised hers was even worse than she'd feared. The most she could congratulate herself on was that it was in one piece. That in itself was a miracle when she considered how flimsy and badly engineered it was. Though she agreed with Corrine about the heat – her construction might not stay in one piece for long if her sugary mortar started to melt. Corrine glanced at Zoe's and then seemed almost embarrassed to remove the wax paper she'd had protecting her own.

Billie almost gasped. 'Corrine! That's so good!'

'Oh, it'll do,' Corrine excused. 'Not my best, but I didn't have time to do another one.'

'You thought you needed to do another one?' Zoe asked. 'What kind of mad perfectionist are you?'

'The worst kind,' Victor said. 'An angel all year, but stay out of her way in the kitchen when she's making her Christmas competition entry.'

'Don't be daft...' Corrine grumbled but looking sheepish enough for Zoe to know there might be a little truth in Victor's statement. She glanced towards the entrance. 'Here come Ottilie and Flo. Wait for the complaining to start.'

'Not by Ottilie,' Zoe said.

Corrine winked at her. 'You're learning fast. Oh Lord, and there's Mrs Icke.'

'Does she even have a first name?' Zoe asked. 'Because I don't think I've ever heard anyone use it since I've been here. I work at the surgery and she's in almost every week, and I still don't know what it is!'

'Do you know,' Victor said, 'it's so long since I've heard it used. I can't remember what it is either.'

'Nobody likes her enough to care,' Billie said, but then flushed as Corrine gave her a look that was gentle but obviously chastising. 'That's what I heard anyway,' she added lamely.

'She's hard work, yes,' Corrine said, 'but she's been through more in her life than any of us could ever imagine. If I get to her age having survived all she has, I hope I can be forgiven for being a bit impatient with folks.'

Zoe watched Lavender greet Ottilie and Flo briefly before taking Mrs Icke over to her space on the tables. The old woman was as combative as always, but Lavender was showing remarkable patience with her. Ottilie went with Flo to put their boxes down a few tables away before coming over to say hello properly to Zoe and her companions.

'These are looking good,' she said, eyeing all three gingerbread constructions. 'Whose is whose?'

'As if you couldn't guess which one is mine,' Zoe said.

Ottilie let out a light laugh. 'I don't like to assume.'

'This is mine,' Corrine said, pointing.

'So that's yours?' Ottilie smiled at Billie. 'That's really good.'

'Can I come and look at yours, Ottilie?' Zoe asked. 'I'm all set here now.'

'If you want,' Ottilie said. 'But prepare to be underwhelmed. And I have to warn you that it also means talking to Flo, who isn't in one of her most tolerant moods today.'

'In that case, consider it a rescue mission.'

Ottilie and Zoe wandered over to Ottilie's bench.

'I can't believe how good Billie's is,' Zoe said. 'Actually, that sounds harsh, doesn't it? I didn't mean I don't think she had the talent, just that I didn't realise she had that much patience.'

'I'm surprised to see she bothered at all. From what you've told me, I wouldn't have thought she'd be interested in this sort of thing. Especially at her age. She's about the same age as Chloe, who told Stacey in no uncertain terms she wouldn't be seen dead at something like this.'

'I know what you mean. I think Corrine's encouragement has helped. I think it's exactly what she's been needing.'

'A sort of mother figure?'

Zoe nodded, and Ottilie shot a warm glance back towards where Corrine and Billie were working out their problem.

'She's that all right. We might have to crown her village mum because I certainly felt that way about her when I first moved here. I don't know what I would have done without her and Victor, but I'm sure I wouldn't still be in Wordsworth Cottage.'

'Me too. They both have this way of making you feel settled and that someone's looking out for you, like they – Corrine especially – have a way of knowing what you need before even you do.'

Flo looked up at their approach. She'd been fussing over a string of what looked like the fake grass you saw on the food trays in delicatessens, trying to get it in the right place around her house.

'It's all wonky,' she grumbled at Ottilie. 'I said we needed to lay it out, but you said no, it'll be fine rolled up in a tub. And now look at it!'

'Want me to stamp on it?' Ottilie asked with such mischievous mock innocence it was all Zoe could do not to burst out laughing. 'The weight of me these days ought to straighten it out easily enough.'

'Don't be daft...' Flo straightened up and tossed the strip onto the table with some disgust. 'I'll have to do without it.' She nodded at Zoe. 'Morning. I see you've come to look at mine. Hoping it'll be bad so you'll have a better chance of winning. I wouldn't bother. We all know who's going to win, don't we? It's a foregone conclusion, as it is every year. I don't know why anyone else bothers.'

'It's really good,' Zoe said, paying Flo's house closer attention. 'Very cute. I like the little snowdrifts around the walls.'

'It's not bad, if I do say so myself,' Flo acknowledged. 'But I haven't got the ear of the judges, have I?'

'I don't think that's the reason Corrine wins,' Ottilie said, clearly trying to keep a frown of disapproval from her features. 'It seems a bit mean to say so.'

'You wait until you've been here a few more years,' Flo fired back, unbothered by Ottilie's faint warning tone. 'We'll see if you still feel that way. All the people in this room come every year, and the same one wins time after time, and if that's not a fix, I don't know what is.'

'It could be that Corrine is just a way better baker than the rest of us?' Zoe offered. 'That's not to say there aren't other good bakers here, only that she's on another level. That's how it is sometimes, right?'

'She gets enough practice,' Ottilie agreed. 'She can whip up a Victoria sponge in her sleep.'

'And it would be the best sponge you've ever had,' Zoe added.

'Hmph,' was all that Flo replied before turning back to her strip of plastic grass and trying again.

Zoe watched her for a moment. Everything about Flo was spiky. She was Heath's grandmother and so Ottilie was forced to spend time with her, and yet Zoe knew that, despite her brusqueness, Ottilie also liked the old woman. Zoe, no matter how hard she tried, couldn't see why. She'd given up over the past couple of weeks, content to imagine there must be hidden depths only Ottilie had seen. *Very* hidden depths, like the sort you'd need oxygen tanks to find.

'I wonder if Emilia will pop in?' Ottilie wondered out loud, interrupting Zoe's thoughts.

'I doubt it,' Zoe replied. 'For one, Lavender's here. And she doesn't seem to be much of a fan of Christmas anyway.'

'I know. Fliss wasn't a fan of village events either, but there were some, like this, she made an exception for. Once or twice she helped to judge. Emilia hasn't said anything about being approached to judge?'

'Georgia hasn't said anything if she has.'

'Simon turned the judging role down. Very politely, of course. It's a shame, but I get why. Said he didn't feel able because he didn't know enough about it. And I suppose he didn't feel he could be seen as impartial when Stacey was putting in an entry. Or Magnus, for that matter, considering he's Stacey's brother-in-law.'

'More like he didn't want to get involved in the village politics,' Zoe said. 'As if you need to know anything beyond "does it look good?" and "does it taste nice?" to judge some gingerbread houses.'

'I'd say that's about right, but...' Ottilie angled her head subtly in Flo's direction. 'You can hardly blame him for wanting to stay out of it.'

Zoe was distracted from their conversation by another thought. 'Georgia said she was going to come and bring a little something.'

'Emilia's sister?'

Zoe nodded. 'At least I thought that's what she said. Last time I saw her, she mentioned joining in. She's not here, though. Hope she's all right.'

'She could be running late. Or she might have decided not to bother in the end. She is almost ready to pop, after all.'

'True. I was hoping she would, though.'

'Why's that?'

Zoe turned to her. 'No reason. Well, there is a reason, but it's nothing important, just that I thought it might be good for her. She seems a bit...' She shook her head. 'I don't know. Sometimes you get a feeling about something, don't you?'

'You think something isn't right with her? It would explain Emilia. Every time I talk to her, I get the sense she's stressed out about something, and it's nothing to do with work.'

'I get that too. It must be a lot, when you think about it, though.'

'Moving to a new place, new job and having your sister and brother-in-law staying with you? You can say that again! I mean, I loved having my sister living with me for those few months, but it wasn't plain sailing.'

'It can't have helped with what happened between your sister and Victor's son-in-law either.'

'The affair, you mean. Well, no, but...' Ottilie paused. 'Has Georgia ever said why? Not that there's any law against staying with your sister, of course, but it does seem an odd way to go about things. Like, sure, you'd ask her to come and stay at some point but maybe not when you're trying to settle in yourself.'

'I'll text her before this starts,' Zoe said, starting back to her own table where she'd left her phone. 'Sorry, you don't mind...?'

'Of course not. I'll catch up with you later.'

Zoe composed her text to Georgia:

> Not sure if you've forgotten but the gingerbread competition is about to start. You've changed your mind about entering?

Zoe paused, watching the screen of her phone as if she might will a reply. After thirty seconds or so, she put it down, close by so she could hear a reply if it came through, and went about making some last-minute adjustments to her own display. Not that it would really make any difference. She had to agree with Flo on one thing – looking at both Corrine and Billie's entries and then glancing across the room to see Magnus's cathedral looking impressive too, there didn't seem any point in fretting about her own entry. The winner was going to be one of those three, and anyone in that room would be forced to agree if asked.

She checked her phone again. There was still nothing from Georgia, and for reasons she couldn't put her finger on, that bothered her. Part of it was the obvious fact that Georgia was now very close to term and the potential for her to go into labour while she was a guest at Emilia's house was very real, but there was another aspect to the situation that troubled Zoe, and it was that underlying, unshakeable feeling that all was not right with her, no matter how happy she tried to look when Zoe was around. Zoe had to admit she could have been mistaken, and perhaps she simply didn't know Georgia that well any more. But even taking that into consideration, there was Brett's unfathomable detachment whenever Zoe ran into him, and Emilia's obvious preoccupation that Zoe was convinced had to be about more than just work. It was frustrating because Zoe hardly knew them, really, and she had no baseline to know for sure that anything was wrong. Her gut was telling her something – she just wished she could be certain of what it was.

'How long do we have before they start the judging?' Zoe asked Corrine.

'Around ten minutes, I'd say, though these things never start on time. Why do you ask?'

'I need to pop out. Could you keep an eye on things here?'

'Yes, but is there anything I can do to—'

'No, no... I don't think I'll be long; I just want to check on something.'

'Something or someone?' Corrine asked with a shrewd look.

Zoe smiled. 'Someone.'

'Go and check on her then,' Corrine said. 'If it will put your mind at rest.'

'I'll try to be back before the judging starts, but if I'm not, would you please apologise to them for mine and let them know I don't plan to subject their eyes to such horrors again next year.'

Corrine smiled, and though it was warm, it was tinged with a hint of concern. Zoe hadn't wanted to worry her, but perhaps her own vague, unknowable worries were tangible enough to spread. She grabbed her coat and headed out into the cold.

15

Zoe knocked at the front door. When there was no answer, she knocked again. This time, Emilia came to the door. It was odd to see her in less formal attire, bundled up as she was in a thick, oversized cardigan and some tracksuit bottoms. She almost didn't look like herself.

'Oh... Zoe... what is it?'

'I came to see if Georgia was planning to bring something to the gingerbread contest. She's all right, isn't she? Only I thought she'd said she wanted to do it, and it's about to start, so...'

'She's fine,' Emilia said. 'Tired but that's to be expected, isn't it?'

'It is. So there's nothing else? Nothing to be concerned about...?'

'With the pregnancy? No, I don't think so.'

'But she's not planning to come... Actually, I don't suppose she's in? I might as well ask her about it myself, hadn't I?'

'She's resting.'

'Oh. Asleep?'

Before Emilia could reply, Zoe heard noises coming from inside the house. A crashing thud, and then Georgia's voice.

With sudden alarm, she looked at Emilia. But just as she was about to rush in, thinking it must be Georgia who'd fallen, Georgia herself appeared in the hallway.

'Em, I need you, Brett's— Oh... hi, Zoe.'

For the first time since Zoe had reconnected with her old friend, Georgia seemed less than pleased to see her.

'Everything all right?' Zoe asked.

'Yes, why shouldn't it be?'

'I don't know, I just... Well, you said you were going to bake for the gingerbread house contest, and it's today, so...'

'I was, but I didn't get time.'

Zoe found that hard to believe, but perhaps she was being unfair. Maybe it was a case of Georgia not having the energy – and that was understandable given how pregnant she was. Something was definitely off here, though – Zoe just knew it. And then Brett emerged from a door in the hallway, blood running down the side of his face, and Zoe gasped, causing Emilia and Georgia to turn around.

'What happened?' Emilia demanded.

'I was coming to get you,' Georgia said. 'He fell.'

Brett was the only person who didn't seem very concerned about his injury. Instead, he fixed a swaying stare on Zoe. 'It's you...'

Emilia rushed to prop him up. After sitting him on a step, she examined the cut on the side of his head that was causing all the blood.

Zoe stepped inside. 'Can I help?'

'No,' Emilia said. 'I can manage. It's not deep.'

'But I could get some water, ring an ambulance or—'

'I said I could manage!' Emilia snapped, hauling Brett up and leading him down the hallway to the kitchen at the end.

Georgia turned a mortified gaze on Zoe, her eyes filling with tears. 'Sorry,' she said. 'She didn't mean it like that.'

'I know. Is he OK?'

'He'll be fine.'

'Look, I know Emilia said... but do *you* want me to stay? I could sit with you, if it helps.'

'I don't think it would be a good idea. I'm sorry about the gingerbread thing.'

'That's all right – it doesn't matter.'

'I was going to do it, but things got in the way.'

'I can imagine.'

There was a heavy pause, so long it became uncomfortable, and then Zoe shook herself, realising there was no point in hanging around. She wanted to help, but she understood that it wasn't necessarily welcome, and whatever the reason for that might be, she had to respect it.

'I hope it's a good day,' Georgia said as Zoe turned to go. 'Hope you win.'

'There's not much chance of that, but thanks,' Zoe said, forcing a careless smile. 'As long as you're OK. Shall I phone you later? I could fill you in on all the gossip that I hear today.'

'I'd like... actually, perhaps I'll phone you tomorrow, if that's all right. It might be a bit...'

Georgia didn't finish, and she didn't need to. Zoe understood perfectly well the meaning from the words she hadn't said.

'Whenever you have a minute,' she said. 'Maybe we'll see you at the carol service next week if you can make it?'

'Hope so,' Georgia said before closing the door.

Zoe stood on the step, thoughtful as she processed what she'd just seen. One thing was fairly clear – Brett had been steaming drunk. It was presumably why he'd fallen and why Emilia was so impatient about it. With a sigh, she made her way down the path. There was nothing more to be done here, and she had a competition to lose.

·   ·   ·

When she got back to the village hall, the judging had already begun. One of the dignitaries who'd come to do the job was apparently some celebrity chef who lived locally. The other two were old ladies, one from the WI and the other someone who volunteered at the church. But as Zoe had never been to a WI meeting or to church, she didn't recognise them either. They worked their way methodically down the row of tables, and when Zoe arrived, they were marvelling over Magnus's cathedral. He was clearly trying not to appear too smug, but his chest was puffed out, and he was smiling broadly, while Geoff looked on with pride.

'I think he's in with a chance this year,' Corrine was whispering to Billie as Zoe took off her coat and rejoined them. 'His cathedral is a stroke of genius. I'm surprised he's never made that before.'

'What is it?' Billie asked.

'A cathedral,' Corrine said.

'I've never seen one that looks like that.'

'It's in Iceland.'

'Is that where he's from?'

'Lord, I'm amazed you didn't know,' Corrine said with a low laugh. 'It's not like he never mentions it!' She turned to Zoe as she finally seemed to notice her arrival. 'Everything all right, my love? If you don't mind me saying, you seem flustered. Nothing amiss, is there?'

'No, everything's fine.'

Corrine looked sceptical at Zoe's reply. 'And your friend is all right?'

'Yes, she hadn't had time to make anything in the end, so she didn't think it was worth coming.'

'I see.'

Zoe faced the front to watch the judges close their discussion of Magnus's entry. They scribbled some notes and then moved on to the next, while people whispered and Geoff gave Magnus's arm a little squeeze before following it up with a light kiss. Corrine was smiling as she watched them. And then she did the most extraordinary thing. She'd framed it as an accident, but later, as Zoe considered it, she was certain it hadn't been. Corrine spun round to her own display and knocked the bell-tower clean off.

'Oh dear,' she said, and it was so convincing that both Zoe and Billie stared at her in disbelief. 'Well, that's torn it, hasn't it?'

'Can't you stick it back on?' Billie asked.

'I could, but it will still look a mess.'

'Better than it does now.'

'Yes,' Corrine said. 'You're right. It will look a bit better, won't it?'

Clumsily, she picked up the chimney and plonked it back on top of her house. But the force with which she did it cracked the roof.

'What the hell?' Billie hissed, her tone so dismayed that anyone who didn't know might have thought Corrine had just destroyed her entry.

'Never mind,' Corrine said. 'Can't be helped.'

By now the judges were appraising Flo's entry. She had her arms folded, her body language daring them to utter one word of criticism. The judges, on the other hand, were perfectly courteous, with smiles fixed to their faces as they made more notes on their clipboards. Then they looked at Ottilie's, giving her the briefest of smiles before moving on.

'They didn't spend long on Ottilie's, did they?' Billie said. Zoe tried not to grin because despite the strange and troubling experience at Emilia's house, it was warming to see how invested Billie was in the events happening right here in the village hall. 'I wonder what score they gave her.'

'We'll find out soon enough,' Corrine said.

They watched as the judges continued along the row, stopping to chat briefly and taste bits from everyone's display. Ten minutes later, they reached Zoe and her little group.

'Hello, Corrine!' the woman from the WI greeted her warmly. 'It's lovely to see you again. What do you have for us this year?'

They crowded round as Corrine moved aside, and then the other woman tutted. 'Oh, seems like there's been a bit of an accident here.'

'Just,' Corrine said. 'Can you believe it?'

'Such a shame,' the chef agreed. 'It's a real masterclass of construction too.'

'Isn't it?' the women agreed. 'Shall we taste it?'

They all took a piece and agreed that it was delicious, congratulating Corrine, and then made notes before going on to Zoe's. The look they gave her was more sympathetic.

'It's a very good effort,' the WI woman said. 'I like the little Christmas trees here... May I?'

She plucked a tiny tree from the garden and lifted it to her mouth.

'Oh no!' Zoe reached to take it from her. 'Sorry, they're plastic!'

'Ah!' The woman put it back. 'Is there something on here we can eat?'

'Here...' Zoe plucked the gate from the wall and offered it to her. 'This is probably the least burned, so try this.'

The celebrity chef was stifling a grin. Zoe shared a look with him and shrugged. There was no point in being anything less than honest because they could all see she'd burned most of her gingerbread. She blamed Alex for that, distracting her while she was baking with his soft lips and lovely eyes. She should have told him to go, but she hadn't, and then she'd run out of time to make more. Then again, would it have been all that much better even if she'd been allowed to concentrate?

In fact, the chef didn't take a piece but made some excuse to look at something else while the two women tried it. They both chewed, forcing bright smiles for Zoe.

'Mm... it's quite... gingery.'

'Fiery,' the other agreed. 'Punchy. You wouldn't need a lot to know you've had it.'

Zoe wondered what on earth that meant but guessed it wasn't complimentary. 'Thank you,' she said, now stifling a grin of her own as they turned their attention to Billie's.

'Sorry,' she said. 'Some of the decoration fell off. We got it back, but...'

'It's *lovely*,' the WI woman said. 'Very sweet.'

'Traditional but well executed,' the other said.

The chef abandoned his pretend distraction and rejoined them, reaching to take a section of the garden wall. 'May I?' he asked Billie.

She nodded, and he bit into it.

'Delicious,' he said, and Billie's face transformed.

'Really?' she asked, beaming.

'Very nice. Caramel, if I'm not mistaken?'

'Yes.'

The other judges followed his lead, and they both agreed with him.

'Congratulations!' the WI lady said. 'That's the best bit of gingerbread I've had in a while.'

Billie smiled but then shot a look that was half apology, half embarrassment at Corrine, who simply returned it with a reassuring wink.

'Didn't I say you had natural talent?' she said in a low voice as the judges made notes.

Billie was glowing. Zoe only wished Alex could be here to see it, but she couldn't wait to report everything to him later. Even better, there was a chance Billie might actually win this. It was obvious the judges had been impressed by her efforts.

There were only a few more people to see, and then there was a pub-style quiz where anyone could take part with a prize of dinner at a pub outside the village, followed by a raffle where various bits and pieces of Christmas fare could be won, and then refreshments, and after that the judges were ready to announce their winner.

'In third place...'

The hush in the room was heavy and crackling with antici-pation. Everyone said they had no care for the result or how well they did, but Zoe would bet a lot of those people were either lying to themselves or to the other contestants.

'In third place is Corrine!'

There was a frisson of shock, a polite round of applause and then new excitement as the implications of this bombshell hit everyone else at the same time. Corrine smiled graciously around before sitting down, and Zoe could have sworn she looked pleased about her loss. She'd won this thing for years, after all, and everyone had expected her to do it again.

'And in second place...'

There was another pause, the room almost feverish this time.

'Billie... *Fitzgerald*? The handwriting's a bit wonky, but I think that's right...'

Billie let out a squeal of shock, and Corrine leaped from her chair to hug her as everyone clapped.

'Did they say my name?'

'They did!' Zoe said, hugging her after Corrine let go.

'Are you sure?' Billie asked.

Corrine laughed. 'Yes! They did!'

And then the applause died down and the smiling faces were turned expectantly on the judges again, and then Magnus let out a yelp as they named him the winner. Geoff grabbed him and kissed him with such passion Stacey yelled, 'Get a room!' and then everyone started to laugh, clapping even harder this time, and Magnus, weeping as if he'd won an Oscar, went to get his prize, which was a hefty wooden spoon, decorated with a gingham bow and the year and details of the contest burned into it. Holding it aloft, he beamed around the room.

'Well, there's a turn-up for the books!' Zoe heard someone nearby say, and when she glanced at Corrine, she could see that her neighbour wasn't a bit bothered by the fact she hadn't won the prize that everyone assumed was hers for the taking. Something had changed between Corrine arriving and now. In fact, Zoe had to conclude that Corrine, for reasons of her own, hadn't wanted to win. Even if it were true, she'd never admit as much because Zoe also realised that it would take the shine off Billie's success, and Corrine would never do that.

'It's only a silly competition,' Billie said as they packed up, although her face was still pink with pleasure. 'It's nice to come second, but you don't need to phone Dad about it.'

'He'll be dead proud!' Zoe said, nudging her with affection. 'He'll want to know.'

'We can tell him later when he's back.'

'We can, but surely you can't sit on that news until then? I thought you were happy.'

'I am, but it's not like I won the lottery, is it?'

'What you've got to remember,' Corrine put in as she folded the tablecloth, 'is that this is your first go. You'll only get better at it from here. Next year I bet you'll win.'

'I don't think so. That cathedral Magnus made was really good.'

'True, but a lot depends on the day, so you never can tell.'

'How are you feeling about it?' Zoe asked Corrine. 'I mean, not the result you were hoping for?'

'You can't win every year, can you? That'd be silly. I'm happy for Magnus – he's been desperate for years to get that

'Are you very much in need of coffee after last night?' Zoe asked.

Magnus grinned. 'Geoff has already worked his hangover magic on me. Now I'm only tired, but I have so much to do I'm making coffee to wake up. How are you both feeling?'

'Surprisingly well,' Alex said. 'We both woke up feeling fine, but, as Zoe pointed out earlier, we had that big walk up the hill in the snow, and it probably sobered us up a bit.'

'I'm not sure it's the cure I'd want,' Geoff said, going to a drawer and taking out Zoe's bracelet. He handed it to her.

'Thank you so much for keeping it safe.' Zoe put it around her wrist and fiddled for a moment with the fastening. She frowned and showed it to Alex. 'That'll be why it came off – the catch is broken. See, the hinge there...'

'I'll fix it later,' he said. 'I've got some little tools somewhere that will do that.'

'Really?' She smiled as she slipped it into her bag. 'There's no end to your hidden talents, is there?'

'I try,' he said with a soppy grin.

'We need to buy some Jack Daniels next time we go to get stock,' Geoff said to Magnus as he sat at the island and beckoned Zoe and Alex to do the same.

'It'll be after Christmas now,' Magnus replied.

'I might go tomorrow.'

'We said we weren't going to do that. We said whatever we have in now will have to be enough. We're closed for two days, and most will go out of the village to get what they want for Christmas. We're not going just for that.' He poured coffee into four cups. 'I can't believe we sold out of what we had. We barely sell a bottle of that a year.'

'Yes, well...' Geoff picked up his coffee, and now the alarm bells were clanging in Zoe's head. 'He had to buy vodka today.'

'*Today*?' Magnus paused. 'What do you mean, today?'

'Today. We had no Jack Daniels, and so he took some vodka

instead. I daresay we might have to get a few bottles of that in too, just in case he gets a taste for it.'

'He buys a lot?' Zoe asked, and then it seemed Geoff realised the conversation he'd started with Magnus might not be one to have in front of her and Alex because he simply spooned sugar into his coffee without a reply.

Magnus had no such reservations. 'I don't want to complain about business, but he drinks too much. Someone should tell him. I wonder if we should stop serving it to him.'

'I don't think that would be a very good idea,' Alex said. 'Not from what I saw today.'

If it was possible to combine the two, Magnus looked equal parts horrified and yet thrilled by the prospect of drama. 'Do you think he may be violent?'

'I don't know about that, but it might get awkward for you. It's not really up to you to police someone's alcohol intake anyway, is it?'

'If it was a pub, it would be,' Zoe said.

'Yes, but it's not a pub,' Alex replied patiently. 'Yes, you could refuse to sell it, but I don't know what grounds you could give. I think he'd kick off.'

'We could stop selling alcohol for a while,' Geoff said thoughtfully.

'You really want to do that?' Alex asked. 'This is your livelihood – do you really want to make less money on a thing you know locals buy for the sake of one man? And at the end of the day, business is business. His money is the same as anyone else's. Like I said, it's not up to you to look out for him.'

'I think it is,' Zoe said.

Everyone turned to her.

'It's not just about whether he likes to get drunk or not, or whether he can afford it. I think there's a moral obligation here. If he likes a drink, that's OK, we all do. But there's a line, isn't there? If someone likes a drink so much they're hurting the people around them, then that's crossing the line as far as I'm concerned.'

'But is it up to us to decide if he's crossing the line or not?' Alex asked.

'It's up to us to find out.'

'And then what?' Alex put down his cup and held Zoe in a challenging gaze. For one moment, she wondered if they were about to have their first proper disagreement as a couple. They'd argued before, and it had been horrible, but since they'd got together properly, it had been fairly harmonious. 'I know you have your concerns, but, realistically, what are we meant to do about it? Georgia and Emilia don't want people getting involved – that much is obvious from yesterday.'

'Yesterday?' Magnus asked. 'What happened yesterday?'

'It doesn't matter,' Alex said, turning to Magnus. 'Sorry, but I don't think it's our place to say.'

'Actually,' Zoe said, a sudden idea occurring to her, 'perhaps it is. Magnus and Geoff might have thoughts about it, and it may be that they decide to stop selling booze to him.'

'Since when has that ever stopped an alcoholic getting booze?' Alex asked. 'He'll just go somewhere else. If he wants it badly enough, he'll find a way to get it.'

'Nobody said he was an alcoholic,' Zoe insisted. 'He might not be yet; he might only have a drink problem.'

'Same thing.'

'It's not. Alcohol dependency can be nipped in the bud before it becomes alcoholism.'

Alex arched an eyebrow. 'Is this your professional opinion or wishful thinking?'

'It's neither; it's fact, and don't patronise me.'

'I'm not. I...' Alex paused, perhaps realising that tensions were building and it wasn't the time or place to have an argument. Zoe wouldn't have backed down if it had come to that, but she was glad Alex did.

'I didn't mean to patronise you. I know you're worried – I went with you yesterday to check, remember? There's only so much we can do, that's all I meant. In the end, it's up to him and Georgia to deal with whatever is going on.'

He was right, to a point, but that was the problem as far as Zoe could see. They couldn't be sure anything was going on, and if it was, they couldn't be sure Georgia was equipped to deal with it either.

'I'm worried as her midwife,' she said finally. 'That's my main concern.'

'I get that,' Alex said, and Zoe could see he'd backed away from the fight entirely now. 'I'm sorry; I didn't mean to sound flippant.'

When she looked around, she could see that both Magnus and Geoff were pretending not to follow the discussion, and she had to laugh. 'Crisis over, you two. We're not going to start a fight, so you can look at us again.'

Magnus grinned. 'Thank goodness for that.'

21

When Zoe got to work the following morning, Lavender was slamming a pen down on her desk, muttering under her breath.

'Good morning,' she said with some caution.

'Is it?' Lavender replied. 'You'd think, the way some people speak to you when you come in early to microwave some potatoes for a nice lunch, that it's the first morning of the apocalypse.'

'Oh,' Zoe said, guessing that the new feud that had erupted between Lavender and Emilia had spilled out from mere disagreements about Christmas decorations to new territory. She decided it was better not to ask.

'I brought tuna with me,' she said instead. 'For the jackets at lunch. And some grated cheese and beans. I think that will be enough, won't it?'

'You'd better go and check with Her Highness that the smell won't be bothering her before you unpack any of it.'

'I'll...' Zoe paused, wondering how to respond, but then Lavender turned to her computer screen and Zoe realised none was needed. 'I'll go and put it all in the fridge then. Did you enjoy the gingerbread day at the weekend?'

'It was fine.'

'And you had a nice Sunday?'

'Yes, thank you,' Lavender said stiffly without looking up. 'You?'

'Yes. You want a coffee?'

'Got one, thanks.'

Zoe decided to knock to see if Ottilie was in yet and to ask if she wanted a coffee. And perhaps she'd get the low-down on just what had happened that morning.

'Come in!' Ottilie sounded distracted.

Zoe pushed the door open and put her head round to see her poring over a diary. 'Want a drink?'

'I'm good; I went to get one a minute ago. Just got in?'

'Yes. What's going on with...?' Zoe hooked her thumb behind her, and it seemed Ottilie didn't need any more elaboration than that.

'I don't know, but I'm keeping out of her way. Both of them in fact. I've never seen Lavender so riled, not since I started to work here. I think' – she lowered her voice – 'our new GP needs to watch her step.'

'Seems like six of one and half a dozen of the other to me.'

'It might be, I don't know. All I know is the other one has got here in a foul mood. She's making Lavender look like a picnic in the park.'

Zoe's mind went back to what she knew of the weekend, and she wondered if there was some connection between Emilia's bad mood and what had happened at her house. She'd been unsure at the time, but since Brett's visit to the shop, she was certain things were not well and that Emilia was having to get involved in his problems. It was no wonder she was tetchy, though Zoe couldn't help but reflect that she might need to get that under control if she wanted to keep her receptionist.

'You know them,' Ottilie said. 'Any hints for the rest of us?'

'Everyone keeps saying that, like we're practically family,

but apart from the last few weeks, I haven't spoken two words to any of them since I was eleven. I don't think that can be classified as *knowing* them.'

'You know more than we do. What's Georgia said?'

'About Emilia? Not a lot. It's not really what we talk about.'

'What do you talk about then?'

Zoe paused. She had to admit, she wasn't sure if anything they talked about was of any consequence. They chatted about things that didn't matter, laughed about old times, and on occasion there might be a glimpse into Georgia's current life, but it was always somehow shrouded, like Georgia didn't want her to see the full picture. Why was that? Was Georgia ashamed? Worried she'd be judged or pitied? It had been clear to Zoe that there was more than she was being told, and yet she hadn't asked. She wondered if she should have done because now she felt the current situation might have been made worse by her neglect. If she'd talked to Georgia properly, found out more, could she have offered advice that might have helped?

'This and that. Whatever people normally talk about. Nothing deep, really.'

'I'm sorry I asked,' Ottilie said, going back to her computer.

'Hey, there's no need to take it out on me! I'm not falling out with anyone!'

Ottilie looked up ruefully. 'I know; I'm sorry. I feel as if all this bad feeling is rubbing off on me, that's all. I was hoping you might be able to help.'

'It's all right. You're bound to be a bit more susceptible to that sort of thing right now. I wish I could tell you something useful, but I can't. Except...'

Zoe paused. Perhaps she could share with Ottilie what she knew. Perhaps Ottilie would have more useful insights than Alex, and given that Magnus and Geoff knew some of it, it was probably only a matter of time before everyone knew anyway.

But before she could frame her next sentence, Emilia's voice was behind her.

'Good morning, Zoe,' she said briskly.

Zoe spun round, trying not to show her mortification at the notion of what she might have heard had she got there only a minute later.

'I'm glad I've caught you both at the same time – it will save me a trip. We're being audited in the new year. I'd be grateful if all your notes could be complete and up to date by then.'

'They're always complete and up to date,' Ottilie said, slightly defensively.

'Yes, but it doesn't hurt to mention it,' Emilia said crisply. 'People sometimes get lax at this time of the year.'

'Not me,' Ottilie replied primly. 'Especially now, as I'm getting closer to my maternity leave.'

'Yes,' Emilia said, 'of course. Which reminds me, we'll soon have the additional headache of your cover to deal with.'

And then she swept out again, leaving Zoe and Ottilie alone once more.

'I'm sorry to have been such a nuisance,' Ottilie said through gritted teeth. 'God forbid I should have a life outside this surgery.'

Zoe gave her a pained smile, and Ottilie tried to return it. 'It's you I feel bad for.'

Zoe frowned. 'Why?'

'Because I persuaded you to come here and take this job and told you how lovely the surgery is – and now look at us. It's not what I promised at all.'

'No,' Zoe said, 'maybe not right now, but I can hardly complain about coming here. I got Alex, for a start. And you, and all the other friends I've made here. I don't think you need to feel bad about that. Things are a bit fraught right now, but I'm sure it will all settle soon. Maybe a bit of time off over Christmas is just what we all need. It might be that we're all tired and at the end of our tethers, and we need a few days to recharge.'

'Ever the optimist,' Ottilie said. 'You always were the sunnier one.'

'I don't know about that. I'd better get on... See you at lunch?'

'Yes, as long as we haven't all been fired by then. Zoe...'

Zoe turned back. 'Yes?'

'I think I might set my mat leave date today. I might not come back after the Christmas break. I know that's going to piss Emilia and Simon off because it will be short notice, and I wanted to hang on until the end, really, so I could have more time with the baby after the birth, but... with the atmosphere around here at the moment...'

'I don't blame you,' Zoe said. 'It's not good for anyone, especially you. It's *really* short notice, though. Christmas is more or less on top of us.'

'Do you think I ought to hang on then?'

'If you're finding it stressful at work, then no, I don't. I'll do my best to square things with them if it comes to it. I can tell them it's under my advice. Then they can take it out on me if they're going to get annoyed at anyone.'

'I couldn't ask you to do that.'

'But it might make life easier.'

Ottilie gave a small smile. 'I can't deny that it would. I'll talk to you about it when we've got time, if that's all right.'

'Let's do that.'

Zoe left Ottilie's room. She passed Simon's and wondered whether to try and air her concerns before surgery began, but she didn't even know where she'd start. Would he think she was speaking out of turn? Uncertain how he'd view it, she decided not to. For now, perhaps the best thing she could do was keep her counsel and see how things went. Then again, perhaps there was one thing she could do.

As she switched on her computer, she decided to speak to Georgia as soon as she could and, for once, to insist on a straight answer. If there was trouble, for many reasons, not just because they were friends, Zoe needed to know. But she'd have to do it away from the house, and as she was here now with a private room, space on her clinic list and the perfect excuse as her midwife to get Georgia in, she decided to take the bull by the horns and phone her before she did anything else.

An hour later, Georgia was in the office with her. Zoe had immediately worried about her decision, fearful of what Emilia might say once she found out, because she'd likely know there was no real reason to get Georgia in for an appointment, or demanding to be told about it if she thought there was.

'What's up?' Georgia asked as she sat down. She looked more worried than Zoe had wanted her to be, and perhaps that had been a mistake too. 'Is there a problem? I mean, I feel fine...'

'It's just... you're very close to term now, and I wanted to know if you were OK. Like no headaches, bleeding... you know, that sort of thing. You're feeling all right?'

'Yes, I'd have told you straight away if I wasn't. I wouldn't mind hurrying things along now. I've read eating a hot curry will do that. Or is it an old wives' tale, like eating pineapples, or the sex thing? Not that we'd be doing that at the moment...'

'Actually, pineapples do have some effect, but I don't think you should be trying to bring anything on just yet. Stress is another thing that might do it... You're not too stressed?'

Georgia's expression was hard to read. 'As much as anyone is.'

'And your plans after the baby is born? I only ask because it's all a bit vague, and if I'm going to hand you over to another midwife out of the area, I probably need to know.'

'Will you have to do that? If I'm here when the baby is born, that's that, isn't it?'

'No, you'll still have visits for a little while to check baby is thriving and you're recovering properly.'

'Oh, well... in that case, you might be doing that too.'

'Might?'

'I don't know. It all depends.'

Zoe sat back and studied her. 'I'm sorry, Georgia, but I'm worried about you. I feel as if things are going on that you're not being honest about. At home, I mean. And that they might have an impact on you and the baby. Ordinarily, it would be none of my business – or rather, sometimes it would be, but that's another story – but you're my friend, Emilia is my colleague and I want to do right by you both. She asked me to care for you, and I want to do that, but I can't do it properly unless you're frank with me.'

There was a blankness in Georgia's expression. 'I don't know what you mean.'

'Georgia, please... You're my friend, and if nothing else, that should be enough. I'm not saying I can help or do anything to change your situation, but at least I'll understand.'

'You know most of it.'

'Do I?'

'Brett and I ran a business together. It went under, we lost everything and now we're here.'

'But why? Emilia said you were staying with her.'

'You know we are.'

'Permanently?' Zoe asked. 'Because Emilia asked me to take on your care, but she couldn't say how long you'd be here and what the situation was with your previous midwife, whether you'd be going home or when. And then there's Brett...'

'He's struggling,' Georgia said.

'I know – that much is obvious. I'm afraid that it might be obvious to lots of people in the village too. He came to the shop when Alex and I were visiting yesterday. Geoff told him they were closed, but he wouldn't leave until he'd been able to buy a bottle of vodka – and Geoff said he buys a lot of alcohol.'

Georgia's shoulders slumped. 'I didn't know that. I mean, I know he's been getting through a lot of booze, but I didn't know he'd gone out after it yesterday. I'll talk to him.'

'That's not really what I'm asking of you. Come on now, Georgia – this is me you're talking to, and we're past pussy-footing around. Is this affecting you to the point where it might be a problem for your baby? For your future as a family? I'm never going to judge anyone because it's not helpful, but I don't want to see anyone's baby – especially yours – grow up in a house with that much tension. If it's this unmanageable now, when you do finally go home and it's just you and Brett, what then? Will it be worse? You have Emilia there now to mitigate, but—'

'I don't know! All right? I don't know! Maybe we'll never go home... We don't even have one of our own right now! We lost everything, and all we have is a few pounds to our name. There... is that what you wanted to hear?' Georgia's eyes filled with tears.

Zoe felt awful for forcing the admission, but she stood by her belief that at least now she knew she could think of ways to support her friend, she could be better and more effective than she'd been so far.

'We're staying with Emilia because we don't have anywhere else to go. At first it seemed like the perfect solution. She was lonely after her divorce, and she'd just moved to this new place where she didn't have anyone, and we needed somewhere to live until we got back on our feet. Brett wasn't happy, but he could see the sense in it. And we didn't think it would be for long. Brett would get a job, and we'd find somewhere to rent, and we'd be on our way again. We'd be bruised and battered, but we'd recover, and things would get better and life would go on. The baby was the one bright spot on the horizon too, a reason for us to try so much harder to get back on track. But Brett hasn't been able to get a job, and his mood has sunk lower and lower. He feels like a failure, living with his sister-in-law, no money to support us. I wanted to get a little job somewhere to tide us over – anything would have done – but he was dead against it. Not that it would have been easy – who's going to employ a massively pregnant woman? I'd hoped I could get some casual work, something I could do from home, but Brett wasn't even happy about that. I suppose it made him feel even worse, being supported by both me and Em and not being able to contribute anything.'

'Is he drinking a lot?'

'Enough,' Georgia admitted. 'Enough to worry me and annoy Emilia. She's being as patient as she can be, but she's got her own stuff going on too, so it's hard. I think she'd like to put us both in a bag and shake us. That or throw us out.'

'It doesn't seem like she wants to do that. She'd have done it already, wouldn't she?'

'Doesn't mean she doesn't want to. We all know Em's conscience is better than that – better than mine would be. I'd have thrown us out, if I was her.'

'I'm glad you're not. I'm glad you've told me. I meant what I said: it comes from a place of friendship first, but it does also help me to care for you as your midwife. I need to be aware of anything that might affect your pregnancy or life after the baby is born.'

'So you can call social services to come and visit?' Georgia asked, and Zoe was stung by the sudden accusation in her tone.

'I'd never do that to you.'

'Wouldn't you? You're telling me that if you thought Brett's drinking was becoming destructive, you wouldn't get the authorities involved? Isn't that your professional code? What you're meant to do? Why would it be any different for us than anyone else?'

'Has it got that bad?'

'I don't know. How bad is that bad?'

'He hasn't... he hasn't got overly angry? Made you fearful?'

'You mean has he hit me? No, he'd never do that. I don't know what's going on with him, but I know that much. Brett's a gentle, respectful man, whatever else he is. You don't need to worry whether I'm safe with him.'

Zoe nodded slowly. It was reassuring to hear, but she wished she could share Georgia's utter faith in her husband. She was no expert, but she'd visited families where there were addiction problems of all sorts, and the one thing she'd found in every case was that nothing was as simple and predicable as Georgia wanted to believe. A loving, caring parent or spouse could do shocking and uncharacteristic things under the influence. 'Georgia...' she said after a long pause. 'Do you think he's an alcoholic?'

'I'd have thought that you of all people wouldn't use that term for it.'

'But do you think he's dependent on it?'

'No,' Georgia said firmly. 'I think it's helping to numb things – that's why he's turning to it, but I think he could quit. Right now he just needs a reason to.'

'And you don't think your baby is a reason?'

'The baby's not here yet. It's hard to imagine what life will be like when it is. He'll come round then.'

'You're sure?'

'He wants this baby more than anything – we both do. I'm sure. In the meantime, whatever he needs to cope, he can have.'

'Sounds like burying your head in the sand to me. He might be able to quit drinking when the time comes, but the more he does it to excess, the bigger danger there is he'll cross the line to a place where he can't quit.'

Georgia held her in a frank gaze. 'Seems like you know everything. So you're an expert on addiction now?'

'Don't... I'm not trying to patronise; I want to help. Surely Emilia's said the same to you?'

'Like I said, Em's got her own things going on. I'm sure if she could click her fingers and have us out of her life, she would.'

Zoe shook her head as she glanced at the clock. Regardless of whether she felt their conversation had achieved anything, she'd have to cut it short if she was going to get around to seeing the rest of her list. 'Thanks for coming,' she said. 'I'm sorry I got you here on false pretences. You understand why, don't you?'

'Yes. I might have done the same. Has it helped?'

'Helped me? I suppose so, but that wasn't the point. Has it helped you?'

'Well, nothing has changed. I still have no money, no house, a room with my sister, a big pregnant belly and a husband who spends his time hating the world. So I don't really know if it's helped.'

'At least you can talk to me now if you need to.'

'Super,' Georgia said wryly as she got her coat on. 'I can talk to you. So that's everything fixed then, isn't it?'

22

Victor was running late. Lavender had just locked up the surgery, and everyone had left apart from Zoe, who was still waiting. Worrying too. Victor didn't have a mobile phone, of course, so there was no way to get hold of him, and she didn't want to call the landline at Daffodil Farm just yet, for fear of worrying Corrine if there was no need. So she leaned against the porch of the locked-up surgery and huddled in her heavy coat as she waited, scrolling through social media on her phone and occasionally looking up to check the sky. There was more snow in the forecast – though she didn't know how that was even possible.

'Hiya!'

She turned at the sound of a familiar voice to see Maisie crossing the lane.

'Hi, Maisie. On your way home?'

'Yes.' She made her way over. 'I'm glad you're here – I was going to text you to say I did the thing you asked. You know, with your boyfriend's daughter. I did it straight away because I didn't want her to be lonely.'

'Aww, that's brilliant. Thanks so much, Maisie. She did say

you two had been messaging and you might meet up. Have you seen her then?'

'Yeah!' Maisie was flushed, though it seemed that it was about more than the bitter wind trying to pierce Zoe's coat. 'She's really nice.'

'You got on well?'

'I think so, yeah. She lived in Spain, you know!'

'I did know something about that...'

'And she can even speak Spanish!'

'I didn't know that!' Zoe replied, surprised now that it had never come up in conversation.

'Her boyfriend died.'

Zoe raised her eyebrows. 'She told you that?'

Maisie nodded.

Things had moved on more than Zoe had realised. Only a few months before, Billie had been closed and secretive, and it had been a while before she'd confided in Zoe what had happened to Luis in Spain. But here she was, first time meeting Maisie and apparently telling her all about it.

'It's so sad for her,' Maisie continued. 'No wonder she needs someone to talk to. I told her I'd split up from mine.'

Zoe frowned now. 'You mean the new one? Not the baby's dad?'

Maisie nodded again. 'Yeah, he said he didn't think he wanted to look after the baby after all. I suppose it's because it's not his.'

'Are you upset?'

'Not really. I liked him, but...' Maisie shrugged. 'If he doesn't want to be around my baby, then I don't want to be around him.'

'I'm glad to see you know your worth. As it should be.'

'Anyway, Billie says she'll help me if I don't get another boyfriend by the time the baby comes. She said we could do it together.'

'Do what together?'

'Look after our babies. I was like, do you think our babies will grow up to be friends, and she said they might.'

'Hold on... you're going to look after your babies together?'

'Well, she said she might be able to help me find a job. She said her dad was opening some camping fields or something, you know, with those little huts... and they would probably need someone to work, like cleaning them and stuff, and I said I didn't have a job, and she said we could both do it and take our babies around with us, and her dad would pay me.'

Zoe was silent for a moment. While she was pleased to hear the young women had apparently got along famously, the things Maisie was telling her didn't sound like the sort of things Billie would say. Especially the bits where she seemed to be planning a future that included the baby she'd said she was going to put up for adoption. And yet, Maisie must have had these ideas from somewhere. Had Billie changed her mind? Had Maisie somehow, without knowing any of the facts, changed it for her? It seemed so unlikely. Zoe hadn't seriously expected Billie to have much time for Maisie, who was not only younger but a lot more immature, and yet it did sound as if they'd got on. What she'd asked of Billie as a favour to help keep an eye on Maisie had seemingly been just as beneficial for her. It was a question Zoe wouldn't have the answer to until she'd spoken to Billie as well.

'She made dinner for me too,' Maisie said. 'I had lasagne. It was really nice.'

Zoe smiled, pleased to know that those calories, at least, hadn't been counted by Maisie. 'She's a brilliant cook.'

'Yeah, she said she'd show me how to cook some stuff. I showed her your leaflets, and she said they were crap but she'd show me better things to make.'

Zoe's smile grew. *That* sounded more like Billie.

'She learned to cook in Spain, you know,' Maisie continued.

'I bet it's amazing, living in Spain. No wonder she was sad coming back to England.' Maisie gave Zoe a bright smile. 'I'm glad you asked me to meet her.'

'I'm glad too,' Zoe said. 'It sounds as if you've cheered her right up.'

'You think? I mean, she was nice to me, but she didn't laugh much.'

'That's just her way. She's still sad.'

'About coming back to England, I guess. And her boyfriend. Her baby is due before mine, isn't it?'

'Yes.'

'It's a shame because if mine had come first, I'd have been able to tell her what it was like to give birth.'

'She'll be able to tell you instead.'

'Yeah, she will.'

'Are you going to meet up again?'

'I think so. We didn't say, but she'll probably message when she's free.'

Zoe reached to rub Maisie's arm with a warm smile. 'That's good. I'm really pleased you two have connected.'

At that moment, the quiet of the lane was interrupted by the growing sound of a rough and ready old engine. Zoe recognised it before she saw Victor's Land Rover turn a corner and come into view.

'Here's my lift,' she said. 'Will you be all right getting home? I'm sure Victor won't mind taking you where you need to be.'

'I'll be fine,' Maisie said. 'It's not that far.'

'But it's dark, and the weather's bad. I'd feel better knowing we'd got you home safe.'

'But what if my mum sees you?'

Zoe held back a frown. 'She can't be mad at me for bringing you home, surely?'

'No, but...'

Zoe gave a sage nod. Perhaps Maisie had a point. Zoe was

sure she wasn't flavour of the month with Bridget. 'How about if we drop you somewhere close but not right outside?'

'I suppose that would be all right,' Maisie said, though she sounded uncertain.

'Your carriage has arrived!' Victor called from the driver-side window.

'Do you think we can drop Maisie home too?' Zoe asked.

'We can do that,' Victor said with an affable smile. 'Your parents still at Stonehouse?' he asked Maisie.

'Yeah,' Maisie said. 'Mum says the only way she's giving up that house is if she's carried out in a box.'

'Well, it's not a bad spot,' Victor said. 'Hop in then, both of you. Corrine's got tea stewing in the pot up at Daffodil!'

Maisie was suddenly far shyer in Victor's company, but Zoe loved that he did his best to put her at ease. He asked after her parents and grandparents and how her pregnancy was progressing and what work she was doing and what her plans were once the baby arrived. Zoe made the odd contribution to the conversation, but she was happy to let Victor natter. It some-times felt too intense when Zoe was talking to her, because it was often about her pregnancy and Zoe's worries on that score rather than simply learning about Maisie as a young woman independent of the baby she was carrying.

Ten minutes later, Victor turned into a lane that was darker than the road that led into it, cast into gloom by dense trees and a streetlight that blinked on and off.

'Someone needs to do something about that,' Victor said as he halted outside a double-fronted house. 'Here you go,' he added, turning his gaze to the house and then smiling at Maisie.

Zoe looked at what she presumed was Maisie's home, hoping Bridget wouldn't see her. Victor had laughed at Zoe's discreet question of whether it would pose a problem for them to be there, saying he knew Bridget of old and she was all bark and no bite, but Zoe had been barked at before by Maisie's mum, and it had been enough for her to know she didn't want it to happen again.

However, here she was, and to be silly about it in front of Maisie wouldn't send a very encouraging message. Maisie had put a lot of faith in Zoe and so she had to at least look like a sensible adult in her presence.

The house would once have been a handsome place, with symmetrical windows either side of a perfectly central front door and a decent-sized garden that was a bit wild with shrubs and trees but still a good outside space. But even in the dark Zoe could see the house was in a state of disrepair, and it looked as if it had been like that for some time. There were slates missing from the roof, chunks of rendering gone from the front wall and one of the windowpanes downstairs had been replaced by a square of chipboard. The presence of an old mattress propped against a rickety lean-to only added to the depressing air of neglect. If this was the outside, it was a fairly safe bet that the inside wouldn't be much better.

Zoe's heart went out to Maisie. Perhaps it didn't bother her because she didn't know any differently, but it seemed to Zoe like a miserable place to live. No wonder her mum, Bridget, was so tetchy all the time. It was just another thing for Zoe to worry about. She was no stranger to caring for young mums in unsuitable accommodation in Manchester, but it was a shock to find one here, in the breathtaking beauty of the Lakes. She hadn't yet made a home visit to Maisie, but when the time came, Zoe wondered how she'd find it and whether she'd be forced to try and do something about it. Those situations were hard – nobody wanted to be told their house wasn't a fit place to bring up a baby, but sometimes it had to be said. And knowing Maisie's mum, she wouldn't take something like that well at all.

'Thank you,' Maisie said to Victor. She turned to Zoe. 'See you soon.'

'You will,' Zoe said. 'And thanks again.'

Maisie smiled. 'You're welcome.'

She hopped out of the car and pushed on an already unlocked front door to go inside.

Victor restarted the engine. 'She's a lovely little lass,' he said. 'Shame about her parents.'

'I've had run-ins with Bridget, but I've never met her dad.'

'Think yourself lucky,' Victor said, pulling away from the kerb.

'They can't be that bad if they managed to raise Maisie. She's so sweet.'

'They're not bad,' Victor said. 'But they have some odd ideas. Not very fond of many in the village either.'

'Oh, so it's not just me.'

'No,' he chuckled. 'Don't worry – it's not just you.'

23

Two days before Christmas, Zoe still hadn't managed to find the perfect gift for Alex. She'd ordered a few things online, but every single one had arrived and was either far less impressive than she'd hoped, damaged or suddenly the stupidest idea she'd ever had. She'd always hated buying gifts online anyway, and this depressing display only confirmed to her why that was. At this point, she'd settle for any gift at all, and so she kept them in reserve and, with time running out, she decided to head to the only town with a late-night opening for the shops, determined to return with something better.

To save time, as soon as the surgery had closed, she changed quickly from her uniform in the bathroom with the intention of going straight to the bus stop from there. While she was getting into her own clothes, her phone bleeped a text message.

Hey, gorgeous, don't know if you've noticed it starting to snow again. Want me to come down and pick you up? X

I'm fine. I'll leave my car here and walk, thanks. See you tomorrow for the carols. X

It looks like it might be bad. Better if I come to get you. X

Zoe smiled ruefully. On any other evening she'd be feeling smug about how lucky she was to have found such a wonderful man, but today his concern was a spoke in the wheel for her plans. She didn't want to tell him where she was going because she didn't want him to know how last-minute his gift had been when he opened it on Christmas morning. She was rather hoping it would look well thought out and expensive (that would be a Christmas miracle because she was fairly broke too), and him knowing she was dashing to a nearby town on a last-minute quest wasn't going to help with that illusion.

I've got some things to do at the surgery, so won't be ready for a while. Just spoken to Simon and he says he can take me home if needs be. X

Zoe hoped her little white lie would be enough and hurried to finish getting changed, shoving her uniform in a locker when she was done. Her phone bleeped again, and she was relieved to see Alex content with her pretend arrangements.

OK. Text me when you're home so I know you're safe and call if you need help after all. Can't wait to see you tomorrow. X

When Alex had messaged to say the snow had started again, she already knew it was in the forecast, but when she stepped outside, she was taken aback by how quickly conditions had worsened. Over the past couple of weeks, it seemed that the cloud of arctic weather was simply stuck over the Lakes, and no sooner did it seem to be clearing than it began to come down again. It had snowed on and off for the past week fairly solidly, and it was only the relentless efforts of those in the village who had tractors and shovels keeping the lanes here clear enough to walk. The roads leaving the village, however, were a different matter. Almost everyone who'd ventured out had reported back that they were virtually unpassable in places unless you had a stout set of tyres and front wheel drive. Aware that she wasn't the most confident driver in the best of circumstances, Zoe was pinning her hopes on a functioning bus service to take her where she needed to go. She could have asked Victor to take her, but she didn't want to bother him when he was busy getting ready for his own Christmas, and even if she did, she wouldn't expect him to wait around for her, so she'd still have the issue of getting back to Thimblebury when she was done.

By the time she reached the bus stop, she was sweating under her layers. She wiped the snow from the timetable pinned up on a post and checked to see how long she'd have to wait. Fifteen minutes. It wasn't too bad on any other day, but once she cooled down from her walk, she might start to get very cold. She glanced towards the shop, a little way down the road, and saw that the lights were on, so they were open, and wondered if Magnus and Geoff had their hot drink machine running today.

Leaving the bus stop, she decided to go and ask. She was hungry too, and so perhaps a packet of sandwiches or a bag of crisps wouldn't go amiss.

Magnus was leaning on the counter staring at the windows when Zoe opened the door.

'I bet this is a walk in the park for you,' she said, stamping the snow from her boots before going in.

'I'm used to seeing it at home, of course, but we're a lot better at carrying on in Iceland than you are here. I hope you're not planning to go far,' he added.

'Into Windermere, actually. I was just wondering if you had

your hot drinks on. I thought I might get a cup of chocolate to see me through while I wait for the bus.'

'The buses are running?' Magnus asked as he went to switch the vending machine on. It whirred and clicked as it set up. 'It won't be a minute. Is there anything else you want while you're waiting?'

'I'll take these,' she said, grabbing a bag of crisps from the stand and putting them on the counter. 'I really hope the buses are running,' she continued as she got out her purse. 'Otherwise I'm sunk. Have you heard anything?'

'We've had the radio on, but there's been nothing on the traffic report – at least I haven't noticed if there has, but I haven't really been listening for that sort of thing. Sorry.'

'That's all right,' Zoe said. 'There isn't one due for fifteen minutes. I'll have my warm drink and my crisps, and I'll just wait. I'm sure it'll be fine.'

'Is it desperate that you get to Windermere?'

'Not life and death, but I could really do with getting there. I need to do some last-minute things for Christmas.' She shrugged. 'Don't mention it to Alex if you see him, but I haven't got his present yet. I'm so annoyed at myself, really, but I've just been so busy, and the time's gone nowhere, and now here I am, two days before Christmas and still not ready. Next year I'm going to be more organised.'

'I say that every year.'

'Yeah...' Zoe gave a rueful smile. 'Me too.'

'Do you know what you're going to get? Will it be easy to pick it up and come straight home?'

'Not really, which is hardly helpful, I know. Don't suppose you have any ideas?'

Magnus pressed the buttons for Zoe's drink. 'I barely know what to get for Geoff these days, let alone anybody else. What sort of things does he like? He has hobbies?'

'I mean, we haven't been together all that long, have we? So

I feel as if I barely know myself. I ought to – we spend a lot of time together – but beyond the obvious, like things for the house or aftershave or whatever, I don't have a clue. And I really don't want to get him something that predictable.'

'I think a well-chosen cologne can be a lovely gift.' Magnus put the lid on her drink and set it down on the counter for her. 'There's nothing wrong with the basics. I think they're only wrong if you choose badly. I'd be very happy with a nice set of pyjamas or some bath salts.'

Zoe smiled as she took her drink. She wasn't going to say so, but bath salts and pyjamas were absolutely not on her list. 'Thanks, Magnus. Well...' she added as she went to the door. 'Wish me luck!'

'Stay safe,' he said, waving her out. 'Will we see you at the carol service tomorrow evening?'

'Wouldn't miss it,' Zoe said before stepping out into the snow again.

With her hands cupped around her drink, Zoe waited at the bus stop. She didn't see a single car pass, and although someone had cleared the road earlier that day, the tarmac was already beginning to disappear under a fresh layer of snow. At this rate, Alex would be opening a ski resort rather than a glamping site.

Twenty minutes had passed, and although she was getting colder now that she'd finished her drink, Zoe didn't worry that there was still no sign of the bus. It was hardly a surprise that it might run late in weather like this, and she was prepared for a delay. But when forty minutes passed, she stamped her feet against the cold, looked up into a heavy sky and wondered if it was going to come after all.

After an hour had passed and she'd started to give up, she heard her name being called and looked up to see Emilia walking towards her.

'Are you all right?' she asked. 'I thought you'd gone home ages ago.'

'I left, but I didn't go home. I was hoping to get a bus to Windermere, but I've been waiting an hour and I'm ready to give up. I suppose they're either hopelessly behind or not running at all. I checked online and I didn't see any notifications, but...' Zoe shrugged. 'Since when was bus information round here bang up to date?'

'I wouldn't know – I don't use them. So you're just going to wait until you turn into a human snowman? What's so important for you to get to Windermere tonight anyway?'

'Would you believe Christmas shopping?'

'I would. I can't remember the last time I finished mine with room to spare. I've still got things to get.'

Zoe tried not to show her surprise, but it was there. The way she'd been acting up over Lavender's seasonal enthusiasm, she wouldn't have imagined Emilia giving Christmas gifts a second thought. She'd given the impression that she didn't celebrate it at all. 'So what are you going to do?'

'I expect I'll do mail order to aunts and uncles and cousins. I know it's a bit late but I can order them next day delivery when I get home. Georgia and I have agreed not to buy this year, so that's one out of the way.'

'I couldn't do that,' Zoe said, and then immediately wished she hadn't, given what she'd recently learned of Georgia's financial troubles. It may have been that Emilia's lack of enthusiasm had her fully on board with a plan to ignore gift buying for her sister, but it was more likely that she'd either agreed or suggested it because Georgia had very little money to spare.

'Well, that's you, isn't it?' Emilia said. 'Everyone views it differently. As far as I'm concerned, I can do without the commerciality. If I have loved ones close, that's all I need.'

Given what Zoe also knew of Emilia's marriage split, and that Brett and Georgia were currently forced to live with her, she also had to wonder just how much comfort the notion of having loved ones close was right now. She was hardly living in a Hallmark movie.

'Georgia said you called her in for a chat,' Emilia added into the gap.

'I wanted to know she was well. I mean, because she's so close to term and she's away from home. It can be stressful, the uncertainty. That's all.'

Emilia nodded slowly, and Zoe wondered how much Georgia had told her. But she offered no more, except for a thank you. 'It's good of you to watch over her so well.'

'It's my job.'

'Yes, I know, but still.' She glanced up and down the road. 'I don't think your bus is coming.'

'I'm beginning to think that too.'

'What's your list like tomorrow?'

'My workload? There's not much on it, to be honest. I'll be done by lunch when the surgery closes for the Christmas break.'

'Can't you take the afternoon to do your shopping then? I don't think it's going to be worth your while tonight. Even if you do manage to get there, I would imagine a lot of the shops will be closing early with the bad weather. You might struggle over for nothing.'

'You wouldn't mind me taking the afternoon? What about paperwork... the audit after Christmas?'

'Not at all. You and Ottilie said the other day you're up to date already, so it shouldn't be a problem, should it?'

'Well, yes, we are...'

'In fact...' Emilia paused, and then said something entirely unexpected. 'I could give you a lift to Windermere and do some shopping myself. That's if you don't mind the company.'

'And Georgia too?'

Emilia was silent for a moment, and then she gave her head

the briefest shake. 'I don't think she's up to it, do you? If she were to go into labour...'

Zoe wondered whether she was being admonished. It was certainly stating the obvious; then again, it wasn't as if Georgia would be without very able help should that happen. She wondered whether Emilia had another reason for not wanting to invite Georgia, but she couldn't think what it might be, only that she might want to get her sister a gift after all, despite what they'd agreed.

'If you're sure it's no bother. I thought you said you were going to do mail order or something.'

'I will for those I won't see, but I'd like to get some food. Better food than I can get at the shop here.'

'Don't let Magnus hear you say that. He prides himself on stocking nice things.'

'Yes, they're fine, but there isn't a lot of choice. I'd like to see what I can get in a bigger town, and I haven't had the opportunity to see much of the area yet, so it would be two birds with one stone.'

'Assuming the weather will let us, I'd love that.'

'My car's pretty sturdy and usually good in bad weather, so I think we ought to make it in one piece. Let's both stop work at lunchtime and go straight off.'

'Lavender was planning to do a special lunch before we all finished for the break,' Zoe said doubtfully.

'I don't think there will be time to stay for that if we're going to get to Windermere in time to achieve anything.'

'She won't like it if we miss it.'

'It strikes me she's too vocal about a lot of things she doesn't like. She's struggling with the change, I think.'

'You mean Fliss retiring? They were close – worked together for a long time.'

'So I hear, but nothing stays the same forever, no matter how we might want it to.'

Zoe was struck by her words and the way she'd said them. Was she still talking about Lavender now, or her own life? As for her offer, it made sense. It looked increasingly unlikely she was going to make the shops tonight, and the only other time she'd get was the following afternoon, sandwiched between her morning at work and the carol service that evening. If she was going to make the best of that window, she ought to get there as soon as she could. Lavender wasn't going to like it, but perhaps when Zoe explained her predicament, she might let her off. It wasn't like they were best friends or anything because Zoe was a fairly new addition to the surgery team, and if Lavender had her very close colleagues there, it was all that mattered, surely?

'If you do decide to go, then yes, I'd love to come along. I'm going to wait for a little longer here, just in case a bus does come.'

'I don't think that's wise. It looks as if the weather is only going to get worse tonight, and when you get back to Thimble-bury – assuming you can – then you still have to get up to your house.'

'In the dark, in the snow,' Zoe acknowledged. She hadn't envisaged being back late or the weather making it impossible to get up the hill, but now that Emilia had pointed it out, she recognised it was a very real possibility. Alex wouldn't leave her stranded if it came to it, but she didn't want to have to get him out, not only because he'd find it difficult but for the same reasons she hadn't wanted to tell him she was heading over to Windermere tonight. She let out a sigh of resignation. 'Looks like I'm going to have to wait. If I don't find anything tomorrow, I don't know what I'll do.'

'I'm sure you will,' Emilia said. 'If I were you, I'd go home and settle down before the weather gets much worse. Will you be all right? I can give you a lift—'

'Thanks, but I'll be fine. I'll take my time, and I have my torch with me.'

'Phone me if you run into trouble. I'm popping into the shop to get some milk, and then I'll be home for the rest of the night.'

'Thanks, but I expect if I got really stuck, Victor would come and get me in Old Banger.'

'In what?'

Zoe smiled. 'His Land Rover. He calls it Old Banger.'

'Right, I see... Well, goodnight.'

'See you tomorrow.'

Zoe watched Emilia go into the shop, and then, with a last glance up and down the road to find only darkness in both directions, she gave up and headed for home.

Annoyingly, the snow stopped falling as soon as Zoe and Emilia had parted and, even more annoyingly, as she made her way to the path home, she saw the bus she'd wanted lumbering through the village, too far away for her to catch, even if she ran. But perhaps Emilia had been right – Zoe would have arrived into Windermere late and would have been rushing around, with no guarantee she would get what she'd been looking for or that she'd have transport home. The winding road up to Kestrel Cottage had been more challenging than normal, though that was to be expected, but perhaps not as challenging as it might have been because someone had tried to clear it.

The following morning she woke to a message from Ritchie, her ex. With a frown, she opened it to find an electronic Christmas card. It was strange because they'd barely spoken since Thimblebury's quincentenary event, where she'd clarified, once and for all, that they were never going to get back together. They'd had essential contact, of course, because they were still going through the process of divorce and settling what to do with the things they'd owned together, but that had been it. Perhaps, she thought with relief that was tinged with some regret for the way things had gone between them, he'd started to forgive her and move on. It would be a nice Christmas gift to think so.

Work had thankfully been low-key. It was a welcome slow down after a hectic few weeks. Most of her expectant mums hadn't wanted appointments on Christmas Eve, and the ones who did come only wanted reassurance that someone would be on call over the festive season should they need it. Zoe's clinic list was done by eleven, and then she spent the next couple of hours making sure all her paperwork was up to date for the audit they were expecting in the new year. She'd managed to schedule a quick catch-up with Ottilie too – she'd changed her mind about her maternity leave and now wanted to wait until the very last minute again before she stopped work. Zoe wasn't hugely happy about it but recognised that if Ottilie felt well – and she insisted that she did – it was her decision to make. She didn't blame her for wanting to save her maternity leave entitlement for after the baby was born, rather than using it up before.

The one thing Zoe had needed to do she'd been avoiding, and that was telling Lavender that she was going out with Emilia once they'd closed the surgery instead of having a last-day-of-work celebratory lunch with the rest of them. She'd mentioned it to Ottilie, who had seemed surprisingly disappointed about it, though she understood the reasons why, but who also warned her that Lavender wouldn't be happy.

'I'm sorry,' Zoe said when she eventually plucked up the courage to go through to reception and tell her, shortly before lunchtime. 'It's just that I really need to get to Windermere, and the shops will probably close early today. So I can't hang around. I'll make it up to you, I promise.'

'Next year?' Lavender's tone was sullen, and she was making no attempt to hide it.

'Yes... well, before then I expect. There's New Year's, isn't there?'

'Assuming I'll be here. I might have given in my notice by then.'

'Lavender...' Zoe tried to pat her arm, but she moved it out of the way.

'Don't *Lavender* me. This surgery is falling apart. I knew it would, the minute Fliss left. We used to be like family, and now nobody cares.'

'But you're the surgery mum.'

'I doubt it. There's no point trying to butter me up. I'm disappointed in you, Zoe. I thought you'd be on my side.'

Zoe wanted to laugh at the absurdity of Lavender's statement, and it wasn't unlike something her actual mum would have said. But she also realised that, though it sounded silly to her, it was important to Lavender.

'I am,' she said. 'But I have to get a present for Alex. You understand, don't you?'

'I suppose so,' Lavender said grudgingly. 'You can't even stay for one drink and a sandwich?'

'I can't, sorry.'

'Hmm...' Lavender looked sceptical but then went back to her computer. 'OK then. I take it you *will* manage to come to the carol service later?'

'Definitely. I wouldn't miss that.'

'See you later then.'

'I'll see you before I go this afternoon,' Zoe added, but Lavender only gave a dismissive nod. She didn't feel at fault, but Zoe did feel bad for letting Lavender down. Maybe she'd buy her a little something in Windermere too as an apology.

'Lavender...' Emilia came to the desk, giving Zoe a brief look before turning back to their receptionist. 'Could you phone this patient to see if he can come in before we close today? I need to see him ideally before Christmas.'

'Yes, Doctor,' Lavender said, viewing Emilia with such reproach that there was no way Emilia could fail to recognise it.

But if she did, she saw no reason to comment. She didn't even look a bit concerned; she only nodded. 'Let me know what he says. Please impress on him the urgency.'

'Is it bad news?' Lavender asked.

'It's not the best.'

'Then surely you should wait until after Christmas to give it to him? There's no point in making him worry over the whole break.'

'Christmas or not, there are time limits that we need to adhere to. I want to see him before we break up.'

'But he's got literally an hour to get here!'

'How far away is his house?'

'A couple of streets away.'

'And he's retired. Shouldn't be a problem.'

'But—'

'If you could,' Emilia insisted before leaving them again.

Lavender glared at her retreating figure, and Zoe decided to get out of the way before she got dragged any further into their feud.

24

The sun was a few hours from setting, but the hills were gloomy as Emilia drove towards Windermere. Gloomy but still beautiful, Zoe reflected as she gazed out of the passenger-side window, like a scene from a gothic classic, snowy peaks scarred by dark cracks and heavy skies pushing down on them. There had been no new snowfall since the previous night, though it had been forecast. Zoe wondered how there could possibly be any more on the way – surely it must end soon? One thing was for certain, they'd get their white Christmas.

Emilia drove without speaking, and she didn't put the radio on. They'd shared some sporadic comments on the weather and the current state of the roads but nothing any deeper than that. Zoe, though, could tell something was bothering her. Emilia was always serious, but this was more than that. She thought about asking, but it didn't seem as if Emilia wanted to talk. Perhaps Lavender's antagonism was getting to her. Or perhaps she was beginning to regret taking the job at Thimblebury surgery. She'd come from Manchester, and it was only natural that some would welcome the slower pace, and some wouldn't. Zoe knew from experience that either way, going from a huge bustling city like Manchester to a tiny village out in the wilds was a culture shock. Then again, it could be any number of things.

'I've got quite a lot to get,' she said into the silence. 'I hope that's OK. I know the shops will probably close early, but I'm hoping I can get everything before they do. So I'll probably let you go and do what you need to and meet you back at the car park.'

'That's fine by me,' Emilia said. 'How long do you reckon you'll need?'

'As long as you can give me, really. Of course, we have the carol service later, so we'll have to be back in time for that.'

'I'll make sure to have you back for that.'

'You're not going?'

'I doubt it.'

'But it's the one thing everyone in the village goes to. Almost everyone. So Lavender tells me.'

'I'm sure Lavender thinks it's very important. She's quite a Christmas fan.'

'When it comes to the carol service, the whole village seems to join in. Fliss used to, apparently. As the village GP, she felt she had to show her face every once in a while, especially to big events. Or rather, *only* big events. Other than those, she mostly kept to herself.'

'Sounds sensible to me.'

'So you might come?'

'I'd rather keep an eye on Georgia.'

'But she's going? I'm sure last time I mentioned it, she said she would.'

'She hasn't said anything to me. I should imagine it depends on what Brett wants to do.'

Zoe didn't think it ought to matter what Brett wanted to do – if Georgia wanted to attend, then she ought to be able to, regardless. But she also recognised that things might not be that simple, given what she now knew about their situation and Brett's issues.

'An hour wouldn't kill anyone, would it? I think it would do you all good to get out.'

'Do you?' Emilia shot her a wry half-smile before turning back to the road.

'It isn't good for anyone to cut themselves off from everyone around them. People want to get to know you.'

'Well, as long as they get what they want, it doesn't matter what I want, does it? I suppose I can't say I wasn't warned when I took the job.'

Zoe paused and then decided she'd had enough of the cryptic clues. 'Do you really hate this village so much? Has it been such a bad move for you?'

Emilia's eyebrows went up. She didn't answer for a full thirty seconds, and just when Zoe had resigned herself to the most awkward car ride she'd ever had, she finally spoke.

'No,' she said. 'It's not that, and if I've given that impression, I can only apologise. Things have been difficult.'

'I know; Georgia told me.'

'Not only for her. I love my job, and perhaps that's why I take it too seriously. It also feels like the only thing I have left that's worthwhile in my life.'

'Why?'

She shook her head. 'I don't know that this is the time to talk about it. All I can ask at the moment is that you understand, perhaps make some allowances for me. If I'm obstructive, I don't mean to be. The only sense of worth I have these days comes from how good a doctor I can be. If people can let me have that, I'll find my way back eventually.'

Zoe was thoughtful, and the car plunged into silence once more. Where did Emilia need to find her way back from? It was one more mystery. Was it because of the split from her husband? It might be, but Emilia didn't seem like the sort of woman to let a thing like that get to her. Unless it had been somehow traumatic? Or perhaps she'd loved him more than she'd even let on to Georgia, who hadn't seemed overly worried when she'd shared her thoughts with Zoe some weeks before.

After a few minutes, she spoke again. She'd been thinking over what Emilia had said about her job and had a sudden epiphany about so much that had gone on over the previous weeks.

'Did you get to see your urgent patient today?'

'Yes.'

'And you told him the bad news?'

'Yes.'

'How did he take it?'

'How you'd expect.'

'Hmm. Do you think Lavender might have been right? That it might have been better to let him have his Christmas first?'

'Would you want that? He'd had his tests on the two-week pathway, so he already knew there was a possibility for bad news. He'd be waiting to hear, and all sorts of disasters would be preying on his mind. Do you think he'd have had a happy, relaxing Christmas if I hadn't told him the results? At least he knows now. He can make his last Christmas with his family count in whatever way he feels matters to him and them. No, I don't think I should have let him have his Christmas first. I think I've made sure it's the most important Christmas he's ever had.'

Zoe had no response to Emilia's statement. She didn't know what she'd do, or whether she felt it right or wrong, but she understood perfectly Emilia's logic. She also felt she was beginning to understand Emilia herself in a way she never had, by the things she did rather than what she said. She wasn't trying to upset Lavender by being so resistant to the Christmas decorations and music and all that other seasonal stuff; she was worried that it would be a distraction from what she felt really mattered, the thing that they were all there for – the patients. Lavender and Emilia disagreed about what the patients needed, and that was the problem as far as Zoe could see. Lavender felt they needed humanity and connection and all the things that gave them a sense of security in belonging, but Emilia saw those things as unnecessary, putting her faith in procedures and knowledge and science, in cold, hard facts and difficult choices. If only there was a way to make both of them see that they were on the same side, but if there was, Zoe suspected it would take a better woman than her to find it.

Coloured lights cut through the gloom of the high street, shining from every shop window, hanging from lampposts and trimming doorways. A brass band was playing in the market square, and a Santa was waving at children from a sled parked a short distance away. Windermere was far livelier than Thimblebury – though that wasn't difficult. The main road through the town was lined on either side by terraces of pale stone with brightly coloured eaves and awnings that might once have been homes but were now mostly shops and restaurants. Some were clad in the Victorian mock Tudor style with little turrets like mini Bavarian castles, but all were lit warmly from within. From the high street, it wasn't possible to see the lake, but Zoe, as she walked from the car park with Emilia, decided she'd take a stroll on the shore before they went back to Thimblebury, if she could squeeze it in, certain that it would look magical, the lakeside cafés and hotels decorated for Christmas and blanketed in snow.

As the shops came into view, they made arrangements to give it three hours and then meet up again for the drive home. Zoe was doubtful it would be enough time, but she was also aware that it was about all she had if she was going to make the carol service. They had one another's numbers if they needed more or less time, and so they left it at that and went their separate ways.

Zoe had visited two shops when the smell of roasting chestnuts reached her from a vendor parked near the main festivities. She was suddenly hungry and hadn't had roasted chestnuts for years, and though she didn't really have the time to stop and eat properly, she could stave off the pangs with a bag of those. And so she dashed over and bought some, and was munching rapidly when her attention was caught by the window of a coffee shop. Sitting at one of the tables was Emilia, leaning in to talk to a man. Zoe hadn't meant to stop and stare, but she couldn't help it. There was something in their body language that was a little off. Troubled, she'd call it, perhaps accusatory. Was this her ex? He was waving his hands around as he spoke, staring her down, while she was measured, as she always was, but her whole body was taut, sprung like a coil welded together, a tension that would never be released.

Suddenly aware of what she was doing, Zoe shook herself and hurried on, her mind full of what she'd seen. Was this the reason Emilia had wanted to come to Windermere? Had she planned to meet him, and Zoe wanting to go too was a fortuitous accident? Or had she seen an opportunity to engineer a meeting out of town, away from gossiping villagers, and had taken it? But there wasn't time to dwell on it like she wanted to because she was already an hour into their allotted three, and though she'd managed to pick up a token gift for Lavender, she hadn't managed to find anything for Alex, and that was the main reason she'd come.

Alex hadn't mentioned much reading, but Zoe had finished her chestnuts and was throwing the bag away when she was drawn to the bookshop. It was worth a try, and if she didn't find anything for him, perhaps she might pick up a cookbook for Corrine.

Inside, she was met by a colourful display of children's

books and hit by a tinge of sadness for her own lost child that kidnapped her attention for a moment. Would she ever get another chance? It felt as if time was running out. Ottilie was older than her, almost forty, but somehow she seemed in a far more stable place to bring a baby into the world. Things were going well for Zoe and Alex, but they were a long way from the point at which they could even discuss settling down together, let alone having a child. And his priority was Billie, the daughter he already had, and Zoe was fully respectful of that. She wouldn't want to change it, and if Billie *did* decide to keep her baby, Zoe would never want to take Alex away from his role as a grandad.

She picked up a hardback with a cartoon dinosaur on the front and stared at it with a vague smile. This book was old – she recalled her mum reading it to her when she was little, the precursor to many bedtimes, and how much she'd loved those moments. She was desperate to buy it for someone, but she couldn't get it for Billie, and despite being incredibly busy in the run-up to Christmas, she had already managed to get a gift for Ottilie: a gift box filled with toiletries for new mothers that she'd seen online a few weeks prior and ordered on the spot. As for Ottilie's baby, she wasn't due for another five weeks. And now that she thought about it, Zoe wasn't sure whether Ottilie was one of the superstitious types who didn't like to have this sort of gift before the baby arrived. Georgia, perhaps? Her baby hadn't been born yet either, but she was a lot closer than Ottilie.

Putting it under her arm, Zoe decided it was too cute to leave behind and she'd find someone to gift it to. Then she went to inspect the cookery section and found something for Corrine featuring baking from around the world, and then she tried to turn her thoughts to what Alex might possibly want to read – if anything at all.

She quickly decided against a novel. He wouldn't have time to read it, and she didn't know what he was into. There were travel books that he might be interested in, but she didn't see him having much time to go to any of the destinations featured in them for the next few years while he got his glamping business up and running. Then her gaze settled on the local history section. There was a book about Bronze Age settlements in Cumbria, as well as two others about uncovering the archaeology of the Lake District. Would he like those? She picked one up and flicked through it. She wasn't sure, but she was running out of ideas and time.

Uncertain, and with a sigh of impatience, she took two of the three and went to the desk to pay for the lot.

'Did you get what you needed?' Zoe asked as Emilia got out of her car to open the boot. Zoe put her shopping in, noting with a vague frown that there wasn't very much of anything else in there, and went round to the passenger side as Emilia shut it again.

'Yes,' she said as she got back in. 'Did you?'

'I got some things,' Zoe said. 'No clue if they're the right things, and I don't think I'm especially happy with a lot of what I've bought, but at this point they'll have to do. I should have started earlier. I say it every year, and every year I'm doing this last minute.'

'There really is too much pressure on people at this time of year. If there's going to be a marriage break-up, a family estrangement, a nervous breakdown... you can almost guarantee it's going to happen around now. In my opinion, this requirement to make everything perfect, regardless of how anyone might be feeling, is unhealthy. People keep things bottled up for the sake of everyone else's good time, and that's when things come to a head in a far worse way than they otherwise would have done. At the end of the day, it's an arbitrary date. It only has the significance we've attached to it, and why should illness and worry choose another day to manifest?'

Zoe had no reply for Emilia's sweeping statement, but the continued anti-Christmas sentiment was beginning to depress her. She'd already been frustrated at her own lack of preparation and at the need for the last-minute rush, and Emilia's opinions were hardly helping.

'Town was busy,' she said instead. 'Nice atmosphere, though. People can get impatient sometimes, but generally they seemed in a good mood today.'

'I can't say I noticed. I mean, it was busy, but I got round as quickly as I could.'

'You didn't see the brass band in the square?'

'Yes, but I didn't have time to watch.'

'I had roasted chestnuts too,' Zoe said. 'Haven't had them for years, and I'd forgotten how much I like them. In fact, I could eat them all over again now.'

Emilia started the engine. 'We'd better get back before the weather gets even worse.'

Zoe took that as her cue to shut up about Christmas. Instead, her thoughts went back to the man she'd seen with Emilia in the coffee shop. She wanted to ask but was afraid she'd start a conversation Emilia didn't want to have. But then Emilia started it for her.

'I met up with Todd, actually,' she said.

'Did you?' Zoe asked with as much innocence as she could fake. 'Who's Todd?'

'Hasn't Georgia told you? I'd have thought she'd have filled you in on my ex and his... well, the trouble he's caused.'

'She mentioned your divorce, but she hasn't told me anything much about it.'

'I find *that* hard to believe.'

'I'd have no reason to keep it quiet if she did – after all, you're telling me now anyway.'

'True. He's come into some money, and he wants to offer me a share.'

'Well, that's...' Zoe began but then ran out of steam.

'Decent of him?' Emilia said, 'I suppose it is, though I think it's to alleviate his guilt.'

'Why should he do that? You're divorced now, so that's it, isn't it? No reason for either of you to worry about the other.'

'Yes, but aside from the things he did to end our marriage, had we stayed together, the money would have been half mine anyway. That's a long story. The reason I'm telling you about it today is because I think you might have seen me. In the coffee shop. And I wanted to explain why I didn't say anything before.'

Zoe flushed and wondered if she would have said anything at all had she not been rumbled, but there didn't seem much point in asking. 'I hadn't realised you'd seen me. I didn't mean to spy or anything – it was just that I happened to be passing.'

'I should have realised the town was too small for you not to be somewhere close by. It's not your fault, but I'd appreciate if you didn't tell Georgia about it. She thinks I ought to stay well out of his way.'

'Depending on what he wants from you, I'd be tempted to say the same,' Zoe replied.

Emilia looked sharply at her.

'I stayed in touch with my ex at first. I wanted to stay friends for the right reasons, but he didn't. We ended up in a much worse place than if I'd cut ties and called it a day.'

'I'll bear that in mind,' Emilia said, watching the road again.

'Sorry,' Zoe said awkwardly.

'What for?'

'I shouldn't have compared my situation to yours. I wasn't trying to make it about me.'

'I didn't think you were.'

Why did Emilia have to be so contradictory all the time?

From one minute to the next, Zoe couldn't work her out. She'd be open, and then she'd clam up. She'd be warm and then ice cold, grateful for help and then resistant to it. Zoe found it maddening and unsettling. As a young girl, she'd always been awed by her friend's older sister, feeling there was some enigmatic mystique about the quiet, hugely intelligent girl who was aloof and unknowable and yet fascinating. But now, she only found Emilia's changeability frustrating and, frankly, rude at times. And she couldn't help but feel that Emilia knew it, and that it somehow amused her to know it.

Zoe turned her gaze to the window, where the beams of the headlights illuminated the falling snow and obscured everything beyond their range, and decided to stop talking because it really was getting her nowhere.

25

Later that day, with half an hour to spare before the Christmas Eve carol service, there was a knock at the door of Kestrel Cottage. Zoe had just fixed her earrings in place and hurried down the stairs to get it. Alex was on the doorstep, snow in his hair and on the shoulders of his coat.

'The Lapland Express awaits you.'

Zoe laughed as she pulled him over the step and into a kiss. 'You look good,' she said. 'You smell even better. Cold and clean and musky. Maybe we won't go to the carols; maybe we'll stay here instead.'

'We could do that,' he said with a warm smile. 'Won't you be annoyed later? You said you were looking forward to it.'

'I did, didn't I? I was silly back then.'

He laughed. 'Come on. I must be mad to say it, but we're not staying in; we're going. You'll regret missing it, and everyone is expecting us.'

'Who cares?'

'Since you, very wisely, told me I ought to make more effort to charm the villagers so they'll be a bit more forgiving when the

campsite opens, I think that's rather a rash thing to say, Miss
Padbury. Get your business head on.'

'Business head, right...' She pulled one of his coat buttons
open. 'Admit it – you want to go more than I do. You actually
like everyone.'

'I never said I didn't. They don't all like me – that's the
problem we're trying to fix, remember? So...' He fastened his
button again, and she laughed. 'Stop trying to tempt me, and
let's go before the snow gets too deep!'

'Spoilsport,' Zoe said, blowing him a saucy kiss and then
leaving him to go and get her boots.

When she returned, he was typing on his phone. 'Just
checking on Billie,' he said.

'Is she all right? You've only just left her, haven't you?'

'Yes, but she frets a bit on nights like this. I told her we
shouldn't be late. The service is only a couple of hours, isn't it?
We ought to be back just after eight, I reckon.'

'Don't forget about the refreshments afterwards.'

'Yeah, but even if we stay for an hour, that should be plenty
of time to do our Christmas Eve presents.'

'Christmas Eve presents?'

'We've always done it. We have a special one for Christmas
Eve – usually a book or something like that, something small but
significant, or something we want the other to try.'

'That sounds cute,' Zoe said, now feeling guilty about the
fact that not only had she rushed buying his actual Christmas
gift, but she didn't have anything to give him for a Christmas
Eve gift.

'I can see the cogs working,' he said with a smile, 'and it
won't matter one bit that you haven't bought one for us – I'm
pretty sure neither of us said, so how would you be expected to
know? Billie heard about how they do it in some Nordic country
in a lesson at school once, and then she wanted us to do it.
We've done it ever since. It means a lot to her, you know – even

more since we lost Jennifer. I think it sort of keeps her connected to us, doing the thing we used to do when she was around.'

Zoe gave him a small smile and suddenly felt guilty for being so flippant on his arrival, for failing to remember that this time of the year was about so much more than Christmas to him. It would be a time to remember, to think back on past Christmases in his other life, the one he'd had before he'd met her. She'd been thrown by a random Christmas card sent by Ritchie – she couldn't imagine what it must be like for Alex. Especially this year, the first year he wouldn't be able to visit his wife's grave.

'Are you all right?' she asked.

He frowned. 'Why wouldn't I be?'

'Because this time of year... seems like it's a time to remember things, and not always things we want to remember. I had a conversation with Emilia this afternoon, and we talked about that, and then you... Well, I just wondered, that's all.'

'I could say the same to you.'

'I have been thinking about it, actually. I went into a shop and there was all this kids' stuff, and I thought about what it might be like to buy it for my own, but...' She gave a small shrug. 'There's no point in that, is there?'

He took her hand and kissed her fingers. 'I wish I could make it so you're never sad again.'

'I wasn't sad; I was just... well, I was only thinking about how things might have been. But they're not like that, and I have this life now, and though what I lost hurts, this life is good. You help to make it good.'

'I feel the same way. Since we met you, you've been so good for us, me and Billie. We think the world of you.'

'Even Billie? I'm sure she just thinks I interfere.'

'Oh, there's no doubt about that.' He laughed softly. 'But

she thinks *everyone* is interfering all the time, so don't take it personally. She likes you, though. A lot.'

The warmth spread throughout Zoe's whole body. 'Really?'

He nodded. 'We ought to go if we're going to make it before the start.'

'Yes, right...' She rushed to collect the gifts she'd wrapped for her friends and neighbours, and Alex angled his head at the bag.

'What's all that?'

'Presents for people I won't see tomorrow.'

'Oh. I haven't done that. I mean, I haven't got presents for anyone but you and Billie. Should I have done?'

'I don't think there are rules. I only got token things for people who've been kind to me since I moved here, but they're not much. It's just to say thank you, really. I can't say I'm entirely happy with most of them, but...'

'Oh.'

Zoe smiled. 'Don't look so worried. You're not going to get chased out of the village for not buying Christmas presents for everyone!'

He held out his hand to take the bag from her. 'I'll carry that for you.'

'Are you sure? I can manage—'

'You can watch your feet, and I'll keep this lot safe. And...' he added with a cheeky waggle of his eyebrows, 'when we get to the church, I'll hand them out and pretend I bought them.'

She laughed. 'Ooh, you would as well! That's ruthless!'

'I know. What are you going to do about it?'

Zoe closed the front door behind them, and they stepped out onto the snow. 'What am I going to do? Don't worry, I'll think of something that will make you sorry.'

'Promises, promises,' he said, laughing, and she gave him a playful shove that almost had him over, and then she was laughing too.

. . .

With banks of snow piled against walls and weighing down trees and shrubs, and the lights reflecting from it, Thimblebury looked like a Christmas card. One of those ones Zoe's gran always sent, with no glitter or jokes or drunken Santas, but with delicate line drawings and soft watercolours that were from a bygone age.

'I haven't been to a carol service since school,' Zoe said as they trudged the lane to get to the church.

Alex turned to her. 'Seriously?'

'Why would I? I'm not especially religious. I was christened, of course, and all that, but I haven't been to church... well, apart from a few times, and the last... It isn't a memory I want to think about.'

'Right...' He squeezed her hand to say he understood. 'If it makes any difference, I know what you mean. My last time in church wasn't great either. But maybe this will make us both new memories, nicer ones.'

'I'm hopeful. Who knows? Maybe we'll have such a good time we'll become converts, and we'll want to come to church every Sunday.'

He laughed. 'Steady on. Let's start with Christmas carols and see how we go. Anyway, we'll be too busy to come to church – in the summer, at least, I hope. If I'm not busy, I'll have done something very wrong with this glamping business.'

'It'll be good; I have faith in you. What did Billie say about doing your social media?'

'She was up for it, as long as she doesn't have to be in it. So I told her you'd be her star influencer.'

'You didn't? Alex!'

'I didn't, but I had you going for a minute, admit it! Seriously, though, it might be nice if you wanted to get involved. It would help to have a friendly face on the business.'

'Put yours on it then.'

'I would, but yours is prettier. I know which would persuade me to book if I was looking.'

'I think photos of the hills and lakes will do that just fine.'

'We'll see. I might persuade you yet, but I'm going to say that's a problem for later. Now we've got a carol service to get through without laughing.'

'Or falling asleep.'

'Right. I can see why Billie didn't want to come – not exactly the hippest place in town, is it?'

They looked up at the tiny church, warm light flooding from the open doors, candles on stands lining the path and ranged along the windowsills. The vicar's robes were flapping around his legs in a stiff, icy breeze that had the flames on the candles dancing as he greeted everyone before they filed in. The shrubs at the entrance were all decorated with messages tied to the branches that the villagers had been invited to write and bring with them – messages of hope, of gratitude, of prayers for souls who'd been lost, and for the coming year. Zoe was all at once affected by the sight, despite all their jokes only minutes before. It might not have been the hippest place in town, but it was rather lovely, a flashback of an older, gentler England that had long since gone, or like the Christmas stories she'd read and watched as a child. There was something inviting and comforting about it, like everyone who entered this church today was under some kind of protection. She hadn't been to church since the funeral for her unborn child, and she hadn't wanted to – until this very moment.

After a quarter of a year in Thimblebury, Zoe recognised nearly everyone going in, though there still the odd surprise. She wondered if people travelled in from outside the village to join them – it was a pretty church, after all, and Christmas Eve was often a special occasion for many that provided a moment of spirituality they scarcely felt during the rest of the year. If they had, she had to admire their tenacity because all the reports she'd heard said the roads through the hills and into the village were treacherous now.

'Have you had your cough sweets?' Alex asked.

'Huh?'

'To get your voice ready for all that singing?'

She smiled. 'You're daft.'

'It's been said. Come on then.'

Among the surprise attendees were Emilia, Georgia and Brett. Zoe did a double take as, after being greeted by the vicar, she went inside and found them sitting on a pew close to the doors. Given the fuss Emilia had made about Christmas – and not in a good way – and the fact she'd told Zoe earlier that day she had no intention of coming, Zoe was especially surprised to see her there. She wondered if it was simply to keep up appearances in the village, as Fliss would have done, though Emilia hadn't been all that bothered about appearances since she'd been here. Perhaps some of what Zoe had said had registered with her after all.

She went over with Alex. There was no room to sit with them, otherwise she would have done. Instead, there was an awkward moment where they all said a courteous hello, and then Zoe waited for a conversation to begin that never came. After a few stilted moments, she gave up. 'Maybe I'll see you afterwards for the mulled wine.'

'No wine for us,' Emilia said with such obvious bitterness that Zoe wondered if she'd heard properly.

Georgia flushed. 'Hopefully. I won't be having any, of course, and Em doesn't drink much, so we might have a quick word with people, but we won't stay.'

'I don't think there's only wine,' Alex said. 'I think there's going to be hot chocolate and eggnog and that sort of thing.'

'I've got things to do,' Emilia said. She looked at Georgia. 'You can stay if you want to, of course.'

So much for the afternoon she'd spent in her company, Zoe thought. She'd left Emilia hopeful they'd bonded somewhat over their shopping trip and the personal things they'd shared, but if they had, it had all been forgotten now. Or perhaps it had never felt that way to Emilia at all.

Georgia gave a small nod but didn't give any clue either way.

'So...' Zoe said into the gap, 'we might see you later...'

Once the encounter was over and they'd walked away, she heaved a silent sigh of relief.

'What was *that*?' Alex whispered as they searched for a seat.

'You saw it too then? I wondered if it was just me.'

'Definitely not just you. If I was a boxing referee, I'd be reading them the Queensberry rules right now.'

Ottilie was further down the hall towards the front, waving them over.

Zoe saw her and waved back, tapping Alex. 'There... I think Ottilie has saved us a seat.'

Ottilie and Heath had Flo with them as well as another couple Zoe had never seen before.

'This is Heath's mum and dad,' Ottilie said. 'Lori and Colin, this Zoe and Alex.'

'Pleased to meet you,' Zoe said, while Alex shook hands, and then they took a seat. 'It's getting full, isn't it?'

'Always is,' Flo said. 'The only time I see all the heathens in church is today when there's mulled wine afterwards.'

'You don't come to church either,' Ottilie reminded her.

'Only because my knees play up when I'm sitting in the cold.'

'Right...'

'I would,' she said. 'But this lot... Christmas Eve and when someone dies, that's it.'

'Well,' Ottilie said with a smirk, 'there's a festive thought.'

Flo folded her hands on her lap. 'Only saying what's what. No point in talking if it's not plain.'

'I like a Christmas service,' Lori said. 'I think all the singing is magical, especially on Christmas Eve.'

'You would,' Flo said brusquely. Zoe tried not to smirk this time. She'd never met Heath's mother, but she'd heard all about Flo's thoughts on her.

'Here's Magnus and Geoff,' Ottilie said. She waved, but Flo seemed as unimpressed by their arrival as by her daughter-in-law's company.

'That puffed up so-and-so,' she huffed. 'Done nothing but crow since he won the gingerbread prize. I can't even go in the shop now.'

'He hasn't been that bad,' Zoe said, but now she had to laugh at the look on Ottilie's face. 'All right, I admit he has been milking it a bit, but he's been waiting a long time to win it, hasn't he? And his entry was actually brilliant, so... Oh, here's Corrine and Victor! Who's that with them?'

Ottilie's face lost two shades. 'Melanie. Their daughter,' she added.

'I thought she'd left the village.'

'She has, but she's bound to come back to see her parents occasionally. And it is Christmas...'

'I wouldn't worry,' Flo said with something that sounded a bit too much like triumph in her voice for Zoe's liking. 'I doubt she'll be coming to talk to you, season of goodwill to all men or not.'

Victor and Corrine's other daughter, Penny, followed them in with her husband Leon. Corrine sent a slightly awkward smile the group's way, and Victor looked even more uncomfortable. It was a shame because they usually all got on so well, but Zoe supposed it was only natural things might be more difficult with the arrival of someone who'd parted from Ottilie on what some would call bad terms. Ottilie had always said she held no grudge, and neither did Victor or Corrine, but Melanie was an entirely different matter.

'As long as Damien doesn't turn up,' Heath said in a low voice. 'That would put the tin lid on things.'

'Damien's the ex, right?' Zoe asked.

'I doubt him or Fion would be that daft,' Ottilie said, nodding to Zoe, though she looked uncertain all the same.

Lavender came in next with her husband, and as Zoe watched, she could see the tension between her and Emilia as soon as they saw one another.

'I wouldn't hold your breath for any improvement in relations there,' Ottilie said, following Zoe's gaze.

'I'm hoping she's forgiven me,' Zoe said. 'She wasn't happy about me going off earlier.'

'She grumbled a bit, but she understood your situation and she seemed to be all right with that. You'll have to make it up to her over New Year's. She'll be having a party, and if I were you, I'd drop everything to go.'

'Otherwise no two-scoop specials afterwards?'

'I wouldn't hold my breath for many more of those anyway. I wouldn't be surprised if one of them isn't gone by the new year.'

Zoe stared at her. 'You think it's got that bad?'

'One doesn't let go of grudges easily, and the other doesn't care who has a grudge against her. Neither of them are very good at backing down. One could probably get a job anywhere at a pinch, and one doesn't need to work really. Why would either of them put up with it?'

'Do you think we have to do something?'

Ottilie shrugged. 'Like what?'

'I don't know. Talk to them both, try to mediate.'

'Good luck with that. I don't think you could find two worse people for that.'

Zoe had to admit Ottilie had a point. It was like Lavender and Emilia were enjoying the conflict because neither of them wanted to give an inch. She might have been tempted to suggest that Lavender should back down because she was, after all, employed by the surgery and, therefore, by Emilia, but Ottilie was spot on – Lavender didn't need that job. She cared about it and she enjoyed it – at least she had when Fliss had been the senior GP – but there had to come a point where it wasn't worth the constant warfare. 'I wish they'd sort it out, that's all. I feel like we're all caught in the crossfire all the time.'

'Maybe it will settle after Christmas,' Ottilie said.

'You just said you think one of them will go.'

'Well, I can only be wrong or right, can't I? For the sake of today, let's choose to be optimistic after all.'

Simon and Stacey came in next. Chloe wasn't with them, but Stacey had Mackenzie in her arms.

'He's getting so big so fast,' Ottilie said, an unconscious hand going to her own belly. 'Right now, I feel like this will never end...'

'And before you know it, you're waving them off to their last day at school,' Lori said, giving Heath a fond look. 'It flies – enjoy every moment while you can.'

'Some of us never had that luxury,' Flo snipped. 'Some of us had their grandsons whisked off to Manchester without a by your leave.'

'Florence,' Lori said, eyeing her solemnly. 'You know I've never said how sorry I am that you missed out. I'm going to say it now. I'm sorry.'

Flo's mouth dropped open, and she stared at Lori. It seemed for the first time in her life – certainly the first time Zoe had ever witnessed – she was speechless. Heath looked quite moved, while his dad gave a vague smile and Ottilie looked confused by the whole thing. Zoe exchanged a glance with Alex, seeing amusement in his eyes. They'd dissect the evening later together, and it would be interesting to see what he'd made of all these interactions, but, for now, it would have to wait.

The doors to the church closed, so all the drama going on along the pews would have to wait.

'Welcome!' the vicar said, holding up his arms like he was playing to a packed-out Wembley. 'May all the blessings of the season be upon you. If you'd like to turn to the first hymn in the programme, we will begin.'

'Hymn?' Alex whispered to Zoe. 'I was promised catchy Christmas carols, not hymns.'

'It's a nice hymn,' Zoe said, looking at the page. 'It's sort of Christmassy. I'm sure the carols will come later.'

They began, and Zoe wasn't a bit surprised to hear Alex had a good voice. She'd already considered him just about perfect, so of course he could sing too. For her part, she could hold the tune well enough, but she didn't imagine anyone would be signing her up for the choir. But what most of them lacked in technique, they more than made up for in enthusiasm. Even Flo was belting it out, despite looking sourly up and down the pews as she did, while Heath's parents seemed to be having the time of their lives. Their voices echoed around the space, and there was an immediate sense of community in the air, so tangible it took Zoe quite by surprise. For a startling instant, she understood how everyone belonged here, how easily the people of Thimble-bury took even those who had only recently arrived to their hearts. She'd never been a part of something so open and welcoming, and for all the problems, for all the drama in people's lives, that warmth was one constant. She'd wondered since her arrival if she could ever feel truly at home here, and not even meeting Alex had completely settled the question. But this evening, sharing this song with the rest of the village in their beautiful church, she finally had her answer.

26

There was no other scent quite like it. Spicy, sweet and heady. Zoe could smell the mulled wine before she could see it. As a teenager visiting a Christmas market in Germany with her mum, she'd indulged far too much, but the temporary dislike that incident had brought on hadn't lasted. Now it was one of her favourite things about Christmas markets, or any other type of festive gathering, for that matter – as long as she remembered she had limits. Easy to think, harder to do when it tasted so nice.

'I'll get it,' Alex said. 'You go and chat. People want you more than they want me.'

'I don't think that's true, but if you say so.'

She let him go to join the polite queue that had formed at a long table where members of the WI were serving and went to find Corrine and Victor to give them their gifts. Ottilie waved at her as she crossed the floor but seemed to be keeping a distance from where the owners of Daffodil Farm were talking to the vicar. Wisely, probably, Zoe thought, because Melanie and Penny were at their side.

'Hello, my love.' Corrine gave Zoe a brief hug. 'Did you enjoy the service?'

'I did, very much.'

The vicar smiled at Zoe. 'We haven't been properly intro-
duced yet, have we? I've meant to call at Kestrel Cottage to say
hello, but with one thing and another... Well, never mind. Here
we are. It's good to meet you at long last, Zoe.'

'You too,' Zoe said. It was probably just as well he hadn't
turned up at Kestrel Cottage, not during the last few weeks, at
least. There had been a lot going on there, and not much of it
holy when Alex was involved. 'The church looks pretty. Did
you decorate it?'

'Oh no, I have a team of able assistants who help me with all
that. My lovely ladies – I don't know what I'd do without them.
I'll pass on your praise. Have you had some refreshments?'

'Not yet, but there's some on the way to me.'

'Good, good... wouldn't want anyone to miss out. If you'll
excuse me' – he nodded at them all – 'I have some more meeting
and greeting to do.'

'No rest for the wicked, eh, Vicar?' Victor said.

'Indeed. It would be lovely to see you all at one of our
regular services. Everyone is always welcome. Merry
Christmas.'

'And to you,' Corrine said. 'We'll do our best to come down
in the new year.'

He left them all with a gracious smile.

'Can't be all that long till he retires,' Victor said, watching
him go. 'Seems like the village is getting old all at once, what
with Dr Cheadle going.'

'I won't be retiring for a long time,' Zoe said. 'I doubt any of
the rest of the team will be.' She smiled at Melanie. 'Hello... I'm
Zoe. The new midwife. I just moved here a few months ago. I
live in—'

'My old house. Yes, I know. You like it?'

'It's lovely.'

'I was happy there. I used to love the view when it rained

hard. Clouds over the hills, you know, so you couldn't see the tops. Still...' she sniffed, 'I'm glad someone is enjoying it now I've gone.'

Zoe didn't know how to reply and suddenly felt very guilty for living in what would have been Melanie's house. She supposed, in a way, it still was. It didn't belong to Zoe at any rate, being only a tenant, though it had started to feel like home. She shook the impending melancholy before it took hold.

'By the way,' she said, turning to Corrine and Victor, 'I wanted to give you these before I forget.' She handed them a gift each. 'To thank you for being so lovely.'

'Oh, love, we haven't—' Corrine began, but Zoe shook her head.

'They're only small. You do so much for me. I just wanted you to know how much I appreciate it.'

Corrine smiled. 'Aww, thank you, my love. You'll come over on Boxing Day, won't you? I'll be doing a bit of food, and you'd be welcome. Alex and Billie too, of course.'

'I'm not sure what we're planning but I'll mention it to them.'

'Tell him we always have too much food,' Victor said. 'If you came, you'd be doing us a favour.'

'Thank you. I will.'

'Look!' Corrine nudged Victor. 'There's Ann! We'd better go and have a word. I don't expect she'll stay long if she's left Darryl at home. Sorry, Zoe love... we'll just have to...'

'Of course! By the way,' Zoe added, scanning the room, 'you haven't seen Georgia and Brett since the service, have you?'

'They slipped out near the end,' Corrine said. 'Perhaps they decided not to come back.'

'Slipped out?'

'Stomped out, more like,' Victor said, but Corrine shot him a look.

'Shush,' she said. 'We didn't ask for any of that. You weren't even looking properly.' She turned back to Zoe. 'All three of them went – Georgia and her husband and the doctor. Sorry,' she said again, her gaze going to the far side of the room, 'we must catch... Ann! Ann, love!'

Corrine hurried away, Victor following, and then Melanie turned to talk to her sister, who was now chatting to Simon. Zoe hadn't expected to be best buddies with Victor and Corrine's absent daughter, but she might have expected a minimal amount of courtesy. On reflection, Melanie would know Zoe was friends with Ottilie, and perhaps she assumed any conversation would be awkward because of that.

Alex returned with their drinks.

'You haven't seen Georgia and Brett come back in, have you?' she asked.

'Didn't know they'd gone anywhere.' He gave her a stout-handled glass. It bore the name of a German town and a date – Christmas 2001. She turned to look at it, and then Alex showed her his. It had a different town on it and was dated 2007. 'I assume someone goes to the markets every year and brings one back. Either that or there was one hell of a niche jumble sale.'

Zoe laughed as she sipped her drink. 'Oh, that's nice!' She gave it an approving look. 'I could almost be in Berlin again.'

'We ought to do that next year,' he said. 'Go to a Christmas market, I mean.'

She smiled, warmed by the wine and his faith that they'd be together in a year's time, like it was a natural assumption to make. He was happy. She was happy too. 'It'd be fun,' she said. 'I haven't been to one in years. We should, yeah.'

Ottilie came over to them, a disappointingly ordinary mug in her hands containing hot chocolate. 'God, I'm so jealous right now.' She pointed at their wine. 'Being pregnant is rubbish at Christmas. No mulled wine, no snowballs, no chocolate liqueurs...'

'It'll be worth it in a few weeks, though,' Zoe said.

'It will, but I intend to remind Fred or Freda of the sacrifices I made every time they play up. For their entire lives, probably.'

Zoe's smile spread. 'Speaking of pregnant ladies, I've still got Georgia's present here, and I wanted to give it to her before she went home. Corrine said they went out before the service was over. I wonder if they've already gone home. They didn't seem keen to stay...'

'I didn't see them leave,' Ottilie said. 'But I haven't seen them since the service finished either. I suppose they must have.'

'That's annoying, but it can't be helped.' She turned to Alex. 'I'll have to call at the house before we go back to Hilltop. Unless they decide to make an appearance here after all.' She turned back to Ottilie. 'What are you planning tonight?'

'After this? Bed, I expect. I'm worn out. All I want to do is sleep at the moment. When's that spring-cleaning phase meant to start? I'd like some of that extra manic energy, please, because my floors are desperate for hoovering.'

'You won't be nesting for a couple of weeks yet, I'm afraid. You'll have to get Heath or Flo to do it.'

'I might as well not bother as ask either of them to do a decent job.'

'Then you'll have to be patient. It'll come.'

'I used to be good at patience, but it's one thing I've lost, along with my energy and my waistline. Well, I would go and get myself with child.'

Zoe raised her eyebrows. 'I don't think you did that all by yourself.'

'Hmm...' Ottilie scanned the room. 'Speaking of my co-conspirator, I'd better go and find him. He may need rescuing from his gran.'

'Come and say goodbye before you go,' Zoe said. 'Don't do a Georgia and sneak off.'

'I don't blame her,' Ottilie replied. 'I expect she's feeling even more knackered than I am by now. I mean, she's due in a week, isn't she? Anyway, I'll see you shortly.'

'OK.'

As Ottilie left them, Zoe turned back to Alex to find him sending a message on his phone.

'Billie,' he said, looking up. 'She wants to know what time we're due back.'

'She's all right?'

'I think so. Maybe fretting a bit about the weather.'

'It can't be that much worse than when we came down here earlier.'

'I don't know about that. She hasn't actually said that's what's bothering her; I'm only guessing. It could be that she's bored.'

'Or desperate to open her Christmas Eve gift?'

'That too,' Alex said with a grin.

'She pretends to be all cool and nonchalant, but she's still your little girl at heart, isn't she?'

'Always,' he said with such fondness it almost made Zoe envy Billie. Alex loved Zoe, and she was in no doubt of that, but Billie would always be the most important woman in his life. Zoe understood that, and she would never get in the way, but it was a fact she was going to have to get used to.

'If it makes you feel better, we won't stay for much longer. Let's finish these drinks, pop over to Georgia's with their presents and then we'll go back up to Hilltop.'

'Thanks,' he said. 'Not that I'm not enjoying this, but I'm getting to the point where I want to be home.'

'Me too,' Zoe said. 'Very much so.'

27

After many complaints that they were leaving, offers of Christmas Eve get-togethers at some house or other, and affectionate goodbyes, Zoe and Alex finally made it out of the church. They hadn't been outside since the service had begun a few hours earlier and were both shocked at just how fast the weather had worsened. Where the snow had been cleared was inches deep again.

'Here's your white Christmas.' Alex pulled his collar up and clamped a woolly hat onto his head. 'This is mental. I don't think I've ever seen it like this.'

'What time is it?' Zoe asked. 'I don't want to take my gloves off to look at my phone because I think my fingers might get instant frostbite and fall off.'

'Just after nine.'

'Later than I wanted to be.'

'Later than I wanted it to be too. Billie won't be pleased, but there's not a lot we can do about it now.'

'I'm sorry, but I still have these presents to drop off at Emilia's house. I know we're already late, but do you mind if we call in? We don't have to stay.'

'You're right, we're already late, so what difference will ten more minutes make? Come on.'

Grabbing her hand, he led the way. It was slow going, and they both walked with their heads down, partly to watch their feet to make sure they didn't slip and partly to avoid a face full of driving snow.

'I'll be glad when we're home and warm,' he said as they arrived at Emilia's gate. 'Next year, don't even think of talking me into a Christmas Eve carol service.'

'You loved it really.'

'I did. I'm just not loving this bit.'

Just as they trudged up the path, the lights went out on the lane. Zoe looked sharply at Alex, barely able to make out his features in the sudden gloom.

'Snow must have brought a power line down.'

Zoe glanced at the house and could see there were no lights on in there either.

'They'll be out to fix it as soon as they can, I would imagine,' Alex said reassuringly.

'How's anyone coming out to fix anything in this?'

'They're equipped for this sort of event,' he said in a voice so confident that Zoe did feel reassured, even if she wasn't quite sure how he'd know so much about it. 'It won't be out for long.'

Almost feeling their way, darkness and snow reducing visibility to a point that made looking useless, they made it to Emilia's front door. Alex gave the knocker a firm rap – a sound that would have ordinarily echoed back through to them but was muffled by the snow.

'I hope they're in and not out in this,' he said with a look of faint worry.

They gave it a minute, and when there was no answer, they knocked again. Nobody came to the door. Zoe went to a window and tried to look inside, but with no lights on, it was pointless. Even if anyone was home, she couldn't see them. When she pressed an ear to the glass, she couldn't hear movement either.

'I don't think they *are* in,' she said, coming back to Alex on the doorstep.

'They picked a fine night to go sledding,' Alex said. 'What do you want to do? You want to go back to the church to see if they've turned up there and we've somehow missed them on the road? I wouldn't be surprised if we had in these conditions.'

'I don't think they will have done. They weren't all that bothered about staying after in the first place, so why would they have gone back this late, knowing the event would be almost over?'

'Who knows? It was a suggestion I made because I don't have anything else. Are you worried about them?'

'Not Emilia and Brett, but I am worried about Georgia. She's really close to term, and I don't like the thought of her being out.' She pulled a glove off and got out her phone. But then she frowned at it.

'What's the matter?'

'I was going to phone one of them to see where they are, but I don't think...' She switched her phone off and then back on, watching the opening logo on the screen for a moment before her usual display appeared. 'I don't think I can get a signal.'

Alex got his out and nodded. 'Me neither. It must be something to do with the weather. Like the blackout.'

'So we can't phone them then. Where the hell could they be?'

'Would they have gone to see anyone else in the village?'

'They don't really know anyone all that well, and everyone they might know was at the church.'

'I don't know what to say. I don't think there's a lot more we can do. If it matters that much to you, Zo, we can come tomorrow first thing and drop their gifts in. Before lunch or something.'

'There's nothing else for it, so we'll have to.' Zoe looked up at the door and knocked one last time in the vain hope they were in after all, but was met with silence once again. 'That's it then,' she said. 'We'd better go home before we get stranded.'

'Stranded in a blizzard with no lights and no phone signal – sounds appealing, doesn't it?' he said. 'I agree – let's get back. I like a bit of festive snow as much as the next man, but once we're home, nothing is getting me out again in this.'

As they started for home, it quickly became apparent that it was going to be more of a struggle than either of them had imagined. Alex was all for going back to the church to see if Victor was still there with his Land Rover in the hopes he could get them back, until Zoe reminded him that doing so might present troubles of its own. Firstly, they were relying on the fact that he would be there and hadn't already left, and, secondly, even if he was there, his car would be too full for them both because he and Corrine had Melanie and their other daughter, Penny, with them. They couldn't even phone anyone to find out if there was someone else who could help, but Zoe had faith that if they took care, they'd be fine. After all, she reasoned, it wasn't as if they lived in the tundra. This was England, and people didn't get lost in the snow or frozen solid where they stood. And so they walked, frustratingly slowly, with numb fingers and toes and dripping noses, feeling their way in the dark.

'I love Kestrel Cottage,' Zoe panted at the halfway point. 'And I love Hilltop, but after this I might move downhill to the village proper because I don't fancy doing this again next winter.'

'We haven't got through this one yet,' Alex replied through gritted teeth. 'One thing at a time.'

Zoe stumbled and then felt his hand close around hers to steady her. 'All right there?'

'I've been better.'

'Me too. Just keep thinking about that wine when we get back.'

'I think the wine we had before we started out is causing more than enough trouble for us now. I might lay off it. In fact, I might just collapse into bed and you can wake me when it's Christmas.'

'And miss all the fun?'

'Right now, sleeping looks like a lot of fun. Ugh...' She gasped as the wind changed direction to drive fat, wet snowflakes into her face.

'I don't know about the mulled wine we had earlier being the problem,' Alex said. 'I'm definitely sober now.'

Zoe had no idea how long it had taken them to get to the top of the track. There was no moon and barely any light at all. Even when the lights of either Hilltop or Daffodil or Kestrel Cottage ought to be visible, they could see none of them. Zoe could just make out a squat, fuzzy shape across the nearest field, which she guessed was Daffodil Farm.

'I think it's this way,' Alex said, pointing to a spot further along the ridge. 'If that's Daffodil, I mean.'

'I think it is,' Zoe agreed. 'We should be able to see Hilltop soon if we walk along a bit.'

'If we don't, we might have to go to Daffodil instead and see if Victor wouldn't mind running us over to mine.'

Zoe hadn't wanted to disturb the residents of Daffodil Farm, especially when they had family visiting, but she couldn't argue with the logic.

A few minutes later, Zoe thought she could see the vague outline of Hilltop.

'Either that's a mirage,' Alex said, squinting against the driving snow, 'or that's home. I'm hoping for the latter.'

'Me too.'

They picked up the pace, despite the treacherous ground beneath them, both eager to be indoors, finally able to get dry and warm. When they reached the gate, they saw a light in the downstairs window, as there had been a few nights before, but this time it came from a group of candles, lit by Billie. There were no other lights on in the rest of the house.

Alex unlocked the door, and they tumbled over the threshold together, both of them laughing with delirious relief.

Billie was in a fleecy dressing gown, sitting in the old rocking chair in the corner of the kitchen with a crossword puzzle and a torch. Grizzle had been at her feet, but at the sight of Alex and Zoe, he leaped up and began to bark, dancing around them with his tail whirring.

'All right, all right...' Alex chuckled. 'Give us a minute!'

'Where have you been?' Billie demanded. 'I didn't know what to do! I couldn't get a phone signal, and the lights went out, and you weren't—'

'The power's gone off in the village too,' Alex said. 'And our phones were out of action. We've had to walk, and it's tough going out there, so... sorry you were worried.'

'I didn't know what to do. I was going to go to Daffodil if you weren't back in the next half hour.'

'No need now,' he said, going over to his daughter and giving her a hug. 'We're all present and correct. I could do with a brew, though.'

'You'll have to boil a pan on the stove,' Billie said. 'I had to earlier.'

'I'm sure there's a back-up generator somewhere in the barn,' Alex said, undoing his boots. 'Ann left it behind. Not sure if it's any good, but I could look. When I've warmed up, that is.'

'Do you even know how to connect it up?' Billie asked.

'Well, no, but there's YouTube. I bet there's something on there.'

'Hmm,' Billie said wryly. 'And how are you going to watch YouTube? We've got no power, no phone signal and no Wi-Fi.'

'Ah...' Alex gave a sheepish grin. 'Looks like we're going back to the Stone Age for a bit then.'

'It's kind of nice,' Zoe said, and both Billie and Alex stared at her. 'Traditional, you know? Like an old-fashioned Christmas before they had electric. It could be fun.'

'At least we're here and in one piece,' Alex said. 'That'll do for me. It also looks as if you'll be staying here for the foreseeable.'

'Looks like it. I was going to go home after the service to do some bits for tomorrow's lunch before we settled down here, but I suppose that's out of the question after all the unexpected drama.'

'We'll manage. It doesn't matter if lunch isn't perfect, as long as we're together.'

'I know, but it's our first one together, and I wanted it to be. I offered, and I'm... well, I'm disappointed. I wanted it to be special.'

'It will be.' He smiled warmly at her before clapping his hands together. 'Right... let's see about this pan-on-the-stove business, and when we've had a cup of tea and warmed up, we'll do the Christmas Eve present exchange, eh, Billie?'

'Yeah,' Billie said, her gaze going to a neatly wrapped parcel on the table. She'd clearly been ready and waiting for some time.

Zoe couldn't help but feel responsible for the delay, but wasn't sure how it could have been helped in the end.

Finally, with the feeling just about coming back to her extremities, Zoe was sitting with a blanket over her lap in front of the fire with a cup of hot tea. Billie had settled down with her while Alex went to get their early gifts from under the tree.

'I saw Maisie,' Zoe said to Billie. 'I think you made quite an impression on her.'

'Did I?'

Zoe nodded. 'Seemed like she had a great time with you. And thanks for cooking for her. It's good to know she's getting some decent food.'

'Well, if she comes over again, I'll cook something else for her.'

'That would be great. And good for her to see you being so sensible about your pregnancy.'

'Yeah, she told me about her mum. What a dickhead.'

Alex burst into laughter as he came over with their gifts. 'Billie! You can't say that!'

Billie rolled her eyes. 'I just did. Anyway, it's the truth.'

Zoe paused, wondering if Billie would share anything more of her afternoon with Maisie. She hadn't yet asked Billie about what Maisie had said regarding supporting one another after their babies were born, and Billie hadn't volunteered any of the details either.

Alex had been an even trickier prospect. Zoe had been desperate to share what she knew with him, but she was painfully aware of the dangers of creating false hope. If Billie was changing her mind about the adoption, the news needed to come from her, and she had to have made her decision without any pressure or expectation from anyone else.

'Well, here you go...' Alex said, handing a parcel to her, and as she took it, Zoe realised the moment had gone. For now, she put it from her mind and smiled as she watched Billie open her Christmas Eve gift.

'It's lovely!' she said, standing to open out a heavily beaded and embroidered wall hanging.

'I had it shipped from Spain,' he said. 'From that shop you loved in Seville – remember?'

'The handicraft place...' Billie gaped. 'It must have cost you so much to get it sent here! You should have saved it for my main present!'

'I was going to, but I was too excited for you to open it.'

'Dad!' Billie laughed. 'You're like a kid!'

'It's been said.'

'Aww...' She kissed him on the cheek, and Zoe wasn't sure she'd ever seen her look so happy. 'I love it! Can you help me put it up in my room later?'

'It would be my pleasure, *mademoiselle*!'

'Right.' Billie nodded at the coffee table, where a neatly wrapped parcel was sitting. 'Your turn.'

He reached for it and undid the ribbon. He was silent for a moment as he opened the paper and studied what was inside.

'Wow...' he said finally.

'You like it?' Billie asked. 'I know it seems a bit random, but—'

'Of course I like it,' he said. 'It's brilliant.'

'I thought when we're all done here and Hilltop is how we want it, it might be nice to have those pictures to look back on. To see how far we've come, you know, remember what it was like when we got here. I took some of the countryside too, when I was walking around those first couple of weeks. I didn't know I was going to make a book for you, but I had some space, and I thought I'd put them in too.'

'Can I see?' Zoe asked, craning to look over his shoulder.

He handed the book to her. Lit by the warm yellow glow of the candles, she flicked through to see photographs of what Hilltop had looked like before he and Billie had arrived and started to transform it. They'd come so far already, she silently remarked as she turned the pages, even though they often said there was a lot more to do.

'I forgot just how run-down it was when Ann had it. I mean,

it wasn't horrible, but she'd said she needed to do a lot of repairs.'

Alex nodded, and Zoe went back to the book to see photos of the hills and valleys around their home, taken at different times of the day where the light was watercolour greys and blues, or where the sun was cresting a hilltop to bathe it in golden rays, or a red and orange sky was fading into twilight. Billie had photographed flocks of birds, and a lone buzzard circling the field that separated Hilltop from Daffodil Farm and Kestrel Cottage. She'd taken shots of the flora and fauna, and there was almost more nature in the book than there were images of their house. Zoe looked up at her with a bemused smile. She hadn't meant to, but she couldn't help it. She'd never had Billie down as someone this connected to the world around them. Alex's daughter was still full of surprises, even now, when Zoe was starting to feel she almost knew her.

'It's gorgeous,' she said, closing it carefully and giving it back to Alex. 'You're really creative. I should have known that already from your gingerbread house,' she added. 'But you're actually good at everything!'

'Not everything,' Billie said, flushing. 'I like taking photos, that's all. I used to do it all the time, and I forgot for a while, but I got my old camera out and started to take some and...' She shrugged. 'I didn't know I'd missed photography until I started to do it again.'

'You'll have cracking shots for your accounts when the campsite is up and running. Your dad says you're taking on the social media.'

'If I have time,' she said, shooting a cautious glance at Alex.

'You might get a job instead?' Zoe asked, her mind going back to what Maisie had told her about Billie suggesting they both work at Hilltop together and the plans for their babies. 'Wouldn't you rather work in the family business with your dad? I mean, it will be sort of a family business, won't it?'

'Maybe,' Billie replied, and Zoe detected that hesitation again. Clearly, she had thoughts she wasn't ready to share yet. Zoe didn't yet know Billie properly, but she knew one thing – she would make her feelings and her plans known when she was ready and not before.

'I have one for you...' Alex said to Zoe, putting his book down and reaching behind the sofa for a small square gift.

'Oh no!' Zoe protested. 'You know I didn't get you anything!'

'I haven't done it for that reason; I just didn't want to leave you out.'

'But I feel terrible I haven't got anything for you and Billie.'

'You've got actual Christmas presents,' he said.

'Yes, but they're at my place for tomorrow.'

'Then we'll have them tomorrow. This isn't about keeping score; we just wanted you to be able to join in our tradition.'

Zoe gave him a warm smile, knowing when she was beaten and touched, despite the gesture feeling one-sided. 'Thank you, but you shouldn't have.'

'I'll take it back then...' he said, and she snatched it from his grasp.

'No you won't! I want to see what it is now!'

Tearing off the paper, she found a small midnight-blue box. Inside, there was a key. She looked up at him.

'It's a spare one,' he said. 'For Hilltop. You can come and go as you please, and maybe, when you're ready, you can come and not go...'

Zoe's eyes filled with tears, and she looked at Billie to see the plan had her approval. Her head wanted to say it was too soon, that she wasn't ready for a move like that, but it didn't matter. He'd phrased his hopes perfectly, so that there was no pressure. She could come and go, and when she was ready, she could come and stay forever.

'Thank you,' she whispered, stroking the key.

'I hope it hasn't freaked you out,' he said, sudden doubt in his eyes. 'That wasn't my intention.'

'Not one bit. We'll need time, but I think... I think I'd love to be here all the time eventually.'

There was silence, and a flood of understanding that passed between all three of them that, somehow, this was a huge moment. The key in her hand and Alex's offer would make them a family. What was bigger and meant more than that was Billie's acceptance.

The spell was broken as the lights went back on. A few minutes later, phones began to beep the arrival of messages.

'There's a lot from you,' Alex said to Billie as he scrolled through his. 'Anyone would think you were worried about us.'

'Very funny,' she shot back. 'It's all right for you – you weren't sitting here alone with no electricity.'

'I think I'd rather have been doing that than fighting my way home in a blizzard.'

'That's not fair. I was scared. I thought something had happened to you...'

Alex's face fell, and Zoe knew what he was thinking. He'd been flippant, but as soon as he'd made the joke, he'd realised that Billie had lost so much, people who were everything to her, so she'd had every right to be afraid for them. He'd allowed himself to forget, for just a second, and it hadn't been fair.

'Sorry,' he said. 'You're right.'

'It doesn't matter now. At least you're here.'

Zoe's own phone updated more slowly, but a few seconds later it did, and she noticed the missed calls from Georgia and Emilia. Lots of them. And then a text came through.

Where are you? Georgia's waters have broken.

It was from Emilia. Zoe looked at the time – it had been sent two hours before, when there had been no signal in the village. Perhaps Emilia hadn't realised until it had failed to go through, or perhaps she'd sent it anyway in the hope it would reach Zoe when her phone came back online, hoping it wouldn't be too long. She looked up at Alex.

'Oh, no,' he said, reading her expression. 'What now? What's wrong?'

'It's Georgia. Her waters have broken.'

'Where is she?' he asked. 'They weren't at home. So does that mean they're at the hospital? I mean, it's only half an hour or so to drive. So they don't need you if that's the case, do they?'

'I don't know; Emilia hasn't said any more than that. It's half an hour in decent weather, but this isn't decent weather, is it? I'm not sure how passable the roads are, but judging by how we struggled to get home, I don't imagine very. If Emilia was asking, she must have wanted me.'

'When did she send the message?'

'A couple of hours ago.'

'She might have got help since then. They wouldn't have waited around for you, would they?'

'I don't know that either. She might not be progressing very fast – perhaps she's just telling me so I can keep tabs on things. It might be hours and hours before she's ready to have the baby, but if her waters have broken, I'd rather be on hand.'

'Can you be on hand tomorrow? Emilia knows what she's doing... enough, surely? Do you have to be on hand tonight? There's no way you can go out in this weather again.'

Zoe shook her head vaguely and dialled Emilia's number. It was answered immediately, but not by Emilia, by Brett.

'Hi... it's Zoe. I've only just got the text... what's happening?'

'Georgia's waters have broken.'

'So the message said. Where are you now? Are you home?'

'We're at the church.'

Zoe frowned. 'But you'd left there...'

'We went back to find you when it happened, and yes, I know we shouldn't have let her go out into the snow, but she wouldn't hear otherwise. Now Emilia doesn't dare move her. She's not doing great.'

'Georgia isn't?'

'She's struggling. In a lot of pain...'

'She's in labour?'

'I don't know. Maybe.'

'Can you put Emilia on?'

'Hang on... She's just....'

Brett's voice faded, and then Emilia's was on the line.

'Hello,' she said briskly. 'She's started. I can probably manage if you can't get here, but I'd be grateful if you could. It's not really my strong suit, delivering babies. Not something I generally have to do a lot of.'

Zoe smiled grimly. 'I don't suppose it is. I'll come. How far along do you think she is?'

'She won't let me look. I think she's a bit delirious, keeps banging on about everyone in the church being able to see.'

'You've got her somewhere private?'

'Heavens, of course I have! There's nobody here now but the vicar. I did ask if he could deliver a baby but apparently not.'

'Hang on,' Zoe said, fighting an irrational urge to laugh at Emilia's statement, despite the situation. Casually asking the vicar if he could deliver a baby like he might whip up a pot of tea and being surprised and annoyed when the answer was no... It was very Emilia. 'Make her comfortable... Sorry, I know, stating the obvious. I'm sure you know all that. I'll be with you as soon as I can.'

Zoe ended the call, and when she looked up at Alex, she could see real concern. 'Surely you're not going out? Can't they call an ambulance?'

'I'm sure they have, but it's got to get here. Come on – you know how long it takes. We had the same thing with Billie not so long ago, when she had her fall and she was bleeding, remember? And you were glad enough to have me on hand then...'

'Sorry...' Alex looked shamefaced, and she realised her tone had been sharper than she'd meant.

'No, I'm sorry. I didn't mean it like that. You have to understand, this is my job. I could never stand by and let everyone struggle down there. How could I sit here and be at peace with my conscience? I could never look another mum in the face again, and what if something bad happened? It would be my fault.' She gave her head a firm shake. 'Sorry, but I have to go.'

'I'm coming with you then.'

'Don't be daft! What about Billie?'

'I'll come too.'

'Absolutely not!' Zoe pulled the blanket aside and stood up. 'There's no way I'm putting you at risk on a night like this. You're staying here, and I don't care how much you argue because it won't change.'

'She's right,' Alex said.

Billie pouted, but she didn't offer a reply.

And then Alex turned his common sense on Zoe. 'How the hell are you going to get down to the church? Or have you forgotten how bad it was underfoot when we came up here earlier? It's snowed more since then as well.'

'I'll walk.'

'You *are* joking, right?'

'We walked up here.'

'Yes, and, again, I'd like to remind you how difficult it was.'

'The car would never make it.'

He was thoughtful for a minute. 'Victor might have snow chains or something. We might get down with those.'

'There isn't time for that.'

'We'll take our chances in the car as it is then. I'll take it slowly. I've driven in snow before...'

Zoe wanted to argue. She didn't want him to come with her because he didn't really want to go, and he didn't really want to leave Billie either. But she could see that if she was going, he was never going to let her go alone.

'All right,' she said finally. 'I'll go and get my coat.'

28

In the end, their discussions had been a waste of time. Alex's car had barely made it out of the garage before it slid down an incline and into some shrubbery. There was no real damage, but as he tried to reverse out, all that happened was the wheels spun, smoke poured from the engine, and it got stuck deeper in the snow.

He pulled on the handbrake and turned to her. 'That's that then. We're not taking the car, apparently.'

Zoe glanced out to see Billie watching them from the window of the house, arms wrapped tight around herself. 'Apparently. So it's walking or nothing.'

'Let me phone Victor,' he said, getting out of the driver's side.

Zoe sat back in the car to stay out of the snow while Alex dialled the number for Daffodil Farm. After a brief wait, he ended the call and stuffed his phone back into his pocket.

'Doesn't sound like there's anyone home.'

'They might all have gone to spend the evening with Penny and Leon.'

'Who knows? Unless they've gone up to check on the

alpaca. I wouldn't blame them for being worried about them in this weather. I wish one of them would join the twenty-first century and get a mobile phone. I don't know how anyone used to manage without them. I don't have a number for Leon or Penny.'

'Sorry, neither do I. I've never had all that much to do with them since I arrived, other than to say hello in passing. They tend to keep themselves to themselves.'

Alex got back into the car and tapped his phone on his chin for a moment as he pondered their predicament. At least, that was what Zoe hoped he was doing, rather than trying to find a way to tell her that she couldn't go down to help Georgia, because nothing he could say would change her mind, and she didn't want to have to fight him as well as the weather.

'OK,' he said finally. 'We're going to have to dig the car out and try again. Hang on here; I'll go and get a shovel.'

While Alex went to find his equipment Zoe texted Emilia to find out how things were there and to explain their delay. Emilia replied immediately.

She's OK at the moment. But we could do with you sooner rather than later. I'm sure I could deliver, but I'd feel better if you were here.

Zoe would feel better if she could be there too. She had no doubt Emilia would be capable enough to get by, but Zoe didn't like the idea of leaving them all to struggle when her expertise could make things a hundred times better. She'd made a promise too, that she would take care of Georgia, and it was a promise she took seriously. Come hell or high water, she was going to get back down to the village to be with her friend when she needed her most. If only she hadn't left before being certain all was well. If Zoe owed Georgia nothing else, she had that mistake to make up for.

A few minutes later, Alex came back.

'You've only got one shovel,' she said, getting out of the car.

'I wasn't going to have you digging.'

'Faster with two.'

'You slide into the driver's seat, and when I say, see if you can reverse.'

Zoe did as she was asked, and through the side mirror, she could see Alex trying to dig around the back wheels. Then he went to the front and did the same before stepping back and signalling for her to start the engine. But the wheels only spun again, and though the car inched back a little, it slid forward again almost immediately.

'Whoa!' Alex yelled, and Zoe killed the engine.

'What about some cardboard?' Zoe asked. 'We could slide some sheets of cardboard under the tyres so they've got something to drive on, and it might be enough to get us free.'

'Cardboard?'

'My dad got stuck once, and someone came out from a nearby house and helped him with flattened cardboard boxes.'

Alex scratched at his neck, studying the car. 'I suppose it's worth a try. Not sure what I've got, but I can look in the shed... might have some leftover from when we moved in.'

Zoe got out of the car and followed him.

They gathered what they could and went back to the car. Zoe went around to each wheel this time, shoving the flattened sheets underneath each tyre to give them a surface to drive on, though no sooner had she done it than the cardboard itself began to disappear beneath a fresh layer of fast-falling snow.

'OK!' she shouted.

Alex revved the engine, and after a few seconds, the car began to move. And then it was free.

Zoe leaped back into the car and slammed the door shut, afraid to lose the momentum. 'Let's go.'

They'd barely gone twenty metres when the car began to slide again. This time it spun straight into a fencepost.

'Shit!' Alex leaped out to inspect the damage. 'It's caught one of the headlights, but it doesn't look too bad.'

'Can we still go?'

'I don't know... Zoe, I think you're going to have to accept that we're going nowhere in the car tonight.'

'So I've wasted all that time when I could have been walking.'

'You can't walk it.'

'Then how am I going to get there?'

'Zoe' – he leaned into her open window – 'they have Emilia, and Simon is close by. If two fully qualified GPs can't deliver a baby between them—'

'It's not that simple!'

'Ottilie did it. You told me she delivered Mackenzie.'

'She was lucky – Mackenzie's birth was straightforward, but they're not always. What if Georgia's is complicated? It's not fair to ask Emilia and Simon to do it.'

'But they could.'

The gaze that met his was challenging. 'Would you want that for Billie? If Billie was in labour and there was no midwife, would you be like, that's fine, as long as someone who knows a bit about medicine is there...?'

'It's not Billie.'

'And that's a *bugger you, I'm all right, Jack*, attitude to have. I'm shocked at you for having it. It's not who I thought you were.'

'Maybe it is, but I'm not going to apologise for it. I want you safe. To me, you're more important than Georgia. I don't care if you don't like me saying it, but it's the truth.'

Zoe folded her arms and stared straight ahead. 'I *don't* like you saying it.'

'Then I'm sorry for that but not for the sentiment. They've called for an ambulance, and they've got Emilia. Leave it – accept that you can't get there, that just this once someone is going to have to manage without you.'

'Do you really think I can sit here and drink wine and not give it another thought? I can't. If anything went wrong and they couldn't deal with it, I'd never forgive myself. I'm going to have one more try. I'll go on foot. You don't have to come with me; you can stay and keep an eye on Billie.'

He paused, holding her in a frank gaze. And then he let out a sigh. 'You're determined to make my life as difficult as possible, aren't you? I can't let you go on your own, and Billie should be safe enough here for a few hours. If we're going, then we'd better go now before it becomes impossible.'

The most difficult thing about going on foot wasn't the snow itself, but the fact that the true path down the hill had all but disappeared beneath it. They made their way as best they could, in visibility that was not only poor from the absent moon and driving snow, but from the glare of the lamps Victor had installed, which now bounced from the frozen ground and threw confusing shadows onto it. Where there was a path looked like a dip, and where there was a fissure looked like it was safe. They'd picked their way down the first slope that led up to Hilltop with relative success – certainly more than they'd had in a car. The ground plateaued for a time, and that seemed straightforward enough, but they'd both been watching their feet and not their surroundings, and as there was little else to orient them, neither Alex nor Zoe had any clue just how badly they'd veered off course until they got into trouble.

As the ground began to tilt again, the incline felt wrong. Zoe had walked this path many times since she'd moved to Thimble-bury and even more since she'd started to visit Alex and Billie, and she could tell her feet weren't feeling the undulations they normally did. She wondered if she was simply on a different section of the correct path than she'd thought she was, and perhaps that was why it felt off. But they'd gone off course, close to where the crest of the hill dropped away to one side, into a gulley that wasn't neces-sarily steep but in the current circumstances was enough to cause a problem if someone found themselves at the bottom of it. If she could have seen what was coming, of course, Zoe would have called a halt to their walk and taken time to reorient. But she didn't see until it was too late. One wrong step, a bank of snow that gave way beneath her and a moment later she let out a squeal as she slid away from Alex, down the ridge and into the shadows below.

29

'Zoe?'

Alex's voice came from the gloom above her as she finally came to a halt. Every rock and stone had knocked the breath from her on the way down, but at least the fall had been cushioned by the snow. Now she was simply wet and bruised, rather than something much worse.

'I'm all right...' she said. 'I can't... bugger... I let go of my bag and I can't see it.' She squinted in the beam of Alex's torch as he shone it down on her. 'Shine it around to see if you can find it, please.'

She watched the light cover the ground, but although it had been bright enough trained directly onto her, it was next to useless trying to cover the terrain that was further away. Her bag might have been there, but there was no sign of it. Though she couldn't see him either now, she looked up at where she thought Alex was with a vague sense of panic welling inside her. Without her bag, how was she going to give Georgia the care she needed? It was about more than the sanitiser and protective sheets and gloves. To do her job safely, she needed other things that were in there, like items for pain relief, a resuscitation kit for emergencies, as well as the usual things like clamps and forceps and postpartum supplies. At an extreme pinch, she could head over without them and make do until somebody could get replacements to her, but she really didn't want to have to do that.

Even then, perhaps a more pressing issue was how she was going to get back up this slope. She took a deep breath to steady herself and then decided that the first thing she had to do was to try to find her equipment. Then she'd worry about getting back to the path.

But when she tried to stand up, there was a pain in her ankle that the shock of the fall had masked, and she realised she'd injured herself after all. It wasn't at the sort of intensity that might have suggested a broken bone, but it was enough to hamper her efforts. And she was cold, so there was no telling if that was helping to numb the pain so that she couldn't correctly identify the severity of her injury. It might be worse than it seemed.

No matter, she told herself, whether it was serious or superficial, she had to get up. She had to find her bag, and she had to find a way to get back to the path.

'Zoe...' Alex's voice was full of concern. 'You've gone quiet... Talk to me.'

'Yeah, sorry. I was trying to work things out. I've... don't freak out, but I've hurt my ankle.'

'I'm coming down—'

'No point. You'll come down and we'll both be stuck.'

'I won't get stuck; I'll take it slowly.'

'Alex... don't. I'll find a way to get back up. Have another look with your torch to see if you can find my bag first. If I know where it is, I can go straight to it and then bring it with me.'

'Can't you leave it and come back for it when the snow's stopped?'

'It's really important. I need it for Georgia, but I don't want all the equipment in it getting soaked – that won't do any of it any good.'

'Right,' Alex said, sweeping the terrain once more with the beam of his torch.

Frustratingly, there was still no sign of the bag. Zoe had to assume it had rolled or slid much further on, or that she simply couldn't see it in the gloom. She wondered whether to take a few minutes to feel around for it. Her ankle protested as she got on her feet, but no sooner had she started to hobble than her feet began to slide away from her again, threatening to take her even further down the slope.

'Alex...' she said slowly.

The beam came back to settle on her. 'Why does your tone worry me?'

'Yeah... I don't think I'm going to be able to get up here, actually. I think it's too slippery.'

'Shit.'

'I couldn't have put it better myself. You might have to come down after all.'

'But...' He was silent for a moment, the torch beam moving away to plunge her into gloom again. 'Stay there,' he said finally.

'It's not like I have a choice.'

'Yes, sorry... I mean, hang on. I'll go and get help.'

'Don't fall down any slopes!' Zoe called after him as she watched the beam of his torch turn back the way they'd come. She let out a sigh and sat down again. It wasn't like her bum could get any wetter, and her ankle was hurting, so why not? She felt around the ground in her immediate vicinity for her bag again, in case she'd somehow missed it, but in vain. That was the most annoying aspect of this whole thing.

Unable to do much about that now, she dug out her phone to check for messages. There were none. Either everyone was too busy looking after Georgia to update, or they were too busy because something bad had happened.

Zoe decided to text Emilia, but when she pressed send, she was met with a notification that told her there was no signal again. The night was getting better and better, she reflected ruefully.

With nothing else to do, she resigned herself to waiting for the promised help, and hoping that Alex wouldn't run into trouble on his way to get it like she had.

Twenty minutes had passed. Zoe was cold, and she was getting stiff and plagued by a vague, irrational worry that if she sat there for much longer, she'd get buried by the snow and nobody would find her until it was too late – for her and for Georgia. But then she heard an engine, deeper and throatier than Alex's car, and was filled with new energy. Surely this had to be her rescue party?

The engine came to a halt somewhere on the track above her, and then Alex called down.

'Zoe? You OK?'

'Better now you're back,' Zoe called up.

'I'm coming down.'

'But—'

'Don't worry!' another voice called, and Zoe took a moment to place it until she realised it was Leon, Victor's son-in-law. 'We've got mountaineering gear fit for Everest, so it should do us here just fine.'

Zoe might have stopped to wonder where they'd come by such equipment, but she was just too happy to hear she was finally going to be rescued. Not only was she now freezing, soaking wet, impatient to get to Georgia and in some discomfort from her ankle, but she felt incredibly stupid too. Stupid for getting into this predicament in the first place, and for the inconvenience she now causing for everyone having to pitch in to pull her free. It was Christmas Eve, and poor Leon had been dragged away from his family celebrations to fetch the silly moo who'd gone and slipped down a hill.

There was some clicking and clanking up above, and then the beam from a much stronger torch than Alex's swept over her.

'Ah, there you are,' Leon said. 'We'll be with you shortly.'

A few minutes passed. Zoe could hear puffing and panting and the sound of a clip against a rope, and then Alex was there, a headtorch – presumably borrowed from Leon – on. He pulled it up so that the beam wouldn't blind her and smiled. 'Hello there.'

'Hello.' Zoe returned his smile, relief flooding through her.

'I'm going to put this harness on you and clip it to me, and then Leon's going to help us... It's mad this, isn't it? Like a disaster film.'

'I feel like a disaster film right now.'

'Don't. It's not your fault. Right... let's just make you safe and secure, and then see if you can grab hold of me...' He took a minute to kit her out. 'Put your arms around my neck... that's it. Leon! OK, we're ready!'

The rope that had them tethered to the top of the slope tightened, and Alex used it to support and steady them both as he climbed, Zoe piggybacking, doing her best to hold on while keeping her strain on him to a minimum. A minute later, they were up, with such surprising ease that Zoe wondered how it had been such a problem in the first place. But when she saw the equipment Leon had brought with him, she had to admit that it was pretty heavy duty.

'Thank you so much!' Zoe said, throwing her arms around Leon with such force he looked faintly shocked.

'How's your ankle?' Alex asked.

'It hurts, but I can manage.'

'We'll have a look when we get back to the house—' he began, but Zoe stopped him.

'When we get to the church and I've seen to Georgia, you mean. We're not going back to the house. I haven't come this far and gone through all that just to go back to Hilltop.' She turned to Leon. 'I'm sorry to ask, but is there any possibility you could get us to the church?'

'Not a problem,' Leon said, throwing Alex a silent look of apology. Clearly they'd had some sort of discussion about Zoe's insistence on getting to Georgia as they'd come to rescue her, and Leon didn't seem a bit surprised by her request. It also seemed, however, that he was aware of Alex's opposition to the plan.

'Thanks.'

'What about your bag?' Alex asked.

Zoe shook her head as she hobbled to Leon's four-by-four. 'I've tried to find it and I can't and now, quite honestly, I'm more worried about how long it's taking me to get to Georgia than what's in there. Midwives managed without bags full of medical gadgets for thousands of years before, so I suppose I'll find a way to manage now.'

30

Emilia hadn't called Simon or Ottilie for help. Zoe couldn't help but wonder why, but assumed it was something to do with the patchy signals they'd all been cursed with throughout the evening. There wasn't time to ask because it would have been clear, without Emilia's quick summary of the events, that Georgia's labour had progressed significantly since Zoe had first been called. Despite being the only medically qualified person present, however, Emilia had done a good job of keeping things under control and Georgia comfortable. Zoe found her doubled over, clinging to the balustrade that led from the church floor to the pulpit, Brett rubbing her back as she sucked in regular breaths. At some point, a bed had been made for her on the tiles, piled up with blankets and pillows, and Georgia must have been on it for a time because everything was in disarray.

The poor vicar flapped on a nearby pew, speaking to someone on his phone. He leaped up as he noticed Zoe.

'Oh, thank goodness!' he cried, rushing to her with the phone held out. 'It's the call handler... the ambulance service. They want to know what's going on, but I don't... Well, perhaps you could speak to them?'

Zoe threw a glance at Georgia, who seemed, for the moment, to be coping better than the vicar was. She had the support of Brett and Emilia and would be all right for the thirty seconds or so it would take to reassure the call handler that she was fully trained and they'd be able to wait for the ambulance now without the need to take up more of their time. She took the phone.

'Hello, yes... I'm Zoe Padbury. I'm the midwife here. Georgia's midwife, actually. I've just arrived, and I should be able to keep things on an even keel until the ambulance gets here.'

'Do you still want an ambulance?' the handler asked.

'I think so. There's no telling what might happen. It's a first baby, wasn't planned for a home birth, I'm on my own with pretty much no equipment and if they're already on the way, I think it might be useful to have them here.'

The handler asked her a few more questions, took down some particulars, and then asked to be given back to the vicar. Zoe had reassured her, but it seemed they didn't want to lose contact just yet.

Then she hobbled over to Emilia, who had left Georgia in Brett's care to come and fill her in.

'What's happened to you?' she asked.

'Fell,' Zoe said. 'Nothing to worry about – a sprained ankle or something.'

'Want me to look?'

'Later, maybe. I'll manage until we've got Georgia sorted out.'

'Right.' Emilia didn't argue because she was far too practical for that, and Zoe appreciated the lack of fuss on her behalf. Her ankle hurt like hell, but it wasn't a case of life and death. She'd put it from her mind and concentrate on what really mattered, and later, when Georgia and her baby were safe, she'd make time to think about it.

'What's the situation?' Zoe asked as she limped behind a striding Emilia.

'It's hard to tell how dilated she is, but I do believe she's started properly. I'm sure you'll have a handle on it straight away. You might be able to get her to sit still a while too. All she wants to do is walk around.'

'It must be what she feels she needs right now. I could do with taking a look to see how far she's progressed, though. If we could persuade her to take a load off for a few minutes, that would be good.'

'I'm sure she'll be more inclined to listen to you than me,' Emilia said.

Zoe didn't know why that would be but, once again, there wasn't time to ask.

Brett looked traumatised as Zoe nodded hello to him, his eyes pleading for her to take the pressure off him. 'Thank God,' he mumbled as he tried to move away, Georgia grabbing for his hand and pulling him back.

'Georgia...' Zoe leaned in close. 'I need to have a look at you, so you're going to have to let Brett go for a minute.'

'No,' Georgia said. 'Not again. He'll leave.'

'He won't.'

'He will. He'll leave me – he said he was going to!'

'I'll be right here,' Brett said. He threw an awkward look at Zoe that was full of shame. Whatever had happened between him and his wife in the time leading up to Georgia's waters breaking had been significant and stressful, that much was obvious. Zoe wouldn't have been surprised if it had contributed to the emergency they were now dealing with, but, as with all her other questions, there was no time to ask now. 'Please, George, you need to let Zoe help you.'

Georgia looked up at him from beneath a curtain of red hair. 'Promise you won't go.'

'I promise.'

Georgia let his hand drop and then took the one Zoe offered instead.

'God, I need a drink!' Brett said under his breath but not quietly enough.

'It's a drink that got us in this mess!' Emilia snapped.

He scowled at her, and then the anger suddenly drained from him, and he sat heavily on a pew, watching as Zoe manoeuvred Georgia onto the blankets so she could examine her.

'Is there any way we can make this area more private?' Zoe asked.

Emilia nodded. 'Give me a second...'

She dashed to speak to the vicar and then returned with another sheet.

'Take the other end,' she ordered Brett, who leaped to her assistance without a single word of remonstration at her tone.

They stretched it out between them to form a curtain that would shield Georgia from the rest of the people in the church.

'Someone's impatient to appear...' Zoe said as she checked Georgia's progress. She pulled one of the blankets over her legs. 'Are you in a lot of pain?'

'What do you think?'

'Sorry. The natural way isn't always all it's cracked up to be, is it? There's not a lot I can do for you now, but hopefully the paramedics will be here soon and they'll have something. If you last that long...' she added in a quieter voice. 'Do you want to be on your feet again, or are you happier staying here?'

'I want to walk...' Georgia held out her hands. 'It hurts less.'

'Don't get walking around. You can stand, though. Holding on to the balustrade there seemed to be working for you when I got here.'

'Do you think that was working?' Georgia started to laugh, but was immediately silenced by a shudder of pain that had her teeth clenched and her eyes screwed shut.

'Contraction?' Zoe asked.

Georgia nodded, her face glistening with sweat.

'Can you remember when the last one was?'

'I don't know...'

'Maybe ten, twelve minutes,' Emilia said. She lowered her side of the sheet. 'I'd say around that.'

'You can drop the curtain for a minute, Brett,' Zoe said. 'We're going to get Georgia onto her feet again.'

'Right.' He let Emilia take it and rushed to help Zoe.

Georgia looked up at him and started to cry.

'Don't,' he said, kissing her head. 'I can't stand it. I'm sorry for before... what I said... it was the drink; it wasn't me. I would never...'

'But you said—' Georgia sobbed.

'I know,' he cut in. 'Please, don't remind me of what I said. I'm a tosser. I don't know what you see in me.'

'That makes two of us,' Emilia said, and this time Zoe gave her a sharp look. Surely she was smart enough to see that her barbed comments were hardly helping. She might feel like sharing her opinions on whatever had happened, and perhaps she was justified in doing so, but now wasn't the time.

'Come on...' Zoe said. 'Lean on us...'

She took one side and Brett the other, and they led Georgia back to her previous perch.

'Floor's nice,' Georgia said.

Zoe glanced down to see she was barefooted. 'Cold?' she asked.

'Hmm. Lovely.'

'Shouldn't she lie down?' Brett asked. 'Will the baby come soon?'

'Not for a bit. Gravity will be her friend for now. It'll help speed things along, and standing up is clearly less painful for her. If she wants to give birth standing up, then it might also be easier on her.'

Brett's eyes were wide in disbelief.

'Did you miss that bit in the antenatal classes?' Zoe asked wryly.

'I didn't... I didn't go to all of them,' he said. 'I should have done, I know.'

'You went to one,' Georgia said.

'I'm sorry.'

'You didn't want the baby.'

'Of course I did! It was only... the timing...' he finished lamely.

Zoe rubbed Georgia's back. 'Do you want anything? A sip of water? A damp flannel? Anything at all?'

'I want this to be over. Can you get me that?'

'We'll get to it, don't worry. It's hard, but you'll have to be patient. Before you know it, you'll be done, and you'll have a beautiful baby in your arms. Did you decide on that name?'

'Not really.'

'All bets are off now, aren't they?' Brett said. 'Christmas Eve, in a church... It's got to be something fitting, hasn't it? I'll have to think of something that suits. Like Noel? Or Holly?'

'A bit predictable, though?' Zoe asked, driving to keep the discussion going to take Georgia's mind off her pain. 'Surely you can do better than that between you. How about something biblical?'

'Hannah...'

There was a shout from across the space, and they were reminded that they weren't quite alone.

'Why Hannah?' Zoe asked.

The vicar got up and walked over with an apologetic smile.

'Sorry to butt in,' he said. 'Only I rather like the name. I had two boys, you see, no need of it. Hannah means gift from God. It seems right, doesn't it? For a baby born in His house.'

'As long as it's not a boy,' Brett said. 'Got any thoughts on that eventuality?'

Georgia let out a growl of pain. 'It's getting worse!' she cried. 'Where are those drugs?'

'They're on their way,' Emilia said. 'They'll be here soon.'

Georgia shook her head desperately. 'I don't think I can hang on...'

'You can,' Zoe said patiently. 'Don't forget your breathing. Was that a contraction?'

Georgia nodded, and Zoe checked her watch.

'Good girl. Let me know when there's another one.'

'Oh, you'll bloody know all right! Sorry, Vicar...'

'I'm not a bit offended,' he said mildly. 'Quite understandable in the circumstances.'

Zoe nodded in thanks as Emilia handed her a glass of water with a straw. She held it up for Georgia to drink. Georgia pushed it away.

'Have a bit,' Zoe insisted. 'You don't want to be dehydrated.'

'I don't want it.'

'Have some,' Brett said, and Georgia glared at him.

'You have it if you're so bothered!'

Brett looked so shocked that in less stressful circumstances Zoe would have burst out laughing.

'Don't worry,' she said. 'Things will be said and done here that might be a bit out of character. Names...' she reminded them. 'We still haven't thought of a name.'

'How about Sod Off?' Georgia shot back, and this time Zoe did laugh.

'Will that be Sod Off as two words or one? What about a middle name?'

Georgia's only reply was to let out another howl.

Zoe grabbed a towel to mop her brow. 'Another one?' she asked.

Georgia nodded, and Zoe glanced at Emilia.

'Do you want to examine her again?' Emilia asked.

'I think we're getting close. I could do with checking.'

Emilia went to get the sheet, leaving the vicar to scurry away again. At that same moment, there was a rap on the doors of the church that echoed around the space. One of the church helpers rushed to see who was there.

'Don't leave the doors open for long!' Zoe shouted.

'It's nice,' Georgia said. 'I like... I'm boiling.'

'I know. Brett, could you...?' ·

At Zoe's bidding, he grabbed the damp cloth and mopped Georgia's face.

Despite having done this many times before, Zoe was relieved at the prospect of the ambulance arriving. She could deliver Georgia's baby, but that didn't mean she wouldn't be glad of some proper equipment to help things along. A heart monitor, blood pressure monitor, maybe some painkillers... all of it would help to make her job easier and to make Georgia more comfortable. Not to mention the reassurance it would give to Brett and everyone else in the church. Perhaps they had unshakeable faith in Zoe, but she realised she was just one person when many births – in hospital at least – had a team in attendance.

She wasn't watching the doors as they opened, her attention wholly on Georgia, but had to do a double take when she heard Victor's voice and turned to see him come in with Billie.

'What the hell...?' Alex leaped up from the seat where Zoe had asked him to wait and hurried over. 'What are you doing here?' he asked Billie. 'How did you get here? I told you to stay home!'

'I know, but I wanted to come.'

'Don't blame her,' Victor said. 'I offered to bring her down.'

Alex looked as if he wanted to have a sharp word with Victor but then seemed to swallow it back. 'How the hell did you manage that?'

'Farm vehicles'll get through most anything. Leon told me he'd brought you and Zoe down. Corrine and me went to see if

Billie wanted to come and sit with us while you were missing, but she wanted to come here to see if she could help. Said I could sort it. It's Christmas, after all – she doesn't want to be sitting all on her own in that house not knowing what time you might be back.'

'I appreciate it,' Alex said, sounding as if he didn't really appreciate it one bit. He turned to Billie. 'There's not a lot you can do here, though. We're all just sitting around waiting – it's Zoe and Brett doing most of the work.'

'I can make drinks. Or hold stuff. Don't be annoyed, Dad.'

Alex held his arms out, and Billie stepped in for a hug. 'I'm not annoyed. I wanted you to be safe, and that's the reason I asked you to stay at Hilltop, not because I wanted to leave you out.'

'I was safe. Victor's really good at driving in the snow.'

'Either way, you're here now, so it's a moot point, isn't it? Come on,' he added. 'Shall we go and see if we can help with drinks or something? We might as well be useful.'

Zoe wasn't annoyed either, and she tried to let Billie know with a look as they walked past, but she could have done with less of a crowd here. Or at least, she could have done with the right sort of crowd. All these people were no use to Georgia and perhaps a bit too distracting. Not only that, but Billie was very pregnant herself, and it was just another thing for Zoe to worry about. Having people to chat and make tea was all very well, but what they really needed was those paramedics with all that lovely equipment.

Georgia slapped a hand down on the wood of the balustrade and began to whimper.

'Another one?' Zoe asked.

Her reply was a sharp grunt, and her legs almost buckled as she gripped the wood. 'Bloody hell!' she wailed. 'I don't know how much more I can take!'

'I know, I know… I think you're getting close. Do you want some more water?'

'No! I want to be done!'

'Sorry, but there's no hurrying. Baby will come when baby is ready. You're almost there, and you're doing so well.'

There was another loud knock on the doors, and this time the vicar opened them to the ambulance team. Zoe looked to see Emilia race over, filling them in on the situation. They seemed mildly surprised to see so many people in the church, and Zoe could see why – she'd have been surprised too. But then, everyone was being so sweet, and they just wanted to help, and knowing that was a reminder of why Zoe was beginning to see Thimblebury as a special place, the likes of which she didn't believe existed anywhere else.

A few minutes later, she had all the equipment she needed. It was basic compared to what she'd have in a maternity unit but perfectly adequate for what she hoped would be a trouble-free birth. Georgia had dilated rapidly over the previous half hour and Zoe was getting her mentally prepared for the big moment.

'Any time now,' Zoe said to her. 'How are you feeling?'

'You're seriously asking me that?'

'Well, yes. What else am I supposed to ask?'

'Ask me if I want to push.'

'Do you?'

Georgia nodded. 'But I don't know how. I mean, when? How do I know it's the right moment?'

'You'll know.'

'Argh, that's such a midwife thing to say! It's all right for you – you know how this all works!'

'Technically, but I've never given birth, so… that bit is where you're about to be the expert.'

If there had been time, perhaps Zoe would have reflected on

her own words. She'd never given birth, but she'd once looked forward to the prospect. But there wasn't, and Zoe had more urgent worries.

Georgia wanted to stay on her feet, and Zoe began to guide her as the final stages of her labour began. The paramedics had erected a proper screen, and they were on hand, but now, as Georgia's baby finally arrived, she had only Zoe and Brett close by. There was a moment of uncertain silence, punctuated only by the sound of Georgia's efforts, and then, a second later, there was a sharp cry, and the baby was in Zoe's arms.

Her eyes were everywhere, practised, making swift observations as she made the baby safe and warm.

'You've got a boy,' she said.

'A boy?' Brett repeated.

'He's all right?' Georgia asked.

Zoe smiled. 'Looks perfect to me.'

'How much does he weigh?' Brett asked.

Zoe laughed lightly. 'Give me a minute! He's only just come out!'

'Right, yes... sorry.'

'You're excited – it's fine, I get it. You want to text everyone to let them know.'

'Yeah.'

Georgia took the baby from Zoe and held him close. And then she looked up at Brett. 'Are you OK?'

'God!' he said, tears spilling from his eyes. 'You're asking *me* that? You've just had a baby!'

'I have, haven't I? *We've* had a baby.'

'You did the work.' He leaned to kiss her. 'You're brilliant. Amazing. I love you so much.'

'You mean that?'

'I've never meant it more. I'm so sorry for how I've been. I didn't realise... seeing him now, our baby, right here... I want to be better. I'm going to be the dad he needs and the husband you need. This is it, today, me, turning over a new leaf. I'll get a job, quit the booze and it'll be fine, you'll see.'

Zoe watched them. She wanted to believe him. She believed his words had come from a place of good intent, but changes were rarely that straightforward to make. She also believed, however, that his words of love were true, and if there was enough love, anyone could do anything.

'So,' she asked. 'Are we still without a name?'

'What's the church called?' Brett asked.

'St Cuthbert's.'

'Bloody hell, we're not calling him Cuthbert!'

Zoe laughed. 'That's probably for the best. Unless you're going to send him to school in 1932. Any other ideas?'

Brett looked at Georgia, and she raised her eyebrows. 'I suppose Miles is still out of the question?'

'I love you but not that much.'

'Come on now,' Zoe said. 'She's done all the work. Let her have it.'

'We'll have a think,' Georgia said. 'Later. Right now, I'll take that cup of tea if it's going.'

31

———

Zoe left some final tasks to the paramedic team, who had notes to write up and a report to send back to base. Georgia hadn't wanted to be taken to hospital, and Zoe was content, after weighing up the risks of her staying in Thimblebury against an arduous journey in an ambulance in the snow, that she'd be better off where she was. She'd stay, so she'd be on hand for any emergency, though she didn't anticipate anything. So they left after having a quick word with her to check she was OK to manage anything that might crop up once they'd gone, and the church suddenly seemed a lot emptier without their high-vis suits and masses of equipment. In fact, as they all settled down with the hum of low conversations here and there, it was quite peaceful. Holy even, Zoe might have said, had she not been far too practical for that sort of thing.

Victor joked that the vicar ought to go and empty out the manger on the nativity display so they could put Georgia's baby in it, but for the first time that night, the vicar looked less than affable at the suggestion. Victor seemed to consider himself told and went to sit in a corner to talk to Alex like a boy being sent to the naughty step.

While Georgia and Brett spent some time alone with their baby, Zoe sat nursing a cup of tea, watching them. Nobody had left the church to go home yet. The vicar had offered the opinion that it wasn't safe for those who lived much further out to leave, and to a point Zoe agreed with him. The church was hardly ideal, but it was better than trying to get home in the blizzard conditions that had caused so much trouble on the way down. Not only that, but there was no way she was letting anyone take a newborn out into the snow.

Georgia seemed content in her makeshift bed, sleepy and comfortable with her baby in her arms and Brett close by, giving her so much adoring attention it was hard to believe there had ever been any conflict between them. Emilia hovered, seemingly not knowing what to do with herself. And while Georgia was here, Zoe wanted to be here too, keeping a close eye on things. Which meant Alex wanted to be here to be close to Zoe, and Billie wanted to be here to be with her dad.

After an hour of hanging around and chatting, Victor and Leon decided to go home.

'We can take you back with us,' Victor said to Billie and Alex.

'Go,' Zoe said. 'I'll see you tomorrow for lunch.'

'You're staying?'

'I'd rather. Georgia might need me again.'

'Oh...' Alex looked at Billie, who nodded. 'Then we'll stay.'

'There's no need.'

'I know, but we want to.'

Zoe raised her eyebrows at Billie. 'I can't see it being a very comfortable night for you.'

'I might be able to help with that,' the vicar said. He disappeared through a side door and then came back with his arms full of pillows and duvets. 'It's supposed to be going abroad for charity,' he explained. 'It's all clean. You're welcome to sleep on it if you want to stay the night.'

'Like a sleepover,' Alex said with a grin.

'The weirdest sleepover ever,' Zoe replied. 'We won't forget our first Christmas together in a hurry.'

'Perhaps someone can come and help me get more out,' the vicar said. 'There's plenty, so you ought to be comfortable enough.'

'Stay there,' Alex said to Zoe. 'Keep the weight off that ankle. It must be hurting.'

'It's throbbing a bit, I won't lie. I haven't really thought about it so much until now.'

'I bet you've been running on adrenaline though. You know, like they say, when the moment is highly stressful and you forget to feel pain.'

'Probably. And ignoring it a bit too, so I could focus.'

While Alex went to help, Emilia sat next to Zoe. 'Want me to take a look at your ankle?'

Zoe glanced at it and then shook her head. 'It's only a sprain; it'll be fine.'

'You're sure?'

'Positive. If it gets worse, don't worry, I'll tell you.'

Emilia nodded slowly and then fell to silence for a moment before she took a breath and spoke again. 'I haven't thanked you properly.'

'I think you have.'

'You absolutely went above and beyond today. I don't know how to express how grateful I am.'

'I'm sure you would have done the same.'

'Still, I appreciate it. We all do. I owe you an explanation—'

'You don't. I mean, I don't know what for, but I don't feel like there's any explanation needed for anything.' She gave the tiniest nod at Brett and Georgia. 'Do you think they'll be OK?'

'I hope so. They had a big bust-up earlier... that's why they left the church during the service and I followed, and I suspect that's where the trouble started with Georgia. But... I think all this has shocked Brett into some kind of epiphany. I've spoken to him – he knows the drinking and the wallowing in self-pity can't go on, not now he has a son.'

Zoe couldn't help but feel that, despite Emilia's good intentions, her intervention was a bit heavy-handed. Georgia and Brett would work things out by themselves, as he'd come to his own conclusions about the changes he needed to make to be the man Georgia and their little boy needed. In the circumstances, perhaps Zoe could also understand why Emilia would feel the need to get involved. They were living with her, after all, and what they did affected her too.

Emilia pulled out her phone. 'Signal's been dropping out all night.'

'I know. It's caused havoc in one way or another. What time do you make it? I'm too tired to get my phone out to look.'

'Almost midnight,' Emilia said. 'Give it a few minutes and I'll be able to wish you a happy Christmas.'

'I thought you didn't like Christmas.'

Emilia gave her a rueful look. 'It's a difficult time for me, but I don't *hate* it... and other people like it. The least I can do right now is respect that.'

'Why is it difficult? Seems like you have a proper love–hate relationship with this time of year. You don't have to tell me, but...'

'I suppose you've earned that much, being such a star tonight. Last Christmas, Todd was having an affair. I'd known about it for a few weeks, but I didn't say anything. I wanted him to at least have enough respect for me to come clean. I waited. He lied all through Christmas Eve, Christmas Day, Boxing Day... and then it got to New Year and I knew he wasn't going to tell me. When I finally confronted him, you know what he said?'

Zoe shook her head.

'Told me it was my fault. I didn't pay him enough attention.

I was always at work. I put everyone else before him. I was possessive and distrustful, and I had no right to spy on him, and that I shouldn't have lied to him about not knowing. Can you imagine that?'

'Wow,' Zoe said. 'No wonder you're not a fan.'

'Perhaps,' Emilia said, her gaze going to Georgia and Brett with their baby, 'I might like it better next year. I've certainly made some new Christmas memories.'

'We all have,' Zoe said with a tired smile. 'We won't forget this one in a hurry.'

'You must be exhausted,' Emilia said.

'A bit, but I'm too wired to sleep at the moment. Give me an hour and I'm sure I'll get there.'

They both looked up as Brett came over with the baby in his arms. 'Georgia's going to sleep,' he said, gazing down at his son with such love that Zoe was almost overwhelmed to see it. 'I said I'd take care of him while she gets her rest.'

'We can make him a little bed,' Emilia said. 'You must be tired too.'

He shook his head. 'I'm not tired. I said I'd watch him while she slept, and I will. If she can't trust me now, she's never going to, and I want... well, I want her to have faith in me again. I haven't given her much reason to over the past few months.'

'She loves you,' Zoe said. 'That much is obvious.'

'I love her too. I've been blinded by...' He let out a sigh. 'I've been selfish, too wrapped up in how our change of fortunes have affected me and not thinking about how they might be affecting her. We both made sacrifices, but to me she'd fallen on her feet because at least she was living with her sister, but... Sorry, Em. I've been an absolute nightmare, haven't I?'

'Yes,' Emilia said. 'But new year, new start, eh?'

'That's the intention,' he said. 'I'm going to swallow my pride, get some work and support this family. It doesn't matter what the work is as long as I do my best to look after them.'

'Good,' Emilia said. 'I'll help, if I can. *If* you let me this time.'

He gave a sheepish smile, and then all three of them were distracted by Alex and the vicar coming out of the store room with more bedding.

'Right,' he said. 'Who needs a bed, and where do you want to hunker down?'

'I'm staying up for a while,' Brett said then looked at Emilia. 'You could go home.'

'You could,' Zoe agreed. 'There's no reason for you to stay, you could probably make it back, and you're not far away if we do need you for anything, though I doubt we will. It'll be nice to be in your own bed, and you look like you need some peace and quiet.'

'It would be nice,' Emilia agreed.

'I could walk you home,' Alex said.

'There's no need,' Emilia began, but Zoe stopped her.

'Let him. We'd all be happier knowing you're home safe.'

'OK,' Emilia said. 'I'll call early in the morning to see how things are.'

'I'm sure you will,' Zoe said. She gave Emilia a quick hug, one that her friend's older sister seemed taken aback by, and then offered Alex a brief, grateful smile as he put down the bedding and went to get his coat, Emilia following.

Zoe noticed Billie have a brief word with her dad, and then she came to get some of the bedding.

'Are you sure you're going to be comfortable enough?' Zoe asked. 'Because I'm sure Emilia won't mind you going back with her and staying over tonight.'

'I want to stay here. I'll be fine – there's loads of stuff here.' She pulled at a duvet. 'I can make a mattress out of about three of these and then put one on top – it'll be warm enough.'

'I can't say I think it's the best idea, but I can hardly tell you what to do,' Zoe said.

'Exactly, so shut up about it.'

Zoe gave a tired smile. It held as she noticed Billie's attention switch to the baby in Brett's arms.

'Have you got the name yet?' she asked softly, peering down at the little boy.

'I'm still working on it, but Georgia's asleep anyway, so I'd have to wait to get her approval.'

'He's cute,' Billie said. 'What's your middle name?'

'Mine?' Brett asked.

Billie nodded.

'I don't have one.'

'Oh, well what about your dad's name?'

'Ah, I see. We've been through all the family names, and Georgia doesn't like any of them.'

'Shame. I think I would have my dad's,' Billie said.

'What about your baby's dad?' Brett asked, and then Zoe watched as Billie instantly disengaged.

'I've got to make my bed,' she said, grabbing a duvet and some pillows and taking them to the other side of the room.

Brett looked helplessly at Zoe. 'What did I do?'

'It's not your fault,' Zoe said. 'You weren't to know.'

'Know what? Shit, have I put my foot in it again?' He lowered his voice. 'He's left her in the lurch?'

'He died.'

'Oh.' Brett looked across the room to where Billie was putting together a makeshift bed.

'I'd leave her if I were you,' Zoe said, guessing that he might want to go and make amends. 'She'll be all right by tomorrow.'

Brett looked doubtful, and perhaps he had good reason. Zoe wanted him to feel better about his faux pas, but the truth was, Billie was still struggling to come to terms with her situation. She was better than she'd been when she'd first arrived in Thimblebury during the autumn, but there was a way to go. And there was also the not so small matter of what she was planning to do when her own baby arrived. Brett turned back to the little boy in his arms, and perhaps he was thinking about how it might be if his son didn't have a father. Zoe liked to imagine this was strengthening his resolve to be the best dad he could.

The vicar came over to her with another duvet and more pillows. 'Where would you like to bed down, Zoe?'

'I'll take those,' she said. 'No need for you to worry. Does it matter where I go? Anywhere out of bounds?'

'Perhaps try not to turf the baby Jesus out of his manger to get in there,' he said wryly, and Zoe laughed.

'Poor Victor. I'm sure he's mortified about his joke falling so flat.'

'Perhaps I was a bit harsh on him,' the vicar said. 'I'm not quite at my best and brightest now.'

'I don't think any of us are. We can look after everything else here if you want to go and get some sleep.'

'I might walk along to the vicarage,' he said. 'If you don't mind. I'll keep my phone to hand so you can call if you need anything overnight. I won't lock up. Of course, anyone who wants to is welcome to come and stay at the vicarage. There's a spare bedroom.'

'I think everyone who is here now wants to stay put,' Zoe said. 'But thank you.'

'Yes, well...' He looked at his watch. 'Merry Christmas then. I'll be back in a few hours to get you up – don't want you sleeping through the Christmas Day service, do we?'

'Oh!' Zoe put a hand over her mouth. 'I hadn't even thought of that! Will it be a problem?'

'I'm sure it won't, but I will need to come and get the church ready.'

'Of course. I'll make sure we're awake and everything is tidy for you.'

'Oh dear, that's not what I meant—'

'I know, but we will. At least we'll do our best. Thank you so much for everything you've done today.'

'I have to say it's been one of my more eventful Christmas Eves.'

'I'm sure it has.'

'Well...' He held up a weary hand. 'I'll bid you goodnight. I hope you have everything you need, but if not call me.'

'Thanks,' Brett said. He turned to Zoe as the vicar left them. 'You should go and get some sleep if we've got to get up early.'

'What about you? Do you want me to switch with you in a few hours?'

He looked down at his baby. 'I've got the rest of my life to sleep; tonight is all about this little one. I'll happily sit and watch him until the sun rises.'

32

Zoe woke at the sound of Georgia's baby crying. With a yawn, she clambered from the nest of bedding she and Alex had been sleeping in and padded over to see if she was needed. Georgia was fumbling beneath the top she'd been wearing since the carol service, now crumpled and sweat stained.

'Does he want more milk?' she asked Zoe. 'He's had loads.'

'Little and often the first twenty-four hours,' she said. 'You're all right latching on now?'

'I think so...'

The little boy wriggled around, trying to get purchase, and eventually his lips found their target, and he began to suck.

Georgia smiled. 'It's amazing, when you think about it. I can't believe my body is feeding his.'

'It's been doing that for the past nine months.'

'I know, but I didn't see it. I'm just making milk, right here. Like I'm a cow. I never thought I'd be able to do it.'

Zoe laughed softly. 'Something like that.' She glanced around. 'Where's Brett?'

'Gone to find the kettle to make me a drink.'

'He's all right then? Not too shell-shocked by all this?'

'It's early days, but I think he wants to change. Or maybe not change; maybe just go back to the way he was before.'

'Is that what you want? I mean, is that good?'

'Yes. It'd be good. We were happy. We'd be even happier now because we'd have this little one too.'

'*This little one*... I think that might end up being his name at this rate.'

'I think it might. How long do I have to decide?'

'I think, if memory serves me, you have forty-two days before you have to register his birth.'

'I'd better get my skates on then.'

'I think you'll manage... unless you're really struggling for a name. Hopefully it won't take you six weeks to come up with one, or it might have to be This Little One. Or Sod Off, which seemed to be in the running a few hours ago.'

Zoe noticed someone else was up. Billie was walking up and down, hands to the small of her back. She came over.

'Couldn't sleep?' Zoe asked.

'Got pins and needles and my back is aching.' She looked at Georgia's baby, content at her breast. 'Is it hard?' she asked.

'Feeding? Not as bad as I thought it was going to be. It pinches a bit at first, but then we get the hang of it' – she stroked a finger over his cheek – 'don't we, sonny Jim?' She looked up. 'Hmm... *Sonny*. What do you think?'

'For a name?' Billie asked, her expression telling them what she was too polite to say.

'Maybe not then,' Zoe said with a laugh.

'I don't know,' Georgia said. 'I think it could be a grower.'

'Can I hold him?' Billie asked. 'When you've finished, I mean? Just to see...'

'Course you can,' Georgia replied. 'Getting in some training, eh? For your own?'

'I just want to have a go.'

Zoe tried not to read too much into Billie's interest. She

tried to contain the hope that was building in her, that Billie might yet decide to keep her baby. Nothing would make Alex happier, and if Zoe was being honest, she'd be thrilled too.

Baby's eyes closed, and he was calm.

'Has he finished?' Billie asked.

'I think so,' Georgia said, looking to Zoe for reassurance.

'You don't need me to tell you,' Zoe said. 'You're doing brilliantly on your own.'

'Can I hold him now?' Billie asked.

Georgia took a closer look and then seemed to decide he had finished his feed. After rearranging her shirt, she beckoned Billie closer before lifting him gently.

'Don't forget to support his head,' Zoe reminded her.

'I know,' Billie said. 'I've got it.'

Her face lit into a smile as she gazed at the little boy. Something had sparked in her – Zoe could see it a mile away. She'd seen it before, that maternal instinct kick in. She'd met mums who would never be maternal, ones who did their best even though it didn't come naturally, and she'd met some who were full of it from the start. And she met some who were like Billie – for whatever reason, whether it was fear or doubt or simply that the reality of motherhood hadn't yet sunk in – who had no maternal feelings for the baby they were carrying, but then there would be a catalyst, something would switch and then it would be on, full beam and all-encompassing. They'd transform from passive vehicles to fierce mother tigers willing to do anything for their child.

Zoe glanced at Georgia. There had never been any doubt that she was a mother tiger, but there was so much love in her eyes now, Zoe almost struggled to believe that so much depth of feeling was possible in one woman. She may not yet have had her own baby, but she knew, from this one moment of looking into Georgia's soul, how it would feel if she ever did.

After a minute where all three women were silent, Billie looked up. 'Do you want him back?'

'Do you mind?' Georgia held out her arms. 'I am quite missing him.'

'Yeah, sure... sorry.'

'No need to be sorry. It'll be your turn soon, after all.' Georgia made the baby comfortable. 'I suppose you have a name for yours already.'

'No.'

'Oh, not even ideas? It's reassuring to know it's not just me and Brett who can't make up our minds.'

'I haven't thought about it,' Billie said, which was a tiny lie, Zoe reflected, recalling that only a few hours before, she'd told Brett she'd want to use her dad's name. But perhaps that had only been an idle comment made in passing. Because Billie, after all, wasn't planning to keep her baby – or so she'd told Alex – so why would she bother to think of a name? It was one more grain of hope to add to the avalanche building in Zoe that she'd started to change her mind about that.

By the time her alarm went off, the church was filled with muted daylight. Zoe was groggy. Her sleep had been broken, getting up to check on Georgia almost every time she woke with her baby, but even when she'd managed to get her head down, her rest had been fitful and uncomfortable.

'Well,' Alex said, stirring beside her, 'now I know what it's like to camp in a church. Can't say I'll be recommending it to my holidaymakers in the summer.'

'I agree; it's crap. I suppose, in a weird way, it was sort of fun, though.'

'You have a strange idea of fun.'

'It's why you like me.'

'It's why I *love* you.'

'Ugh...' Billie sat up on her bed a few feet away. 'Get a room already.'

'We tried,' Alex said, 'and look where we ended up.'

Zoe let out a tired giggle. Then she sniffed the air. 'Can you smell bacon?'

'I can...' Alex looked around. 'I'll go and see what's going on. Do you want a cup of tea?'

'I'd kill for a cup of tea!'

'Me too,' Billie said. 'If you can manage one for your daughter as well.'

'He's good, isn't he?' Zoe said, watching him head towards the church's kitchen.

'He's all right, yeah,' Billie said, reaching for her phone. 'All the bars.' She held it up for Zoe to see. 'Do you think the snow has stopped?'

'I hope so; I don't think it could snow much more.'

'We've been saying that for two weeks.'

'Three, I think. Anyway, it looks bright enough through the windows, so we might be in luck.'

Alex came back with three mugs and a plate of sandwiches on a tray.

'Vicar's come up trumps!' he said with a grin. 'Bacon sandwiches! He came in early to make them!'

'That's so sweet of him!' Zoe took the mug he offered and a sandwich from the pile. 'I'm starving!'

'Me too,' Billie said as she did the same.

Alex sat down with his own and stuffed it into his mouth, chewing with a look of great contentment. 'Nothing quite hits like a bacon sandwich when you've had a long night. I feel sorry for vegans.'

'I'm pretty sure they're at peace with their choices,' Zoe said, 'but I know what you mean. This is just what I needed.'

A thin wail went up from where Georgia had been sleeping with the baby.

Zoe grinned. 'Looks like someone else is hungry.' She got to her feet, and Alex grabbed her hand.

'Where are you going?'

'To see if Georgia needs me to help.'

'If it was me,' Billie said as she munched, 'I'd want you to stop interfering.'

Zoe frowned. 'I'm not—'

'What she means is you're fussing,' Alex said. 'In the nicest possible way, of course.'

'She's got to do everything for the baby when you're not there,' Billie continued. 'She needs to get used to it. If she wants you to help now, she'll shout. But she's probably already working it out.'

'It's hard with a newborn,' Zoe insisted. 'You need support.'

'Yeah,' Billie said, 'and she's got Brett.'

'He's got to figure out how to look after a baby too,' Alex agreed. 'I'd give them some room, like Billie says. If they need you, they'll shout.'

Zoe realised that as they'd been talking the baby had stopped crying.

Alex raised his eyebrows. 'See?'

Sheepishly, she sat down again. 'Don't mind me – I'm still on high alert after last night's drama.'

'You didn't get much sleep either, so that's not going to help.'

The doors to the church creaked open, and Emilia slipped in. Her footsteps echoed on the stone floor as she went straight to Georgia and Brett. Zoe watched her. She was bundled up in a thick coat and hat, and looked tired and pale. Zoe guessed she probably hadn't slept well either, despite going home.

As Zoe finished the last of her sandwich, Emilia came over.

'How are you?' she asked.

'All right,' Zoe said. 'A bit stiff but not too bad.'

'What about your ankle?'

'Oh, that's a bit stiff too, but it'll be fine. How about you?'

'Fine. Georgia wants to bring the little one back to the house. I think it should be all right if you're in agreement. It's stopped snowing. In fact, it's quite bright out there. I don't think we'll have any more today.'

'Of course we won't,' Alex said wryly. 'Why would we now the emergency is over?'

'I've got a pram and blankets etcetera back at the house; I could pop over for it.'

'What about Georgia?' Zoe asked. 'I'm not sure it would do her much good to walk that far right now.'

'No, of course not. I'll bring the car; if I drive slowly, it should be all right now. I think they'd all be better at home.'

'Yes,' Zoe said. 'I'm not going to argue with you there if you can manage it. We'd have to go soon anyway, unless we wanted to join in the Christmas Day service from our beds.'

'I'll give you a hand,' Alex said, getting up.

'I think we've got it,' Emilia said. 'There's no point in us all getting cold.'

'Well, let me know if there's anything,' he replied. 'I'm right here.'

Emilia went back to Georgia, and Alex turned to Zoe. 'I suppose, as we're here, we could stay for the Christmas service if you fancied it. I'm not usually a massively religious person, but I'm feeling it today. I mean, if you want to go home, of course we can, but I just wondered.'

'It *will* be hymns today,' Zoe said. 'Not cheery carols.'

'That's all right. Sometimes hymns are quite cheery, aren't they?'

'I guess that means I've got to stay,' Billie said.

'Ah...' Alex was thoughtful for a moment. 'We could ask Emilia if you could go with them for a while until we've finished.'

Billie glanced in the direction of Georgia, Brett, Emilia and the baby. 'I don't think so,' she said finally. 'They'll be busy. I'll stay. It won't be that long, will it?'

'I shouldn't think so,' Zoe said. 'People want to get their lunch on the go, so they wouldn't come if they thought it was going to take up all their day.'

Alex nodded. 'Even the vicar knows if you give people a choice between hymns and a turkey dinner, the turkey is going to win every time.'

Zoe gave a tired grin and drained the last of her tea. 'I wonder if there's somewhere we can freshen up? I don't want the vicar to think we're treating it like a hotel, but I could do with washing and brushing my teeth.'

'What if we go with Emilia and use her bathroom, and then come back?' Alex suggested. 'It would probably suit the vicar anyway because he could get ready for the service without us in the way.'

'And I can be on hand in case there are any niggles with Georgia or the baby when they get there,' Zoe said. 'Good plan.'

'Zoe...' Billie glanced uncertainly between Zoe and Alex. 'I want to... Can I talk to you?'

'What's the matter?' Zoe asked, her stomach suddenly knotted at Billie's tone. She wasn't sure she had it in her to deal with another drama right now.

'Nothing's the matter. I only wanted to ask about something.'

'Sure, fire away.'

Billie glanced uncertainly at Alex again.

'I can take a hint,' he said. 'This is women's stuff, right? I'll go and get our coats – shout me when you've done.'

Zoe wondered what Billie had to say that couldn't wait as she watched Alex leave them. 'Is it something I should be worried about?'

'I don't know. I'm so confused right now and think I might feel better if I talk about it. I know it's not the time, but—'

'If you need to talk, you know I'll always make time.'

'I don't know if I want to give my baby up. I know I said I did, and I feel like it's for the best – for the baby, you know – but every time I try to think about what it would be like not having them around, it makes me feel like crying. But I don't know whether that's just my hormones. And then seeing Georgia with her baby...' Billie fixed Zoe with the most pleading, most vulnerable look she'd ever seen on the young woman. 'What should I do?'

Zoe had fallen into this trap once before. She'd advised Billie to make the decision she felt was right, and it had thrown her into a conflict with Alex that had seemed impossible to resolve. She didn't want that to happen again, and yet it was clear Billie was desperate. In the end, however, Zoe could only be honest, no matter what it meant for her.

'I wish I could tell you. I can only say trust your gut.'

'I don't know what my gut is telling me.'

Zoe gave a small smile. 'I think you do. I think the answer is there, but you're afraid to look. I think that's why you're asking me. You want me to tell you you're right. I'm not going to do that, but I am going to tell you to trust yourself. Have more faith in yourself to make the choice real.'

Billie gave a thoughtful nod.

'But,' Zoe added, a note of caution in her voice now, 'please be sure about it before you tell your dad. Don't mess him around again – I don't think his heart could take it.'

'I know,' Billie said. 'I do feel bad about last time.'

Zoe paused, holding her in a steady gaze. 'Billie, you're not thinking of changing your mind because you think it's what your dad wants?'

Billie shook her head. 'I don't think so. A bit, but I think it's a bit me too. And...' She almost smiled with hope at Zoe with her next sentence. 'The first time, when I made up my mind to have the baby adopted, it was just me and Dad. Now we have you. I think, if I decide to keep the baby, it will be better with you around.'

Tears welled in Zoe's eyes. Billie had well and truly accepted her into their family, and it made her happier than she had words for.

Emilia was happy to oblige their request. After a brief word with the vicar to thank him for everything, they tidied after themselves as best they could and then walked slowly over to Emilia's house, Zoe leaning on Alex for support, her ankle still throbbing. She found it hard not to keep checking on Georgia, but she was pleased to see that Brett was attentive enough for her and everyone else there. He barely let Georgia and the baby out of his sight, while discussions about names were still ongoing, though they didn't seem to be getting anywhere.

Eventually, Emilia put a hand up to stop them. 'Here's a thought... and you can throw it out if you want to, but we're in the Lake District, right?'

'Thanks for pointing that out,' Georgia said.

Emilia frowned at her.

'Sorry...'

'So think about famous locals.'

'I didn't know there were any,' Brett said.

At this, Emilia let out an impatient sigh. 'Where does Ottilie live, for a start?'

'Wordsworth Cottage!' Zoe squeaked. 'Oh yes!'

'William?' Georgia was silent for a moment before screwing her face up. 'It's a bit... ordinary.'

'Why don't you google to see who else there might be?' Zoe said. 'It might spark a bit of inspiration even if you don't like anything you see.'

'That's not a bad idea,' Brett said. 'We'll do that later when we have a minute, eh?'

Georgia nodded.

'You'll have to think of something soon,' Emilia said, 'because we can't keep calling him *the baby* for ever.'

'It'll be unique,' Brett said.

'With good reason,' Emilia shot back, and for the first time since they'd arrived, Zoe witnessed them share a genuine smile.

33

It was funny, but Zoe had to agree with Alex. While she wasn't especially religious and never went to the Christmas Day service ordinarily, something about this one touched her in an oddly spiritual way. Perhaps it was the drama of the night before, the fact that she'd helped to bring a life into the world in this very building, or the deep sense of community that she'd simply never experienced anywhere before, but something was different. She felt safe and loved and part of something far bigger than a tiny village full of people who were all as different as they were the same.

It wasn't until the service had ended, however, and people were drifting away that she noticed some absences. The vicar stood at the doors, issuing his blessings for the season and the coming year, and Zoe scanned the congregation as they waited their turn to speak to him.

'I wonder where Victor and Corrine are,' she said to Alex.

He shrugged. 'I suppose they decided not to come.'

'But...' Zoe shook her head slightly. 'I always thought they were regulars. I mean, not regulars all year, but I imagined they'd be here for special things like this. No Magnus and Geoff either.'

'I don't have them down as churchgoers.'

'But they came yesterday.'

'So, one is enough for them? I don't know.' Alex allowed his gaze to wander too. 'See, not everyone is here anyway. No Ottilie and Heath, no Stacey and Simon...'

'But I'm not surprised by them – I know they wouldn't want to come anyway.'

He shrugged. 'I don't know what to say. We'll see Corrine and Victor at their Boxing Day thing tomorrow, so I wouldn't worry.'

'I'm not. I just thought it was odd.' Zoe let out a sigh. 'I imagine this all means we're going to be eating our lunch a lot later than we'd planned. I haven't even got the turkey on yet.'

'That doesn't matter. We'll eat when we eat.'

'I know it doesn't really, but I wanted our first Christmas to be perfect...' She looked up at him. 'It's far from perfect. Everything's gone wrong, and I know it can't be helped, but it's still not what I wanted for us.'

'It's only lunch.' He stroked her hair with a warm smile. 'And it's not like we won't eat it at all.'

'My presents for you are crap too. I ran out of time, and I didn't know what to get—'

'I don't care about that. Having you with me is enough.'

'And I look like crap. And the cottage looks like crap because I haven't been there to get it ready. I mean, we did the tree and some other bits, but I was going to do some extra cleaning, and I haven't had time, and I wanted to, you know, make it perfect.'

'We don't care if it's perfect, and I bet it is anyway, but if it bothers you that much, then grab everything you need and come to ours. It doesn't matter which house we spend the day in.'

'But that means you'll have to do the work and make the mess at yours, and I wanted it at mine so you could have a break and be spoiled because I know Christmas can be hard for you. I wanted to make it lovely for you and Billie.'

'You already have! Stop worrying!'

'I'm not worrying; I'm just... disappointed. I wanted more for us.'

'How much more do you want from this Christmas?' he asked with a light laugh. 'You delivered a baby! By yourself in a church!'

'Not exactly by myself—'

'Zoe, stop! Would you listen to yourself for one minute? You don't owe one word of apology to anyone! We will have an awesome Christmas – I've already had the most amazing Christmas and we're not even past lunch yet! I love you, you loon! After yesterday, I don't think I could love you any more! You showed everyone just who you are, and it's the most beautiful person. We'll have lunch when we have lunch, and I'll love my gifts, and everything will be perfect as it is.'

Zoe still felt sceptical, and she wondered if her face showed it. Of course, his words meant more to her than anything, and she loved that he was so content with the Christmas they were having, but she'd wanted so much more. She couldn't help but feel that if she'd simply been a little more organised in the weeks leading to it, if she could have managed better, made more sensible decisions, things might have been perfect. Perhaps, she reflected, a little common sense managing to break through, she only felt so disappointed because she was so tired, and it was hard to feel anything but negative when someone was as exhausted as she was.

'Come here...' he said, pulling her into a hug. 'I don't want you to worry about anything for the rest of the day.'

'I'll have to worry about lunch – I did promise to cook, after all.'

'We'll work something out,' he said.

When it was their turn to speak to the vicar, he had plenty to say about the drama that had unfolded in his church overnight, and Zoe could see people listening in with shocked expressions. It led to many of them coming to her and Alex afterwards to ask about it, and all they did for the following half hour was relay the story again and again.

It was as their audience finally dispersed that Zoe realised she hadn't seen Billie in a while. Alex's daughter had been at the service with them, but when was the last time Zoe actually remembered speaking to her? Certainly not as they'd waited their turn to wish the vicar merry Christmas or when they'd been chatting to members of the congregation outside.

'Where's Billie?' she asked sharply, surprised that Alex hadn't already said anything about her absence.

'Oh, she's gone over to Emilia's,' he said.

'When did she do that? Why didn't she say anything?'

'She did... You weren't looking.'

'I thought she might have said goodbye, though.'

'She did. She said it to me.'

Zoe tried not to frown, but there was something evasive about Alex's excuses. Yes, that was it – they *sounded* like excuses.

At the gates to the church, they were met by Leon, who hadn't been to the service. He was jangling a set of keys in his hand and whistling as he watched everyone disperse.

'Merry Christmas!' Alex said, leading Zoe over.

'Same to you. How did you manage last night? Nice and comfy?'

Alex grinned. 'It wasn't too bad. I wouldn't call it five star, but we managed to get at least half an hour's sleep.'

'Need a lift up the hill?' Leon asked. 'I've got the four-by-four parked over there, and it's not too bad going underfoot now.'

'For your jeep, maybe,' Zoe said. 'Not so much for my feet. I'd love a lift if we could have one.'

'No problem,' Leon said. 'Ready when you are then.'

The trip back up to Kestrel Cottage was tough going, but a world away from the journey they'd endured to get down the hill the evening before. At least the relentless blizzard conditions had stopped. The sun was shining, throwing bleached light across the glittering landscape, and the scattered clouds that dotted the sky did their best to wring a few more flakes out, but they were gentle, barely there, fluttering ineffectually to the ground to catch the sun like dust motes in an empty room.

Zoe felt Alex's hand wrap around hers as she watched from the window of Leon's four-by-four. She turned to see him smiling.

'All right?' he asked.

'Yes. I don't feel as tired as I did. I think maybe I've pushed past it.'

'Like jet lag? You don't want to have a nap then?'

'No. I don't want to waste any of what we have left of the day in bed. I want to spend it with you and Billie. Will she come back up from Emilia's before lunch?' Zoe added, suddenly troubled by the notion that Billie might not want to have lunch with them.

'I expect so,' he said cheerfully.

Leon pulled up outside Kestrel Cottage.

'Are you going back to Hilltop first?' Zoe asked Alex.

'I don't think so.'

She'd assumed he'd want to get freshened up, perhaps change his clothes and pick up any gifts he had left for her, and so she was vaguely surprised to hear him say he wasn't going to go home before their lunch. She had a lot to do too, and she'd been hoping for some time without distractions to get things on the go ready for him and Billie to come back. But, she supposed, it was still treacherous underfoot, and perhaps the amount of snow that lay between his place and hers was enough of a deterrent. She didn't know how staying would work for any of his plans, but he didn't seem concerned. She was also surprised to see Leon get out of the jeep and come to meet them at the gate, giving every impression he was expecting to stay too.

Zoe got out her key and opened the gate. Someone had cleared the path to her door. She couldn't imagine who, unless Victor had called and decided to do it, but that seemed unnecessary on Christmas Day when he ought to be enjoying it with his family. Then again, she mused, Leon was here.

As soon as the front door was open, she could see the lights were on in the kitchen. And a second later, the aroma registered. Many of them, in fact – cooking meat and warm herbs and things she couldn't quite place. But the house was quiet. She turned back to Alex with a puzzled look. Had the oddest burglars in the world broken in? Ones that cleared the path, cooked lunch and then scarpered?

'Go on into the kitchen,' he urged her with a grin.

Zoe did as she was asked and was greeted by a roar.

'Surprise!'

Corrine and Victor and their daughter Penny, Billie, Magnus and Geoff, Ottilie, Heath and Flo, and Stacey and Simon were in the kitchen. The table was dressed and laid with crockery, cutlery and crackers, and at the centre sat a row of bowls containing vegetables, roast potatoes, gravy, a selection of garnishes and, of course, a vast, bronzed, steaming turkey.

Zoe's mouth opened and closed, but no words would come out.

'We thought you'd be exhausted,' Alex said. 'And Corrine

wondered if you might want some help. And then it sort of snowballed from there. If you'll excuse the pun.'

Zoe stared at everyone as they beamed at her, unable to take in just what she was seeing. And then she began to cry.

In the next second, everyone was gathered around her, hugging her, apologising for being there uninvited, wondering if they ought to leave, wondering if she needed to rest. But she wasn't crying for any of those reasons. She could barely articulate it, but she was crying because she was overwhelmed by their love. Because that was what she felt – loved in a way she'd never felt before, and certainly not by so many people who hadn't even been in her life a year.

'I'm sorry...' she stuttered. 'I didn't mean... It's lovely... I don't want... I don't want to sound... ungrateful...'

'Give her some room!' Victor said finally.

Everyone moved away, and Alex took her out into the hall while the rest of them stared at one another and wondered what to do.

'Are you angry?' His face was full of doubt and concern. 'I should have realised. I should have asked if you wanted all these people in your house. You're tired. I'm sorry – I thought it might—'

'I love it!' she said, cutting off his apology. 'I love that everyone wanted to do this for me. I don't know how to react to it because it's never happened to me before, that's all. Nobody's ever taken the time to think about me like this.'

'Nobody? Not ever?'

She shook her head. 'Not like this, not so many people. I don't know what to say.'

'I do,' he said. 'If nobody has ever thought you deserved a fuss, then you haven't had the right people in your life. You deserve so much more than this. You give and give and never ask for anything in return. So it's about time someone showed you how loved you are. That's all everyone wanted to do, but if you want them to leave, nobody would be upset. We'd absolutely understand.'

'God no! I want everyone to stay! It's the best...' She gulped back fresh tears. 'It's the loveliest thing anyone has ever done for me. It would be the best Christmas... yes' – she gave a firm nod – 'I want everyone to stay.'

When they went back to the kitchen, the mood was far more subdued than it had been on her arrival, and Zoe hated that her reaction was the cause of that.

'I'm sorry,' she began, and there was a chorus of people telling her she owed them no apology at all. As it quietened, she began again. 'Thank you so much. This is all so lovely, the nicest thing... I don't know what to say, but thank you! And I hope you're all staying. I mean, I'm sorry for taking you away from your own Christmas dinners—'

'Put a sock in it, Zoe!' Ottilie rolled her eyes, and then everyone started to laugh. 'If we didn't want to be here, we wouldn't! So shut up, sit down, and eat your dinner – because I don't know about you, but I'm starving so I'm starting with or without you!'

Zoe laughed through new tears. She wished she could stop them, but she was simply too happy. Instead, she kept on explaining to anyone who would listen that she wasn't sad, quite the opposite, as the dishes of vegetables and potatoes were passed around and Victor took on the carving of the biggest turkey Zoe had ever seen.

'Merry Christmas.'

Alex's voice was in her ear, his head close as she turned to him.

'Thank you,' she said.

'That's it now,' he said. 'You've used up your quota. No more thank yous. You've done so much for everyone else, this is the least we could all do for you. I know you'll be tempted to forget that, or you won't believe me, but it's true. You're quite the woman, Zoe Padbury. Meeting you was a day I never saw coming when I first clapped eyes on Hilltop, but the best surprise ever.'

Hilltop... The key Alex had given her the night before was sitting on his kitchen table where she'd left it when Emilia's text had come through. Kestrel Cottage had become home for her, quicker than she could have imagined, but Hilltop was beginning to feel like the place she'd always been destined for. As for home, perhaps it wasn't really Kestrel Cottage. As she looked at the faces gathered around her table, people who'd become her best friends almost overnight, perhaps *they* were home. The people of Thimblebury, the very best of people, a community unlike any other.

In a few days, a new year would begin. There was no way of knowing what it held, but Zoe was hopeful. As long as she had Alex and this village, she was sure everything else would work out just fine.

A LETTER FROM TILLY

I want to say a huge thank you for choosing to read *Christmas for the Village Midwife*. If you did enjoy it and want to keep up to date with all my latest releases, just sign up at the following link. Your email address will never be shared, and you can unsubscribe at any time.

www.bookouture.com/tilly-tennant

I hope you enjoyed *Christmas for the Village Midwife*, and if you did, I would be very grateful if you could write a review. I'd love to hear what you think, and it makes such a difference helping new readers to discover one of my books for the first time.

I love hearing from my readers – you can get in touch with me on social media or through my website.

Thank you!

Tilly

https://tillytennant.com

facebook.com/TillyTennant
instagram.com/tillytennant6000
threads.com/@tillytennant6000

ACKNOWLEDGEMENTS

I say this every time I come to write acknowledgements for a new book, but it's true: the list of people who have offered help and encouragement on my writing journey so far really is endless, and it would take a novel in itself to mention them all. I'd try to list everyone here, regardless, but I know that I'd fail miserably and miss out someone who is really very important. I just want to say that my heartfelt gratitude goes out to each and every one of you, whose involvement, whether small or large, has been invaluable and appreciated more than I can express.

I don't usually go into the specifics of how I write my books at this point. I rightly or wrongly assume that most people are more interested in the end result than the process, but this time I'd like to say a few things about the research for the Village Midwife series. Having worked alongside nurses, healthcare workers, midwives and many other amazing health professionals during my ten years as an NHS employee, I'm forced to acknowledge here that there is a lot more protocol and many more rules and regulations than my stories might have you believe. I know that many things are not as straightforward in real life as they are in my books, but I also ask for a little forgiveness for my creative licence. My aim is to tell a tale unhindered by such boring things as paperwork, public health directives, shift patterns, uniform complexities, recruitment processes and a million other issues. So, while I know these things exist, sometimes I choose to gloss over them for the sake of the plot. For anyone well acquainted with the workings of our healthcare system, I hope you won't be too cross with me!

With that out of the way, back to the thank yous! It goes without saying that I have to highlight the remarkable team at Bookouture for their continued support, patience and amazing publishing flair, particularly Lydia Vassar-Smith – my incredible and long-suffering editor. I'd also like to thank the wider team, including Peta, Kim, Noelle, Sarah, Mandy, Lizzie, Imogen, Sinead, Alex, Louisa, Occy, Nadia, Laura, Ann and Alba. I know I'll have forgotten somebody, but I hope they'll forgive me. Their belief, able assistance and encouragement mean the world to me. I truly believe I have the best team an author could ask for. Signing with them changed my life, and I don't think I'll ever be able to thank them enough for taking a chance on a daft little woman from Staffordshire.

My friend, Kath Hickton, always gets a mention for putting up with me since primary school, and Louise Coquio deserves a medal for getting me through university and suffering me ever since, likewise her lovely family.

I also have to thank Mel Sherratt, who is as generous with her time and advice as she is talented, someone who is always there to cheer on her fellow authors. She did so much to help me in the early days of my career that I don't think I'll ever be able to thank her as much as she deserves.

My fellow Bookouture authors are all incredible, of course, unfailing and generous in their support of colleagues – life would be a lot duller without the gang.

There's also an honourable mention for my writing retreat gals: Debbie, Jo, Tracy, Helen and Julie. I live for our weeks locked away in some remote house, writing, chatting, drinking and generally being daft. You are the most brilliant women, and my life is better for knowing you all.

I have to thank all the incredible and dedicated book bloggers (there are so many of you, but you know who you are!) and readers, and anyone else who has championed my work, reviewed it, shared it or simply told me that they liked it. Every one of those actions is priceless, and you are all very special people. Some of you I am even proud to call friends now – and I'm looking at you in particular, Kerry Ann Parsons and Steph Lawrence!

Last but not least, I'd like to give a special mention to my lovely agent Hannah Todd and the team at Janklow and Nesbit. I'm so lucky to have an agent who not only champions my books but is also hard-working and absolutely brilliant fun!

I have to admit I have a love–hate relationship with my writing. It can be frustrating at times, isolating and thankless, but at the same time I feel like the luckiest woman alive to be doing what I do, and I can't imagine earning my living any other way. It also goes without saying that my family and friends understand better than anyone how much I need space to write, and they love me enough to enable it, even when it puts them out. I have no words to express fully how grateful and blessed that makes me feel.

And before I go, thank you, dear reader. Without you, I wouldn't be writing this, and you have no idea how happy it makes me that I am.

PUBLISHING TEAM

Turning a manuscript into a book requires the efforts of many people. The publishing team at Bookouture would like to acknowledge everyone who contributed to this publication.

Audio
Alba Proko
Sinead O'Connor
Melissa Tran

Commercial
Lauren Morrissette
Hannah Richmond
Imogen Allport

Contracts
Peta Nightingale

Cover design
Debbie Clement

Data and analysis
Mark Alder
Mohamed Bussuri

RAISING READERS
Books Build Bright Futures

Dear Reader,

We'd love your attention for one more page to tell you about the crisis in children's reading, and what we can all do.

Studies have shown that reading for fun is the **single biggest predictor of a child's future life chances** – more than family circumstance, parents' educational background or income. It improves academic results, mental health, wealth, communication skills, ambition and happiness.

The number of children reading for fun is in rapid decline. Young people have a lot of competition for their time, and a worryingly high number do not have a single book at home.

Hachette works extensively with schools, libraries and literacy charities, but here are some ways we can all raise more readers:

- Reading to children for just 10 minutes a day makes a difference
- Don't give up if children aren't regular readers – there will be books for them!

- Visit bookshops and libraries to get recommendations
- Encourage them to listen to audiobooks
- Support school libraries
- Give books as gifts

There's a lot more information about how to encourage children to read on our websites: **www.RaisingReaders.co.uk** and **www.JoinRaisingReaders.com**.

Thank you for reading.

Printed in Dunstable, United Kingdom